The General's Wife

SARA R. TURNQUIST

If you would like to stay up-to-date on this and other series from Sara and receive a free ebook, sign up for her newsletter:

https://saraturnquist.com/list

For my Lord,
who has sustained me through much.

And for my children,
who give me a reason to laugh.

Prologue

ALEXANDER III WAS A KING OF MACEDON, A STATE IN northern ancient Greece. After receiving the generalship of Greece, he used his authority to launch a military expansion plan. In 334 BC, he invaded Asia Minor and began a ten-year series of military campaigns that broke the power of Persia. He became known as Alexander the Great.

When Alexander the Great died in 323 BC, Ptolemy, one of his generals, was appointed governor of Egypt. In 305 BC, he declared himself King Ptolemy I. He founded both the Ptolemaic Kingdom and the Ptolemaic Dynasty. The Ptolemies were soon accepted by the Egyptians as successors to the pharaohs and ruled for two hundred and seventy-five years.

In 289 BC, Ptolemy I Soter made his son, Ptolemy II Philadelphus, his co-regent a few years before he died in 284 BC at the age of eighty-four. At the end of forty years of war, he had a well-ordered realm to pass down to his son. He also founded the Great Library of Alexandria.

CHAPTER 1

A Journey Must Start Somewhere

"Ismene, look!" Alonah said, pointing out the window of the carriage.

Ismene leaned over to Alonah's side of the carriage and allowed her gaze to follow where her handmaiden pointed, but she couldn't get excited. Her eyes had been watching the sloping topography of the countryside for days now as the carriage drew them closer to her destiny. The noble chariot had long since passed the familiar sites of her native land, and this new world around her was harsh. There was no comfort to be found here for her despondent spirit. Suitable, since the life awaiting them at her final destination offered no consolation either. She had left Greece, her home, far behind. And for what? To become an Egyptian? A bitter taste filled her mouth at the thought of it.

"Have you ever seen anything like it?" Alonah did not turn her gaze away from the window.

The sand sparkled and shimmered as if a hundred-thousand tiny diamonds were hidden there. Still, she mused, the waters around her village were just as captivating. And the landscapes outside her bedroom window in Greece were lush, green, living.

"No, I haven't," Ismene admitted.

She peered over at her handmaiden who was so captivated with everything around them. How she longed to share her fears with Alonah! But could she trust her with these secret thoughts? Dare she speak her true feelings about the life that lay ahead for her?

It was not the life Ismene had planned or even wanted for herself. If only it were possible to command the caravan to turn around and return her home. She did not want what lay ahead: a wedding. Her wedding. Ismene's father had arranged for her to wed Pharaoh Ptolemy II's highest general. She had always known her noble station would require her marriage to be strategically made. It was always to be a political maneuvering for her family and an unavoidable reality for her.

Even knowing this, she had done something quite senseless—she had fallen in love. Yes, this was the worst thing of all about her predicament. Bitter tears stung her eyes as she knew she could never be with him—her Thelopolis. Thelopolis had been her childhood playmate, her most trusted friend. And that caring friendship had grown into adolescent love. It was a comfortable love that she had found stability in. For just one moment, she allowed herself to remember the details of his face —details she could have traced blindfolded. His deep hazel eyes were full of life and happiness. They had darkened when she had told him she would be leaving for Egypt, for a new life, and a husband.

"Please," she had cried, unable to contain her overwhelming sadness. "Say something!" She desperately needed him to find the words to assuage her grief.

He had remained silent. Wasn't his heart breaking too?

Wrapping her arms around him, she had clung to him. "I need you to say something!"

"I know, Ismene." Thelopolis wouldn't even turn to look at her. He wouldn't move. "I am sorry, my beloved." He had choked on the word. "I have nothing to say that could bring you comfort."

But she would not let him escape her. She had turned his face to look at her. That's when she saw the tears that were escaping his eyes. He had twisted away.

"Tell me you love me. Tell me your heart is breaking as much as mine. Tell me we'll be all right!" she said, tears streaming down her face. She didn't even bother to wipe them away.

He then moved so she could see his tears. "My heart *is* breaking,

Ismene. No ocean has known the depths of my love for you. But I will not lie to you. I cannot say that we'll be all right."

Fresh tears poured out of her eyes and sobs racked her body. He had then pulled her into a firm embrace and held her so tightly she feared she couldn't breathe, but she didn't care.

The carriage hit a bump in the road, and it pulled Ismene from her reverie. There was moisture on her face. Ismene raised a hand to her face and felt the tear that had escaped.

Alonah was looking at her, an eyebrow raised. "Milady, are you unwell?"

"I'm all right, Alonah. Perhaps a little sand in my eye."

Alonah seemed satisfied with her response and returned her attention toward the carriage window.

Ismene, too, let her gaze wander across the waves of sand and tried to clear her mind. It wouldn't be right for her to be in tears for the first meeting with her husband-to-be. She had allowed herself much of this trip to mourn the loss of what was and what would never be. Today, she was to face her destiny.

"It's all so fascinating!" Alonah was so taken with their surroundings.

"Yes," Ismene said, somewhat distracted. She was glad Alonah had a pleasant attitude about their venture.

"And all so different!" Alonah took a deep breath. "It even smells different."

Ismene crinkled her nose, trying to draw in the scent of this new place. She couldn't discern what Alonah was talking about.

Alonah was more of an adventurer than Ismene had thought. She had been Ismene's handmaiden for years, but they weren't as familiar with one another as one might assume. In general, Ismene preferred to do most things for herself. So Alonah had never been necessary, in Ismene's opinion, or, for that matter, utilized. Still, Ismene's mother had sent Alonah with her for good measure. Her mother had insisted that it was only proper of her station that she take at least a handful of servants, lest her future husband think his wife a pauper. An argument had ensued about the logistics of taking a small entourage with her on such a lengthy journey. To which Ismene's mother relented, only because

Ismene would have more servants in the house she was to run than were in the one she was vacating.

After the lengthy journey, Ismene was already quite glad to have Alonah with her. This would be the first time she had ever been thankful for her mother's advice. Alonah was a pleasant companion, and Ismene welcomed having a familiar face by her side.

"Oh! I almost didn't believe they were real!" Alonah shrieked.

Ismene's gaze was again directed to where Alonah's attention lay. There, in the distance, was one of the pyramids she had heard so much about. It was majestic and mysterious at the same time. As chilling as the idea of mummifying a person for the afterlife was, a part of her wondered what lay behind those bricks, encased in that magnificent tomb. So captivated was she that she didn't even realize they were fast approaching Alexandria.

This city would be her new home. It was as alluring as it was huge. Large brick buildings lined the streets of the marketplace. They were most likely the homes of the merchants and middle classes. Their close proximity, making the best use of space, reminded her of homes in Athens. However, these homes had converted the lower floor of the two- and three-story buildings into stores. The roofs were flat, too. Intriguing. It must be one of the idiosyncrasies of their architecture.

As if reading her mind, Alonah leaned over. "I've heard tell that the Egyptians sometimes sleep on their roofs. Do you think that's true?"

"I don't know," Ismene's voice trailed off. That would make sense of the flat roofs and would, for certain, make for a more pleasant sleeping environment during the hotter months. Ismene pursed her lips. It was a smart idea.

The streets were alive with people and vendors. Many things among the wares were novel to her. There were beautiful cloths, strange-looking fruits, baskets, art, jewelry, carvings, and much more. She did spot a few things she had seen before, but only as priceless souvenirs displayed in the wealthiest homes of Athens. Her thoughts drifted once more to the vistas of her homeland that she had left behind. That was where her heart lay...with Thelopolis. And again, her heart was sad.

This will not do! She chided herself, *This is your home now and Thelopolis is not to be your husband.* These words had been her constant companion on this long journey. But she vowed to him and to herself that she would never love another. Her heart was his and his alone. Of this, she was determined.

Passing out of the most clustered part of the city, they pulled through the outskirts where the houses were bigger and more dispersed. From the placement of the houses and the grander size and detailing, she guessed them to be upper-middle-class and wealthy homes. She was surprised, but pleased, to note that many had gardens. There wasn't much time, however, for her to muse over the prospect of visiting a garden in this desert as the carriage had halted in front of one of the more spacious structures. Would she truly be calling this small palace home? It was hard to imagine.

Though she was the daughter of a nobleman who held an important station, her home in Athens was closer to the size of the middle-class homes she had seen in the city. There wasn't much difference in size between the homes of middle and wealthy classes in Greece. Wealth and station were determined by *where* your house was in relation to the marketplace and other conveniences, as well as what was *in* your house, such as gold inlaid in the furniture, precious gems, and so forth.

Turning her attention back to the grand estate in front of her, she tried to take it in. A wall surrounded the entire exterior of the home with a large gateway to greet visitors. The sides of the gateway rose high above the wall and bore an intricate design with bright reds and greens. She couldn't see much beyond the wall, only making out the top of the massive structure that lay beyond. To her delight, she did see that there were, indeed, gardens within the safe confines of the walls. Nothing about this house or its appearance indicated that a native of her own land called this home. *Was she to live as an Egyptian? To abandon all Grecian ways?*

Alonah's hand touched her arm, pulling her from her distracted thoughts and drawing her attention to the kind face of a man. This strange man's hand was extended to help her out of the carriage. Almost as an instinct, she drew back. She had seen Egyptians before. As a child of privilege, she had accompanied her parents to gatherings that included political heads and other people of importance to the Greco-Roman Empire. Indeed, she had been in the same room with Egyptians, but never so close. In her younger years, she had been rather interested and quite curious about these people who looked so different. It had never occurred to her that, as a woman, she would not be able to contain that curiosity.

The man's skin was dark, tanned and worn by the sun and harsh winds, and his hair was jet black and straight. His eyes were more almond shaped and set farther apart, and his features as a whole seemed quite smooth and angled toward the sun. Those eyes were deep brown and kind, his nose long, and his mouth small. She was surprised at her overwhelming temptation to just stare at this man. Shaking herself from her trance and gathering her wits, she took his hand and averted her eyes to the ground in order to step as securely as possible on the warm, brown sand.

The Egyptian then turned to assist Alonah, who was more able to disguise any trepidation she might have had about these strange people. Once again, Ismene was thankful for another Grecian face in the midst of these foreign ones.

The Egyptian gentleman led them through the gateway opening and onto the grounds. A few things took Ismene by surprise. One was a pool located to the right of the gateway entrance. Even from her vantage point, she could see that the pool was stocked with colorful fish. The other thing that struck her was the crowd of people between the entrance to the house and herself. They must be the household servants, come out to greet her. Her eyes scanned the area, looking for any sign of her husband-to-be. None among the group appeared the least bit Greek to her.

Ismene gazed down the line of household servants who had come out to greet the woman who would become their mistress. They seemed just as intrigued by her as she was by them. Some of their faces were filled with anticipation, eager for her to say something. No one there seemed above the station of the man who helped her from the carriage, and he was neither Greek nor a general.

Ismene was rather confused by the absence of her husband-to-be. Was he going to make a grand appearance once she was established properly? Was she to be escorted to him as a common guest? Was this a show of power—his way of letting her know who was in charge? *Just as well*, she thought with a sigh. She had no intention of making his life difficult with any semblance of a power struggle. It was her full intention to let him be and avoid any more contact with him than absolutely necessary.

The man who had first offered her his hand was, to her understanding, a station above the other household servants. He stepped in front of her again to greet her in a more formal manner.

"I am Neterka," he offered, bowing. "My master, General Merenre, regrets that he cannot be here to greet you himself. He is appearing before Pharaoh as we speak. But he wishes that I extend apologies and see that you are settled in your accommodations."

Ismene was surprised by the man's Greek. She didn't know what she had expected. And, though it was a bit broken, she was pleased to know that she would be able to communicate with someone here.

"I thank you, Neterka. This is my handmaiden, Alonah. I would like to greet the others of the household, if I may." She indicated the line of servants.

His face brightened. Ismene found that she was somewhat put to ease by his kind smile.

"Yes, they would like to meet you also, but they do not know your language. They are learning well, but they do not know it much." He gave her an apologetic look. His own grasp on Greek was still limited and full of pauses and altered patterns.

"I see." She had not considered what she would have to do in order to communicate. Would she need to learn their language? That hadn't occurred to her. She hadn't thought on much but her sadness on the journey and now wanted to kick herself for her lack of foresight. As she rolled it over in her mind, she decided that she was grateful for the challenge—something to look forward to.

"I can translate for you, if you wish," Neterka offered.

She nodded, turning toward the line of eager faces. Trying to be mindful of Neterka, who was translating a sentence behind her, she kept her word choice simple and paused often, so he could keep up.

"I am the Lady Ismene of Greece. I am honored by your warm welcome as I have entered this strange land to make it my home." She moved to indicate Alonah. "This is my trusted maidservant, Alonah.

She, too, is excited about our new life here. I hope someday soon she and I can both speak to you ourselves and you to us."

When Neterka was finished, Ismene nodded to the small gathering of smiling faces. She lowered her voice, turning back toward Neterka. "What should I do now?"

"May I escort you to your rooms, Lady Ismene? After your journey, you are certainly in need of rest."

Ismene nodded; she had to admit that she was tired.

Neterka faced the congregation again and spoke. A couple of manservants came forward to assist in unloading their possessions. As they came near the carriage, the two Greek manservants in Ismene's party started pulling the chests free of the carriage. There were also three Egyptian female servants who made their way into the house while the rest remained as they were, heads bowed for Ismene to pass before them and into the house.

Neterka nodded to Ismene and led both her and Alonah into the peculiar structure that would, from now on, be their home.

As Nassor moved down the busy streets of the marketplace of Alexandria, he had the distinct feeling that everyone's eyes were on him. But every time he glanced in the direction of the other patrons on the street, their eyes were on the vendor's carts, each other, or the path ahead of them. Was he so nervous that he was conjuring ghosts? Or was someone following him? He had been playing this game with himself for quite some time, and so, for the tenth time, he jerked his head around to look behind him. Nothing. There was nothing to be concerned about. No one knew of his errand, no one knew of their plans, no one knew...

Nassor slowed as he approached his destination—one of a handful of jewelry shops on the strip. Sefu and his wife sold many kinds of jewelry here, from beads to metal, some simple and priced for a pauper, some fit for the queen herself. Sefu's wife made it all. Making his way through the familiar shop, Nassor dodged customers and counters, moving toward the stairs at the back of the structure. Sefu's wife glanced up from her current sale and nodded in his direction, indicating that it was clear for him to proceed up the stairs.

Taking a deep breath, he took the first step. He was tempted to take the stairs two at a time to remove himself from all onlookers and into the seclusion of Sefu's home quarters with greater speed. Also driving him was the knowledge that it was not like Sefu to not be out here helping his wife sell her creations. Nor was it like him to summon Nassor so hastily or before nightfall. He calmed himself to take the stairs one step at a time—he did not wish to draw attention to himself from the customers in the store or passersby on the street. The stairs at length opened into the living quarters of the family, but the room was empty. Moving farther into the area, his eyes darted about the room, looking over the simple furnishings and utensils for any clue as to where he would find the master of the house. As Egyptian houses were quite open, the only place not within his visual range was the bedchambers, and he did not wish to invade the privacy of that area.

"Sefu?" he called out. "Sefu, I have come."

No response. If Sefu wasn't able to hear him on the main living level, then he must be on the roof. He found his way back to the stairs and could find no reason not to take them in twos.

As he reached the roof, the sun once again bore down on him, and he was hit by a breeze which had been blocked earlier by the many buildings lining the streets. It didn't take long to find Sefu, though. The roof was unhindered by structures or furniture save some cooking appliances and rolled up sleeping mats.

Sefu was on the opposite edge of the roof, looking down on the street that Nassor had just come from. He was silent and still, watching over the people below as if he were a guardian angel, ready to swoop down and rescue them from some unseen danger.

"I have come, Sefu, as you requested." Nassor broke into his vigil.

"Do you not wish to come over and enjoy the view?" his friend asked, turning to him, beckoning him to come stand next to him.

"I do not wish to be seen here!" Nassor countered. "Do you not think it too dangerous for us to be spotted together like this?"

"I don't think anyone looks up at the roofs to spy on their countrymen, Nassor. And if the people know, so what? It is we who are fighting for them. Let them know."

This was all quite strange to Nassor because it was usually Sefu who was the picture of discretion. But Sefu still stood there, gesturing for Nassor to take the spot next to him. In the end, he acquiesced, coming up alongside his friend and gazing down on the people below. Sefu seemed to be right—as much as Nassor's eyes moved over the people there, he did not spot one looking up at the rooftops. Everyone was too caught up in where they were going, what they were doing, and never on what may be going on around them.

"They have no idea the dangers that are around them," Sefu said.

Nassor nodded his head in agreement.

They stood for a handful of moments in silence.

"Why have you summoned me?" Nassor asked after some time.

"It has begun," Sefu said simply as he shifted to face Nassor.

Nassor was silent again; he had known this day was coming, but he wished he could have put it off longer. Now that it was upon them, he wasn't sure he was prepared. But he had made a commitment. And he believed the ends would justify the means.

"What would you have me do?" he asked.

"You know what you must do," Sefu said, his voice firm.

"It is time to gather the others."

Sefu nodded. He put a hand on Nassor's shoulder. "Never forget. What we do, we do for Egypt."

CHAPTER 2

Meeting Destiny Head-On

Unpacking was well underway, but Ismene had to sit by while Alonah directed the flurry of activity generated by the female servants. They seemed quite eager to please Ismene with their diligence and efficiency. Alonah had but to make the slightest indication for clothes or perfumes or other things to be moved out of their trunks, dusted, and set in place. It was a bit unsettling for Ismene to be a bystander, but she knew this was what the ladies-in-waiting expected. She did not want to dishonor Alonah's position by stepping in and declaring Alonah so unfamiliar with her mistress that she could not discern how to set up her living space.

Ismene tired of being still and made her way over to the desk. She could no longer sit by and do nothing, but found herself at a loss as to what she could or should do. Her parents would be expecting word of her safe arrival. As much as she dreaded that task, it was *something* to do. It was but a brief search to find papyrus and writing elements. Then, with hesitation, she began the unpleasant chore of the obligatory letter.

What to write? I am well? We arrived safely? It was all so trite, but she knew her mother would enjoy hearing those pleasantries and relish telling her friends about the house her daughter now lived in. So, Ismene would do her mother the favor of writing about it. Well, as much as she had seen. As best she could determine, the rooms were arranged around an inner courtyard. The house had high ceilings with pillars, tiled floors, walls that were beautifully decorated with paintings and hieroglyphics, and she had spotted a staircase. There must be an upper story. She wrote about the two pools she had seen, the one with fish and the one which was adorned by trees, and the gardens that she had yet to explore.

Ismene had only made it halfway into the note when there was a knock at her door. Alonah didn't give the other servants the chance to take the call upon themselves, but rather moved through the bedchamber to the door without pause.

"I have come to collect the Lady Ismene," Ismene heard Neterka's now familiar voice explain his intrusion to Alonah. "The general has returned and requests an audience with the lady."

Ismene glanced up from her writing just as Alonah escorted him into her bedchamber. Alonah came around next to Ismene's desk to stand in front of her and bowed.

"Milady, the general is home and wishes to speak with you."

Her breath had caught in her throat when she'd heard Neterka's request at the door, and she hadn't found her voice quite yet to answer Alonah. This was the moment she had dreaded for so many weeks.

Compose yourself! an inner voice of clarity came through the emotions. She laid her writing tool to the side, rose to her feet, calling upon all of the training her mother had instilled in her as a lady of politics, and nodded to Neterka. "I am ready."

Ismene moved toward Neterka, who was looking over her appearance with a critical eye. Was he hoping to catch any flaws that may be noticed by his master and thus displease him? She was quite different from Egyptian women. Her hair was raven all the same, but it fell in curled ringlets pulled back and unadorned by gold. An Egyptian woman of her position would need time to position her best wig and administer makeup before such a meeting. The features of her face were softer than the angled faces of Egyptian women and her skin was an ivory cream, not tanned by the warm sun in the daylight. Her clothes were another issue altogether.

Though sure she was not an Egyptian beauty, she hoped she was not unpleasant to look upon. And, she reasoned, the general was Grecian born. With any luck, she would be acceptable to his eyes. Either way, she did not seem to exhibit any imperfections to Neterka. Smiling, he motioned for her to proceed toward the door.

Alonah had been performing the same examination of Ismene and halted her as she stepped toward Neterka. Pinching some color into Ismene's drained cheeks, Alonah's hands worked some magic before allowing her to proceed.

"Thank you," Ismene whispered. She did not want her future husband to see her paled by the prospect of their first meeting.

Alonah's face broke out in a slight smile as she moved to follow Ismene.

"It is not necessary for your maidservant to accompany us," Neterka said.

Ismene fought down the wave of discomfort that rushed through her. Making every attempt to hide her immediate rise of emotion, she turned to her side. "Alonah, please stay and continue with the unpacking. I would like for some of my books to be available upon my return."

Alonah nodded and took a step back.

Moving again to follow Neterka, she stepped through the door and into the massive corridor beyond, leaving behind any semblance of familiarity. It was more difficult than she had imagined to face what lay before her without the comfort she had come to find in Alonah. Her thoughts were running rampant, threatening to overtake her calm demeanor. She needed to get a grip on these emotions before she was presented to the general.

Ismene's mother had spent quite some time preparing her for this first meeting. She could remember those "training sessions" rather well. At this moment, she was thankful for them as they calmed her and helped her focus. She could almost hear her mother's voice now, "He will be your husband, but he is also your master and is near royalty in station. You *must* bow. Do not give him any reason to suspect you do not submit fully to him. This is the role of a woman, Ismene. We are to be keepers of the home, bearers of the legacy, and subservient in all things. Conduct yourself as such."

With the little amount of contact she was expecting to have with the man, Ismene had decided that she would not have a problem being acquiescent to him in everything. Her guide halted and Ismene all but stumbled into him. It seemed so abrupt in her mesmerized state, but the near miss jerked her from her reflections soon enough. They had stopped at a room that was, as best she could discern, off the courtyard. Neterka nodded to a servant at the door to let his master know that his requested guest had arrived, but the servant shook his head and spoke to Neterka in their tongue. They conversed for a handful of seconds before he turned back to her.

"Fenuku offers most sincere apologies from General Merenre. He was called out for a moment by a most urgent message that demanded immediate response. The general will only be a little longer, and he wishes for you to wait here for him. Please understand, the general is a rather busy man...especially during times of conflict."

Ismene wasn't sure how to interpret that last sentence. She gathered that he was busy and perhaps there was conflict in Egypt somewhere. It was of little consequence to her at the moment except that she was waiting yet again. Fenuku opened the door to allow them to enter. Neterka led her into the rather spacious lounge connected to another room which was not illuminated enough for her to discern. Assuming that it was the general's bedchambers, she reasoned that this must be a more private receiving room of sorts.

Neterka indicated for her to sit on any of the lounge pieces within. "This is where I must leave you. I cannot stay any longer."

Panic gripped her. Couldn't stay? She was to be left alone with him? Was it to be now? Was that why he had summoned her? The wedding ceremony who knows how many days yet, still he would...?

"Do not fear, lady," Neterka's voice interrupted her thoughts.

She glanced up at him, still disturbed by her thoughts and surprised that her trepidation was written on her face.

"You will find that the general is not a harsh man."

That was all he was able to offer before turning and leaving her alone in the room with her worries and speculations. So, now she was alone and anxious and afraid. What was she going to do? This was unexpected. Her mother never warned her about the possibility of this turn of events. There wasn't a lecture to recall from her memory on this subject. And so she remained there for several seconds, standing where Neterka left her, mind reeling, pulse racing. Ismene began to feel light-headed and forced herself to sit, close her eyes, and take some deep breaths. She needed to find something to focus on in order to stay calm. Whatever was going to happen would unfold for her, and she would have to deal with it as it came. All of her worrying would not affect anything except her heart rate between now and then.

Ismene opened her eyes, attempting to clear her mind of unsettling thoughts. She made her eyes move about the room to take in her surroundings in more detail. The room proved to be quite interesting indeed—both the decor and furniture layout. It was obvious that someone had taken great care to blend Grecian and Egyptian influences, specifically in the artwork. There were statues that alluded to some of her favorite pieces back home and murals surrounded by hieroglyphics that were foreign to her. Everything was put together in such a way that was quite appealing. *A few well-placed plants and this room would be perfect.*

Standing, she walked over to the largest mural, studying it with an appreciation of the hand that had created it with tools that were for certain not as sophisticated as the ones Grecian artisans enjoyed. Her hand drifted up to trace one of the more complex, intriguing hiero-glyphs with her fingertips.

In that moment, whilst she was entranced in her musings, the door opened. She spun around in time to catch but a glimpse of the tall, regal man as he entered the room. So caught off guard, she did the only thing she'd thought far enough in advance to know to do—she dropped to her knees and bowed in submission.

He closed the space between them faster than she'd thought possible.

"Are you...?" he started, his voice betraying his alarm. Then his voice became softer. "No, milady." He knelt next to her. "Don't bow to me." His voice was a strong baritone, both firm and gentle at the same time.

"But you are my husband, my master," she said, not even willing to lift her eyes from the spot on the floor she had found to focus on. Her apprehension had gotten the better of her.

"No, I do not deserve this," he insisted. "Please, don't."

Her mother had not warned her about this either. She had imagined that her mother's lectures would be quite comprehensive due to number and duration, but she was once again lacking in instruction. What could she do, but obey? So, she moved to stand. He was directly in front of her, himself rising to his feet.

Ismene had intended to avert her eyes out of respect, but found herself unable to tear her gaze away from him. The thing that struck her first was his age. He was no more than ten years her senior. How unusual for a man of his military rank. She had expected someone much older and more established. Merenre was tall, tanned from long days spent out in the sun, and muscled from the hours of intense physical activity required of a military man. This was all quite evident in his Egyptian garb that covered less than Grecian robes would have. And his eyes. His eyes were quite captivating, especially in contrast to his browned skin. They were as blue as the sea near her home in Greece. They reminded her of those pools of water that she would dive into, allowing the cool water to wash away her worries. Unbidden, an image of Thelopolis appeared in her mind and she averted her eyes at last, backing away from him.

"I apologize for making you wait not once, but twice today. It was my plan to have been here to greet you upon your arrival. And I would have preferred to not have detained you yet again just now. Often times my personal life must accommodate my station. I wish it could have been avoided."

She nodded, comforted by the familiarity of her native tongue spoken fluently in this strange place. "It did not trouble me," she lied.

He moved around the lounge piece toward what seemed to be laid out as a conversation area with three lounges forming a large *U* shape.

"I trust that your trip was well?"

"Yes, General, it was. Thank you." Still uncertain, she watched him as if she were a caged cat, ready to leap at any threat of harm or promise of escape.

He indicated the seat she had earlier vacated on the lounge next to the one he intended to sit on. Ismene took the seat, her eyes on him as he sat a comfortable distance from her. A servant entered the room just then with *kopte sesamis* and wine. Merenre spoke to the servant girl in

Egyptian after she had filled their cups. She nodded, bowed to Ismene, and backed out of the room.

"For you, milady," he said, handing her one of the goblets.

It took her a handful of seconds to reach for the cup so shocked was she that he would lower himself to serve her. But she held her composure as if it happened to her every day. She had never seen her father or any man, except for servants, *ever* serve a woman. Taking a sip of wine, she was thankful for the opportunity to break eye contact. When she peered toward him again, he offered her a smile, warm, harmless.

"Usually, the best way to do this is to start with names," he said, leaning forward.

She felt her lips spread into a smile despite her trepidation.

"I am Alistair. And, as you already well know, I am a general of Ptolemy II's army."

"Alistair," she tested the familiar Grecian name for *avenger* on her lips. It was a strong name and she decided that it suited him quite well. But she had never heard him referred to in this way; both her parents and everyone she had encountered in Egypt called him Merenre.

"Neterka called you 'Meranrah,'" she tried the unfamiliar word.

"Merenre?" he offered.

She nodded, her face warming at her gross mispronunciation.

"'Merenre' is my Egyptian name. It means 'always honor the king's royal power.' Ptolemy's intent is to rule Egypt as one of them, to separate himself from the Roman Empire and become one with this culture. That is why he, like his father, took the title of 'Pharaoh.' Likewise, it was his desire that I take on an Egyptian name. 'Merenre' was chosen for me so that is what the people call me. Only my closest servants and aids have ever even heard the name given to me at birth."

"Merehnree," she tried again.

His smile widened. "It can be a difficult language, but you will get it in time."

They were in silence again. Surprising herself, she broke it. "I am Ismene Gina."

"That is a lovely name, Ismene, and it suits you well."

"Thank you."

The servant girl returned with a plate of fruit. Alistair spoke but a few words to her and she nodded, bowing, and left again.

"Egypt has an amazing capacity to produce fruit despite how dry it is compared to home. The land may not be as lush as Greece, but there is a good variety of fruit upon your desire of it."

"Thank you." Ismene nodded, reaching to sample the grapes that lay before her on the plate. She was becoming much more comfortable now, but her guard was still up.

They ate in silence. She chanced a glance at him to find that he was watching her rather intently. Somewhat unnerved, she turned away.

Alistair let out a breath. "There is something of utmost importance I need to discuss with you."

She gulped audibly, her stomach turning, and she forced herself to face him again.

"I wish that such a conversation could wait until we have had time to get to know one another better and feel more at ease around each other." He appeared to be a bit nervous, but only allowed it to show for a few seconds before he faced her with a confidence she was beginning to identify as one of his more notable qualities.

He cleared his throat. "I want to know that you agree to this marriage. As it was arranged by your family and myself, I do not wish anything to be forced upon you."

Of anything she had encountered thus far in this strange land so different from her own, this was the most foreign concept of all. Was he insane? Perhaps he had decided he did not want to marry her, but felt obligated to honor their arrangement and his last hope was that she would free him of his attachment to her. That must be it, she decided, dejected. That was the only thing that made sense to her.

Lowering her eyes, she stared at the floor. "Are you not pleased with me?" Of course she would release him from his promise, but it would be humiliating for her family if she were to be sent back, an unwanted bride.

He raised a hand toward her, but stopped short of touching her. "No, please don't think that. I have no reservations about this arrangement," he said quickly. He paused, drawing his hand back and licking his lips as if trying to find the right words. Then he spoke again,

"Ismene, I just meant that I had more say in this arrangement than you did. I understand that marriage matches are made by men back home. Things are so different here on that account. Egyptian women get to take part in the betrothal negotiations, and I see merit in that. I think it only fitting that you should have that opportunity with an arrangement that concerns your life and your future."

Ismene didn't know what to say. Of course she wanted to refuse the whole thing! She wanted to load herself and her things, leave this strange land behind, and return to her home that she loved so dearly, to her Thelopolis. Yet, the right choice seemed clear to her. This was the honorable thing to do. She had to push thoughts of home and Thelopolis from her mind if she were to do it.

Allowing herself to look at him full on for the first time, she tried to exhibit all of the confidence she didn't feel. This was her fate and there was no escaping it. She was going to face it head-on. Now set on her decision, she held his eyes. One stray thought ran unbidden across her mind, *I am so sorry, Thelopolis.*

"Yes, Alistair, I agree to this marriage. I would be honored to be your wife."

Then he looked at her in a way no one ever had and she couldn't quite decipher it. There was admiration in his eyes, even appreciation.

Another smile spread across his face. Then his smile fell and he became more serious. "Then we shall begin the preparations."

Alistair got to his feet and took the open seat beside her, taking her hand in his.

"There will not be much freedom for our own discretion in the ceremony, I'm afraid. "Ptolemy wishes us to have an Egyptian wedding. Our house, servants, and neighbors would be most honored by that. And considering my position with these people, it is best overall." His eyes were affixed to her facial features, watching for her reaction.

Confusion filled Ismene. The type of ceremony had never entered her realm of thought. It had not occurred to her that Egyptians married in a different way than her people did. What was the wedding ceremony like if their funerals included mummification? She caught her rampant thoughts and pushed them down so she could answer her soon-to-be husband. It didn't matter anyway.

"Of course. I will comply with your wishes."

He smiled at her again. His smile was warm and already comfortable to her. She was beginning to like it.

"We must begin arrangements for the engagement party. Egyptian customs dictate that the engagement be quite lengthy under normal circumstances; however, in our situation, it would be most advisable that we rush everything along. Ptolemy and his wife have requested that you stay in their home until the wedding to avoid any talk about you that would happen if we resided under the same roof before the wedding."

Her eyes widened. Move yet again? And to Pharaoh's house?

He must have misunderstood her reaction. "No, I don't want gossip questioning your virtue either. I'll have Neterka let it be known that the *mahr* has been sent to your father and has been accepted, and we shall set the date for the banquet. I will arrange for someone in Pharaoh's house to receive you and to have someone appropriate prepared to educate you on the wedding customs."

"Mayer?" she asked, still stuck on that earlier part of his explanation. The rest was lost to her.

"*Mahr*. It is a gift of money that is required before an engagement can be officially announced."

She nodded, almost thankful for something new and interesting to occupy her mind in the coming weeks.

"That should be enough for now," he said. By all appearances, he was glad to move past talk of the wedding. "Have you seen the house?"

"Yes, it is lovely." It was true. What she had seen of it had impressed her.

"I am glad that you are pleased. Have you seen the gardens?"

Her eyes widened as she shook her head. She had forgotten about the prospects of a garden.

"I would love to show you," he said, smiling.

She noticed that he had a dimple on one side of his face when he smiled.

"Shall we go while we send for some of your things to be packed?" He rose and offered his arm.

She was getting to her feet when a servant knocked on the door.

Alistair called for him to come as Ismene slipped a tentative hand onto the crook of his arm.

It was Neterka who entered the room with haste, speaking in hushed tones to his master. He need not worry about his volume if he was going to speak in Egyptian. Alistair frowned and conversed with him for a moment. Ismene was beginning to hate not being able to understand everyone and became all the more determined to begin her language study.

Neterka excused himself and Alistair moved toward her, placing a large, warm hand on hers. "Again I am apologizing. I regret to do so, but I must take my leave of you. There is something of great importance that I must attend to at once. Perhaps you and your handmaiden would enjoy the stroll through the gardens yourselves?"

"Yes, that would be nice." She was surprised at the twinge of disappointment that sprung up within her.

He nodded. "Neterka will make sure you have a proper guide. If you need anything, just call."

She started to remove her hand from his so he could take his leave of her, but he slid his arm so her hand fell into his. He brought her hand to his face and kissed her wrist before he allowed her hand to drop.

"Milady," he said, as he bowed before turning and exiting the receiving room.

Ismene stood rooted to the spot for several moments after he disappeared through the door. Her mind reran their conversation. What had transpired here today? She had agreed to marry him. So, she would be marrying a man she knew but for a few moments, yet already found herself admiring and respecting. Yes, this day was turning out to be every bit as interesting as she had expected but perhaps in a more positive light than she had thought. She found herself regretting that he had been pulled away by business. But things were not so bad, she decided. After all, there was a garden that awaited her. And the master of the house exhibited such pride in it. This made her all the more anxious to see it for herself.

It was then she realized she was alone. No servant had shown up to escort her back to her room. If only she'd been able to pay more attention on the walk here. Stepping into the inner courtyard, she tried to make her way back to her room as best she could. As she peered around pillars and made turns, her thoughts drifted back to her husband-to-be. Where was it that he'd had to run off to with such urgency? What had caused his mood to shift? Whatever it was, it had disturbed him. She could already see that he had great compassion for the people he was charged with protecting.

After looking into several rooms, none of which were hers, she bumped into a maidservant. "Please," she said, hoping against all hope that the girl spoke some Greek. "I need to get back to my room."

The girl looked at her confused, not understanding what she was saying at all.

"My room," Ismene said. She thought about how to communicate her request in a nonverbal way and moved her hands to make a pillow under her head and leaned over. "My bed. I need my bed."

The girl's face lit up in understanding. She indicated for Ismene to follow. They walked a couple of doors down and the girl stopped, motioning for Ismene to go in.

Surely not. I wasn't that close, was I? She glanced through the door. It was her bedchamber. Smiling sheepishly at the maidservant who was beaming back at her before taking her leave, Ismene rushed into her room, quite embarrassed.

As Alistair entered Pharaoh's court, he didn't bother to stare at the beautiful gold statues, the ornate works of art, or any of its other exotic features. As was most always the case, he was deep in thought and more concerned with matters of state. Garai, one of Pharaoh's aides, stood in front of the doors which led into Pharaoh's primary receiving chambers, the place Alistair was always called to.

"Pharaoh summons me," Alistair declared, his impatience evident in his voice.

"General Merenre, my liege awaits you." This servant opened the grand doors, and stepped just inside the entrance way. As Alistair passed him and came into the chamber, the aide's voice boomed, "General Merenre!"

Sometimes this was all too much pomp and circumstance. This wasn't a royal state dinner after all. He shrugged as he approached the Pharaoh.

Alistair made a sweeping bow before Pharaoh. "I am summoned, my liege."

Pharaoh nodded and waved his hand, granting Alistair permission to rise.

It did not escape Alistair's notice that Pharaoh's brother, Meleager, was also present. Meleager served as special counsel to Pharaoh. Ptolemy trusted him with many things, but thankfully not with the final call on military decisions. Prince Meleager had brought them a lot of information over the short time Alistair had commanded Pharaoh's armies. Some of it had turned out to be good information, some faulty. Alistair was never quite sure if the faulty information had been delivered on purpose or not. There was something inherent in the man that Alistair didn't quite trust.

"General, I wish I didn't have to summon you, but there is growing discontent among the people. They worry that we are going to war with Syria," Pharaoh spoke as Alistair stood.

"That subject matter is secret. How can the people know of this?" Alistair asked.

"It could only have become this widespread at such a rate by way of the mob. If that is the case, you must realize the issue we face." There was tension in Pharaoh's voice as he uttered those words. "If something small like this could leak out, what other more dangerous information is at risk?"

"It is obvious, General. We must find this connection to the mob," Meleager said, serious concern on his face. "We cannot risk more sensitive information getting out. We must launch an investigation at once."

"That has already begun," Pharaoh said. "The head of the secret police has been given much leeway to track down this traitor and bring him before me."

"Begging your pardon, my liege, but what do you ask of me?" Alistair was hesitant to ask that question, for fear of where the answer may lead.

"Anyone who had access to the information that has been dispersed will be subject to investigation."

Alistair recoiled. "My liege, surely...surely you don't think I..." He took a step away from Pharaoh in shock.

"No, no, no. Your allegiance to Egypt and to me has been proven many times over. What I fear is that someone in your household has mixed loyalties."

The general relaxed at these words, but soon stiffened again. "Everyone in my abode is true and honest. They have never served me ill." Alistair was ready to defend his staff with strength and conviction.

Pharaoh leaned in toward him. "I hope this remains the truth. As I have said, my chief investigator has been given broad leeway to track down this criminal. I suggest you give him everything he requires."

A crooked smile crossed Meleager's features as he glared down at Alistair. Sometimes these men were on the same side, sometimes at odds, and sometimes it almost seemed as if they were vying for Pharaoh's support. Theirs was indeed a strange relationship. In this case, he seemed to enjoy watching Alistair squirm a little. Meleager was a member of Pharaoh's house, and, while the palace was being investigated, Meleager would not have to be called out like this.

With those words, it was clear that the audience with Pharaoh was over. He stepped back and lifted his staff back to its traditional pose, indicating no more words would be spoken. Alistair bowed before Pharaoh and retreated back to the entrance, leaving the room in the traditional way, without turning his back on his master.

Alistair could never have predicted this meeting with Pharaoh. It wasn't a meeting to discuss war policy, but to indicate that Alistair better not get in the way of Pharaoh's investigator. As he walked out to his horse, he grunted at the thought of having to deal with a member of the secret police in his own home. Someone of the high court, turning everything upside down in pursuit of some fool? *Bah!* They never did work with any politeness or grace. Instead, speed and harsh results were the probable outcome.

Ismene didn't have to wait long before there was yet another knock on the door. This time she was prepared to see Neterka when Alonah let him in.

"The general says you wish to see the gardens?"

"Yes! So much!"

"And I have heard that I should perhaps help you familiarize yourself with the house."

Ismene felt her face heat. The sweet little maidservant had snitched on her! No matter, it was true she needed a more thorough tour of the grounds than what she was getting as she was shuffled from place to place.

"I apologize that I did not see to that sooner, milady," he said, turning away from her as if prepared for a reprimand.

"It is all right. I'm just glad that we'll be taking care of it now," she said, smiling. "I would like for my handmaiden to accompany us, if she may."

"Of course. Shall we begin?"

The house was laid out exactly as she had suspected. An inner courtyard was at the center of the house and all of the rooms came off of it. There were the master bedchambers, her bedchambers, the sitting room, the bathroom, where Neterka noted that Alistair had a Grecian tub put in, causing her to wonder how Egyptians bathed, and a "Grecian," again as Neterka put it, dining room. All of the rooms were decorated with similar style and taste as Alistair's outer bedchambers—Egyptian décor with touches of Greek influence. Indeed, it was growing on her. The color and artwork were fascinating. She could spend hours just examining the paintings inside the house.

Next, they toured the outer structures. A small private chapel stood outside the main house. Did Alistair worship Greek gods or Egyptian gods? Not that either mattered to her, she would comply with whatever his wishes were for her. She had long since stopped believing in any of those sorts of mystical things.

They were now on the west side of the home. Through the small opening in the yard, she saw the granaries where servants were hard at work checking and filling small silos. The gardens at the south end of the home extended along the entire width of the great wall which made up the living quarters. This green space separated the main house from another long structure that ran along the entire south side of the great wall. Ismene assumed that this structure held the stables, servants' quarters, and the kitchen.

Traveling through the amazing gardens, Ismene saw clusters of Egyptian lotus, immortelle, lychnis, jasmine, and narcissus bulbs filling the western side of the gardens with color and beauty. As her eyes continued to scan over to the eastern side, she found blossoms of chrysanthemum, cornflower, red poppy, arum, iris, and crinum. It was breathtaking. The garden couldn't have been better arranged if she had planned it out herself. Some of these were flowers she'd had the privilege to see, touch, and smell. Some she had only seen or heard about in books. A covered patio sat off the back of the house. It would provide a nice, cool place to gaze over the gardens in the heat of the day, should she so choose. Another pool was featured in the center of the gardens.

Ismene longed to spend more time in the gardens, and assured herself that she would once the tour was over. Coming around the back of the house, through the gardens to the east side of the house, they came first to the cattle yard, which was walled in. Beyond that was the well which supplied water to the house.

In truth, it was a grand estate, and she couldn't fathom that she would become the mistress of all she had seen. How did one look after such a house? But in a matter of days, this would be her home. The irony was that her mother would have longed to care for such a large property and boast of being its mistress. Ismene cared nothing for the status, and found the prospect of taking on all of this quite intimidating. And so her mother would forever be bound to her townhouse in Greece, while Ismene was here in this expansive abode.

Returning to her bedchambers, she found maidservants packing the things she would need during her stay at Pharoah's palace. If this was the home of a general, she could only imagine what the palace of the pharaoh looked like. She was quite relieved that Alonah would be going with her to yet another strange place with strange people. Alonah was becoming not only a familiar face, but a sense of stability amidst all of these changes.

"Thank you for seeing me," Nassor said to his cohort as he was escorted into the living quarters of a house he had never been in before. "Is it safe for us to speak candidly here?"

"Yes," Fadil said. "My wife is out at the market and my children are at school."

As was his habit, Nassor glanced around the living quarters anyway, looking and listening for any sign of life. "Sefu has contacted me," Nassor went right into it. "It is time."

"I see." Fadil's reaction was difficult to read, but whatever the initial reaction was, it was replaced with determination. Was Fadil as hesitant as he? It was hard to say.

"We must be prepared and in place to watch their movements with sharp eyes and look for opportunities. Especially *her* movements."

"And what is the plan?" Fadil asked, his face expressionless.

"It's no secret your greatest value is in your familiarity with all the members of the mob. You seem to know how to find each and every one of us. There must be some link in that house, someone who may be willing to work with us."

Fadil thought for a moment. "There is someone I know of who is already inside, but I'm not sure if he will see things the way we do. I cannot be certain. Would it give us away if I approach him and he is opposed?"

"Perhaps. Let us think if there is someone else. If not, there may be someone who is willing to help us at the right price even if they are not already aligned with the mob."

Fadil agreed that this was a good possibility. "I shall continue to think on the prospect of another person already stationed on the inside. Gahiji has been known to be quite...convincing."

Nassor nodded; Gahiji was one of their men. "Then we shall set him to finding a weak link to be turned. Only if you are not able to find someone already in place."

It was agreed between them that this was a good plan and that Fadil would speak with Gahiji. They also agreed that Nassor should not linger lest Fadil's wife come home early. The less they had to explain away, the better. So Nassor gathered himself and went about his way. He let out a deep breath. The first part of the plan had begun.

As the chariot drove on, Ismene got her first glimpse of Pharaoh Ptolemy's palace. If she had thought Alistair's home was large, she was in for quite a surprise. Pharaoh's palace was enormous even by comparison to the vast estate she would call home. It was comparable to the size of the city they had passed through. The wall surrounding the palace seemed to stretch for miles. And the gateway that greeted her stretched high to the heavens. Instead of having colorful paintings, the columns boasted statues of Pharaoh and the queen standing guard over the entrance to the palace. It was magnificent and overwhelming.

They passed numerous outer buildings, some which were the size of Alistair's entire house. It was difficult to distinguish what they were, but she was sure they represented some of the same outer buildings on her own property—a temple instead of private chapel, kitchens, barracks instead of servants quarters, and so on. The chariot moved closer and closer to the main building which was detailed and ornately decorated with the finest craftsmanship she had seen thus far in Egypt. It was fitting, she decided, for the home of their pharaoh.

The chariot halted by the main entrance which boasted smaller statues of Pharaoh Ptolemy and Queen Arsinoe plated with gold. They guarded the entrance again, looking down upon those who would enter their private abode. Ismene was intimidated, but she remembered who she was: the daughter of a nobleman, the soon-to-be wife of the highest general of Pharaoh, and welcome visitor to the palace of Pharaoh. She gathered her wits about her and entered through the main entrance, stepping into a grand vestibule.

The vestibule blended into the main inner court. The ceilings were high, held up by huge pillars that were decorated with grandeur befitting the palace, and there was a small garden in the center, sporting mostly palms and ferns. The walls told stories of the Ptolemies' rise to power and of Ptolemy I Soter—his military conquest and how the people of Egypt embraced him as Pharaoh. There were also scenes of

Ptolemy II's rule, his competence as a military leader and philosopher, and his establishment of the great library. Ismene had heard stories about the Library of Alexandria. Perhaps someday she would be able to lay eyes upon it.

They were not waiting long before one of Pharaoh's aides came for them.

"Lady Ismene," the man said, approaching them. "I am Paki. I am to announce you."

Ismene nodded, then motioned toward Alonah. "This is my lady-in-waiting."

He nodded, but gave no indication that he cared. "Please follow me."

Paki led them through the inner courtyard and down a large corridor, decorated much the same as the courtyard they had just passed through. The walls continued to display stories in hieroglyphic depictions, and pillars lined the walls, holding up the massively tall, tiled ceilings. As they approached Pharaoh's court at the end of the corridor, two guards opened the large doors ahead of them.

Paki went ahead, indicating for them to linger for a moment.

"The Lady Ismene Gina of Athens, Greece."

Having been announced, Ismene and Alonah entered the great hall that served as Pharaoh's throne room. Pharoah's court was designed with white marble, boasting gold accents. The theme of the high ceilings with large pillars continued. In the center of the wall in front of her were two huge thrones. On one sat Queen Arsinoe. Behind her were three ladies-in-waiting, and to her left, seated in a chair on a lower level, sat another woman.

The queen appeared in all the finery Egypt had to offer. Ismene was sure her shoulder-length black hair was a wig with her golden crown perched on top. Her face was painted with thick black lines over her eyes and some color in other places. It appeared as if the face paint was designed to angle her features a bit more, but there was no disguising her Grecian appearance to a fellow native. Ismene recognized her countrywoman right away. Queen Arsinoe wore a large gold Egyptian collar over a dress of fine white linen held together at the waist by a golden belt. She was beautiful.

Ismene, with Alonah a couple of steps behind her, stopped a reasonable distance away from the throne. They bowed before their queen.

She extended her staff to indicate that they should rise.

"Lady Ismene, welcome to the palace," she said, her voice smooth and melodic.

"I am honored by your invitation," Ismene said in a simple, but sincere tone.

The queen motioned to someone in the distance that a stool be brought for Ismene and at once someone was behind Ismene, preparing for her to sit. Alonah assumed her place behind Ismene and to her right.

"I wish to introduce you to the Lady Naeemah," the queen said as she gestured toward the lady seated down a step and to her left.

Naeemah bowed her head. This woman was Egyptian. Her features bore the same angles Ismene had come to associate with the natives of this land. She was also painted for the occasion and was lovely to Ismene's eyes.

"Naeemah has been selected to assist with your education of Egyptian wedding customs. We hope she will serve you well."

"I thank you. I have no doubt she will be valuable to me," Ismene said, smiling with gratitude up at her queen.

Queen Arsinoe nodded, then leaned forward, crossing her legs and propping her elbow on them. "Now, tell me how things are in Athens."

This took Ismene by surprise, but she soon smiled and spent the next several minutes telling Queen Arsinoe the state of things politically and socially when she had left Athens. The queen drank in every word, commenting here and there if Ismene mentioned a family that she knew of.

"I understand," the queen interjected, "that you have a great love of botany and gardens."

"That is true." How had this little tidbit of news traveled so fast? Was nothing a secret?

"It would be my pleasure to show you through the gardens here on the palace grounds."

"That would be a real treat for me, Your Majesty," Ismene said, thrilled at the prospect.

Queen Arsinoe rose, then Naeemah followed suit, as did Ismene.

This allowed the ladies-in-waiting to then stand. The queen walked down off the dais to join Ismene before they moved out of the court room and back out into the corridor. They were flanked by Naeemah and then by all of the ladies-in-waiting. As it turned out, the corridor gave way to another interior courtyard that was only slightly less grandiose than the previous one. That courtyard led them to a passageway that took them out of the palace and into the lush green setting that was the gardens.

This must be what a jungle looks like! Ismene thought, amazed at the variety of plant life and how mature it was. The garden was not overgrown, though; it was still quite well manicured.

"The previous queen had a great love of gardens. This was her private sanctuary," Queen Arsinoe explained.

"What she accomplished, and you continue to keep up, is magnificent!" Ismene managed to get out after several seconds of stunned silence. Her eye did not know where to look first.

"Please allow me to show you one of my favorites," Arsinoe said, reaching out to touch Ismene's hand to direct her attention elsewhere.

"Of course, Your Majesty," Ismene said, pulling her eyes away from the massive plants with reluctance. She longed to just stare at the greenery.

They walked a short distance into the garden to a patch of colorful blooms that Ismene had never seen before. One grouping that was of particular interest to Ismene was orange with black dots. She had never seen such a flower before.

"These are some of the more prized flowers here—they are called tiger lilies," the queen explained. "They were a gift from another land, so the former queen took the utmost care with their tending, and I continue to do so, as I appreciate how difficult, and quite impossible, they would be to replace."

Ismene dropped to one knee to better examine the flower.

"Please," Queen Arsinoe said as she raised a hand, inviting her to smell the rare bloom.

Ismene drank in its perfume, memorizing its scent, cataloging it in her mind. She returned to a standing position and shook off any dirt on her toga.

"If you so desire, I shall have a couple prepared to transplant to your garden," the queen's voice said as if to a tune.

"Oh, Your Majesty, I could never ask such a thing!"

"But you didn't. I am offering."

"You are most gracious, but..."

"Then it is settled," the queen interrupted. "I shall have some bulbs prepared to be sent to your home. They will be in pots for optimum survival until you have a chance to plant them."

"To say thank you seems...well, it's not adequate for this gesture, Your Majesty."

The queen's smile was understanding enough.

They wandered through the gardens for a while. It seemed like hours and mere minutes at the same time. As they reached the other side of the gardens, Ismene began to feel a familiar rumbling in her stomach. She needed food.

"I know the garden paths can be somewhat confusing, but we are near where we entered." She motioned to her right through some bushes where a door must be hidden beyond. "Just so you have some sense of direction here," she said, smiling at Ismene. "Because we have arrived at your rooms."

"My rooms are right off of the gardens?" she asked, pleasantly surprised. She had died and gone to Elysium. Not even Mount Olympus could tempt her with better accommodations.

"Yes. Hearing of your love for gardens, we thought these guest quarters might suit you best."

"Your Majesty does not know the kindness she has bestowed upon me."

"You are most welcome," the queen said. "And I hope that one day, we shall come to call each other friend."

"I would like that." Ismene met the queen's eyes.

"I will leave you here to get settled and rested before the evening meal. Someone will come to collect you in an hour."

"Thank you," Ismene said, bowing.

"Of course." Queen Arsinoe then took her leave of Ismene, walking back out into the gardens and disappearing from sight.

Ismene was thrilled at how her first interaction with the queen had gone. It could not have been better. She couldn't even imagine that Queen Arsinoe would be gifting her a rare bloom. And those gardens! How amazing! How splendid! Her heart still leapt for joy as her spirit was absorbing all she had just seen.

Alonah cleared her throat, snapping Ismene from her thoughts. Spinning toward the sound, she saw that Alonah had opened the door to her quarters and was waiting for Ismene to proceed. Ismene's half smile was an unspoken apology for her daydreaming. She moved into the bedchambers.

This room was built to coincide with the gardens that lay beyond. The gardens were directly connected to the inner bedchambers, while the outer chambers were connected to the rest of the house. It was a garden-lover's dream abode. Large windows faced the gardens to bring them in and make them part of the room, but draperies covered the windows for privacy. Each corner in the room had potted palms and ferns to continue bringing the outside in. Even the walls had been painted with murals of branches, flowers, trees, and leaves. A large bed sat in the middle of the room with ivy growing up the posts and a blanket of greenery overhead. Fresh flowers adorned the side tables and the vanity. Ismene could not think of a thing she would have changed. She felt her stomach rumble again. Well, maybe one.

Alonah came back from the outer bedchambers with a bowl of fruit.

"I could have heard that rumble from a mile away, milady. There was some fruit left out for you. Please have some."

Ismene reached for a piece. Never mind...the room was perfect.

CHAPTER 3

Expect the Unexpected

ALISTAIR FOUND IT DIFFICULT TO KEEP HIS ATTENTION ON Captain Ptah as the man was giving him a rundown of troop maneuvers that day. When would these reports be over? Exercising the troops had gone long today and, of course, reports *always* seem to run long. Even more so these last few days. Or was it because Alistair was all the more anxious to get home? He glanced up at the sun in the sky. Frowning, he realized he would have already missed Ismene today. Strange that this should bother him so.

Ismene had been coming to the house each day in the afternoon to check on the progress of a transplanted flower the queen had gifted her. She came without fail, but did not linger. So he would have already missed her. The disappointment was almost a tangible thing.

It did please him that Ismene was enjoying her time at Pharoah's house. She and Queen Arsinoe were getting along well. As were he and Ismene. That pleased him too. Maybe too much.

Alistair shook his head, turning his attention back to Captain Ptah just in time to hear the man's wrap-up. More than a little embarrassed to have missed most of the man's presentation, Alistair made short work of dispersing orders for morning training and dismissing the men.

What was going on in his head? He needed to get past this. It would not do for this woman to fill his thoughts like this. No, he had a responsibility to Pharoah, his army, and to the whole of Egypt. They relied on him to be focused and ready at all times. A general did not have the luxury of daydreams. It was imperative he stay grounded and keep his mind on his job.

Shifting from one side of the overlook that served as his office to where a large map of the kingdom was laid out, Alistair returned his attention to his final task of the evening. He looked over the map, reviewing where they had been reinforcing their borders and sending troops to relieve other troops.

Just then, a large shadow was cast over his map. He glanced up to discover who would disturb him at this hour, mere moments before he was to retire for the evening.

"Meleager," he said, his voice even. He afforded the man but a brief look before turning his attention back to his map. "What can I do for you?"

"Oh, I was stopping by to see how you were doing." The intruding prince leaned over the map, peering at the troop alignments for himself. "Perhaps more troops near Macedonia?"

Alistair glared up at him, letting a breath escape through his clenched teeth. Troop assignments and all military decisions fell under his purview, and he did not suffer the king's brother's interference as easily as Ptolemy did. They'd had this conversation on a few occasions. However, when his eyes met Meleager's, he saw only a genuine desire to help. So he made the proper alterations on the map. *Sometimes, his advice is sound.*

"It must be such an inconvenience," Meleager started in a large voice, walking around the table as if he owned the space. "Planning a wedding with the investigator in your home."

Alistair chose to ignore the bait. "All is well," he said, trying to stay focused on his map. "He is doing a thorough job despite the staff's preoccupation, I assure you." Alistair lifted one eyebrow as he raised his eyes once again to meet Meleager's leering face. "And the investigator in Pharaoh's house? Has he questioned everyone yet?"

Meleager shrugged the question off, placing a finger on one of the figurines that represented a company of soldiers. "He is making his way through the ranks. Hasn't made it to the top yet, though." Then a spiteful smile spread across his face. "Have you ever been questioned by a chief investigator?" Meleager made a gesture with his hand over Alistair's troops near Persia. Alistair pushed his hand away.

"No, I can't say that I have." Alistair sighed. He grew tired of this back and forth with Meleager. More than anything, he did *not* want to have the time for a conversation with the prince right now. What he wanted was to finish this and get home. "My Prince, please do not think you need to keep me company. I was about to quit for the night myself..."

"I certainly haven't been questioned," Meleager continued as if Alistair hadn't said anything. He continued to circle the table, now passing by Alistair. "But I don't think any of us will escape it this time, friend." There was something odd about the way he said "friend." The word came out almost as a curse.

It was true that the investigator's presence in Alistair's home had already become an annoyance. The thought of having to deal with him in any direct way was more than a little irritating. None of this changed Alistair's opinion of Meleager's dabbling in troop deployments and other military details. It was just fine to listen to his opinions when discussing policy in Pharoah's council and, truth be known, several of his points made sense. But when orders were given to Alistair, it was *his* duty, not the prince's, to draw up the details. Meleager's attempts to insert himself into Alistair's personal affairs were even more bothersome.

"You know, I think it is time for me to retire," Alistair said, yawning for effect. He wanted to wrap up this discussion that Meleager had seemed to foist upon him. "I'm sure if you have any further opinions about military operations, Pharoah will be glad to hear them at the next council session." Alistair stood to his full height, which put him a few inches taller than Meleager. Then he went about gathering the things he would need to take home with him.

The prince was never the best at recognizing a polite brush-off. He started to open his mouth again, but Alistair knew this game all too well. If he didn't start walking, he would never make it out.

He cut Meleager off with a slight bow. "I thank you for your concern, Prince. But the hour is late and I must take my leave."

Meleager could do nothing else but nod his head in response as he watched Alistair turn and walk away.

Ouch! Ismene's hair was being pulled this way and that as Naeemah was preparing her for the engagement party. It had at last arrived after all the long days of lessons and preparations. Now she had just one last prep session. A beautification session.

"You use the *kohl* to make marks over the eyes like so," Naeemah was saying to Alonah when Ismene refocused on their conversation. How much more of this torture was she to endure?

Alonah, as usual, was ever the eager pupil in the study of Egyptian fashion and makeup trends. She kept a watchful eye over every stroke Naeemah made with the cosmetics and comb.

Then they were pulling at her hair again.

"Now what are we going to do with this hair?" Naeemah was quite exasperated. She pulled at the mass of dark curls. The comb wouldn't slide through Ismene's hair without snagging.

"Let's try to pull it back first and see if the wig will work." Alonah picked up the wig Naeemah had brought for the occasion. Egyptian women wore their hair straight or, for more formal occasions, in a wig.

Naeemah pursed her lips and tipped her head to one side, but shrugged her shoulders. She was willing to try it.

Working together, they pulled some more at Ismene's hair. She was clinging to the chair so tightly her knuckles were turning white. The air was more humid this time of year, so it was proving rather difficult to tame the hair so that a wig could sit on her head.

Ismene breathed a sigh of relief when Alonah at long last held up a hand to halt Naeemah. "Wait. I have an idea." She then ran out of the room.

Biting at her lip, Ismene was not sure how much more of this she could take. She was quite sure they must have pulled half of her hair out by now.

Alonah returned with a bottle of oil in her clutches. Dumping a small amount into her hand, she ran her fingers through the dark curls.

Ismene squeezed her eyes shut against more discomfort, but was surprised when there was none. Opening one eye, she watched in her reflection as the frizziness began to calm. Only then did Alonah begin to pull Ismene's hair back again. This time, there was no pain.

"Grab those gold pieces," she called to Naeemah.

Naeemah nodded her understanding, picking up the gold-plated clips and combs, using them to hold Ismene's hair in place. The pieces also added decoration to her appearance with an Egyptian flare. By and large, Egyptians measured and displayed their station with the amount of ornamentation they wore.

Ismene took that moment to let her gaze wander over the whole of her appearance. She wore the traditional blue silk dress that was indicative of an Egyptian bride-to-be. It was not altogether different from Grecian clothing, she mused. Well, except that it was a lot more revealing than she would like. Silk bands crossed in front of her torso, leaving an open triangle of skin on her chest. This provided a place for Naeemah to display a simple piece of jewelry. Past the belted waist, the cloth fell in rivulets like blue waves down to her feet. Ismene had mixed feelings. The dress was becoming, but she had not been so happy about the low V-neckline. Naeemah had insisted that it must be so, and Ismene did not want Naeemah to have to drag Alistair into their dispute, so she relented to wearing these ceremonial dresses as necessary.

As she allowed her eyes to take in the entire picture of the dress, she noted that it did accent her figure. Perhaps a little too well, in her opinion. But Naeemah and Alonah raved about how becoming she was in it. For her part, she was counting down the moments until this was all over and she could return to her more practical clothing. Still, she had to admit that the way the silk was cool against her warm flesh was a pleasant change.

Ismene sighed then, her mind turning toward home. As much as she and her mother were often at odds, she did wish her mother, father, and brothers could be here for this momentous occasion. But travel between Egypt and Greece was such a long, hard journey. She did understand the impracticality of them traveling such a distance for a ceremony that wasn't such a production in Greece, certainly nothing worth coming such a far distance, risking life and limb for. In her own lands, the wedding ceremony was but a few beautiful words passed between the two intended. No, her family wouldn't have understood a wedding, much less an engagement, to be such an event.

Naeemah drew Ismene's attention back toward the mirror. Her makeup was complete, and she could not believe her eyes. The way her face had been done, she almost appeared Egyptian! Creamy skin and curled locks set her apart, but aside from that... This realization caused a lump in her throat and a knot in her belly...not pleasant. But she admired her image all the same.

Alonah and Naeemah were also admiring their work. They took turns complementing each other's care in their preparations. But something was missing. And though Ismene was quite intent on trying to figure out what was nagging at her so, her thoughts drifted to the place they had been stealing away to as of late—Thelopolis. What comments he would make if he could see her now!

Naeemah's voice broke into her thoughts. She was delivering last-minute reminders.

"At the banquet hall, before the celebration begins, he will put the ring of immortality on your finger and offer the *shabka*."

"Yes, yes," Ismene piped up, rolling her eyes. "And then the music and dancing and feasting and drinking will begin." Sighing, she feigned boredom with the whole thing. She had to admit that Naeemah had done her job well. Yes, she had been a great asset to Ismene these last few days.

"Oh, milady, it will be so much fun!" Alonah said, the words spilling out of her mouth.

Ismene was pleased to see Alonah becoming more comfortable with her life here. She had been every bit the lifesaving friend to her that she had imagined. This past week had been no exception. All of the lessons and information, combined with the newness and grandeur of this place...Ismene had been in dire need of a friend with whom to share all of it.

"It is time, Lady Ismene." Naeemah wet her lips in anticipation. "Let us get you to your general." She then moved toward the door and called for a servant girl to come.

Ismene was to be the last to arrive at the banquet hall. Alistair was already there, in the palace, probably at Pharaoh's common banquet hall. Upon her timed arrival, the engagement ceremony would begin and then the party. Naeemah rang for another servant as Ismene checked herself once more.

"You are beautiful, milady," Alonah reassured her, reaching out a hand to touch her arm.

The servant Naeemah had summoned appeared at the door and Naeemah spoke to her in Egyptian. She would be sending an alert to whomever it concerned that they were prepared for Ismene to make the short trip across the palace for her grand arrival.

Naeemah finished speaking and motioned to Ismene. "Lady Ismene, we must go now."

Ismene moved to obey, but stopped in her tracks. She whirled around and grabbed a lotus flower off of her cosmetic table. This was the final piece! Alonah helped her secure it in her hair.

"There, that's better," Ismene sighed. "Now I'm ready."

Naeemah nodded her approval and they moved out into the hall.

"The banquet hall is magnificent and inviting this evening. It looks quite grand!" Alistair boasted to his companion, Pharaoh Ptolemy II. "Your staff has outdone themselves with the preparations for this evening. If I didn't know any better, I would think it was Your Majesty that was getting married."

"Did you expect anything less for my great general?" Ptolemy smiled as he waved an arm to indicate the grand hall.

It was true that Ptolemy was happy for him and had been eager for him to pick a bride for quite some time. All Egyptian men of power had at least one wife. Alistair, for his part, would have preferred his life as a bachelor. He enjoyed not being committed to any one woman and, well, everything that came with the lifestyle of a single man—no one to answer to, no one to worry with. But he was willing to do this to satisfy his pharaoh and friend.

Even now he was enjoying this opportunity to be in Pharaoh's company in a social setting. Their relationship was rather unique. On anything involving matters of state or military issues, their relationship was all business, and Alistair embraced their roles. But he relished the times, like tonight, when they were just Alistair and Ptolemy. Times when Pharaoh, though still king, was more laid back.

Ptolemy had been generous to Alistair. Alistair enjoyed serving the man as his general, occasional advisor, and friend. There was, however, one desire of Pharaoh's that Alistair could not adhere to. In keeping with his assimilation into the Egyptian culture, Ptolemy would have preferred Alistair choose a bride from among the noblewomen of Egypt. If it were not for a deathbed promise, Alistair would have been all too happy to comply. Alistair's mother had always wished a bride of Greco-Roman descent for him. She had made him swear to her before she passed away that he would choose his wife from among their people. He had no intention of conceding on this point, lest she come back from whatever afterlife and haunt him...or worse.

After meeting Ismene, he knew he had made the right choice. Her father enjoyed a good reputation among the nobility of the empire. In truth, he felt fortunate to have been the best offer for her hand. He was somewhat surprised that her father had regarded him well enough to send his daughter away to a foreign land. To part with her, perhaps never to see her again, all for the sake of an advantageous marriage. It was all rather strange to him. Nevertheless, here she was and she was prepared to become his wife. Even if it was with a little reluctance that she had accepted the arrangement.

Yes, it did not escape his notice that, while she bravely accepted his offer, she had hesitated. There was something in her eyes in that moment that he had not been able to identify. Then again, he couldn't ever quite figure out what was going on in that head of hers, but it intrigued him. Alas, he hadn't the time to spend trying to figure her out. That would not change. He hoped she would adjust to the life he led.

How much demand would marriage place on him? How much would she interfere with his comings and goings? He hadn't given it too much thought, always assuming there would be little change. Many of the marriages he had observed seemed to be for the purpose of stability, society, and children. For the most part, there was not much difference between the married troops and single troops. There were a few men whose wives seemed to place any demand on them and fewer who spoke of their wives and children. For some men, they were a bigger part of life. That would not be him. His work was too demanding and she would have to get used to that.

Ptolemy drew Alistair's attention back to the present, "Has Naeemah served you well?"

"I think the Lady Ismene could better answer your question, but I have been quite pleased. She has helped with the planning to be sure, and her service in educating Ismene has made it possible for me to concentrate on other, more important things." Alistair was responding to Ptolemy, but his eyes were gazing off into the crowd.

Ptolemy nodded, his eyes were on Alistair. When Alistair afforded him a glance, he could see that Ptolemy was giving him a rather odd smile.

"You have not yet told me what you think of your bride-to-be," Ptolemy said, his voice a bit quieter as if they shared a secret.

Alistair's gaze again scanned the room, giving him a few moments to think about a response. What could he say about her? He didn't know much. "My first impressions are good. I am pleased and impressed with what little I know of the Lady Ismene. By all appearances, she will serve well as the wife of a general. She is brave and has the strength of character to make this journey and still face life in a strange place with determination of spirit. A lot of things have been thrown at her in a short amount of time and she has held up quite well. And she is a lovely woman, graceful. I don't think I could have picked a better bride."

He closed his mouth, realizing that he had begun to ramble. But as his thoughts continued to dwell on her, he became all the more perplexed by this woman who was still a mystery to him. Ismene had made some extended day visits to his house to become acquainted with the staff she would be interacting with and to set up her living quarters to her liking. He could tell when she was there or had been there by the demeanor of his staff. His home would become more alive, more exciting. At first, he had credited it to the excitement of the coming nuptials, but it was more than that. It was as if fresh sea air had blown through the house with promises of a good harvest. Once again, he regretted that he had not been able to spend more time with her in order to decode this mystery.

After some moments, Ptolemy broke into Alistair's musings. "Then I can't wait to meet her."

Alistair nodded, still in his thoughts. He was somewhat embarrassed that he had not been paying attention to Ptolemy, so he forced his mind back to the present. When he glanced over at Pharaoh, he had that same odd smile on his face.

"Something I said, my liege?" His face warmed.

"No, not at all," Pharaoh said, but a slight laugh escaped his lips.

Alistair knew the shade of his face deepened, but he shifted his focus elsewhere. He wanted to run a last-minute mental check. Where was Neterka? Dutiful and faithful as ever, he remained stationed by the door awaiting his future mistress's arrival. He held the two precious pieces that would be key in the ceremony.

In that moment, Paki, the servant Pharaoh had chosen to perform as master of ceremonies for the evening, stepped closer to the door and rang a bell to draw everyone's attention.

"The Lady Ismene Gina of Greece," he announced in the loudest voice he could manage.

The doors opened ever so slowly, everyone craning their necks to get a glimpse of this woman who had been the center of so much rumor and speculation.

Alistair made eye contact with Neterka and they moved to the dais. Once the doors were at last opened, Ismene stepped into the light. Every thought flew out of his mind. She was beautiful to behold, even more captivating than he had first thought upon their initial meetings. He noted that the drapes of the Greco-Roman robes had downplayed some of her physical attributes which were now quite well accented by the Egyptian dress.

Pulling his eyes off of her for a moment, he watched as the crowd parted for her to make her way to the dais. His eyes wandered over the crowd. She was, of course, the focus of everyone's attention. He was all too aware of the looks of appreciation she was getting from other men in the room. Seething, he found himself a bit angered at some of the leers. Protective jealousy? This Grecian beauty in all Egyptian finery was stunning, to say the least. And she was walking toward him.

When she lifted her head to meet his eyes, a smile graced her lips—a smile just for him. It took his breath away. There was a desire, a hunger sparked deep within him like he had never known. In that moment, he was struck with the realization that she was going to choose to be his. All of his earlier thoughts of duty and station were but a distant memory as he was overcome with this new feeling. He was honored and amazed that she was to be his wife.

Alistair was not ignorant to the desirable nature of women, but this longing he felt in that moment when her smile reached him went beyond anything physical. It was a strange sensation. Was it the early stirrings of love?

The things he had just finished speaking to Pharaoh about her seemed so insignificant compared to his widening perception of the woman who was drawing ever closer. He felt only *her* in that moment. In a split second this was no longer an arrangement to appease his pharaoh, it was becoming more and more real with every breath he took. Before he knew it, she was but a few breaths away, taking her place opposite him on the dais. Attempting to clear his head of these stray thoughts, he prepared to move into the ceremony.

Alistair stepped forward to address Ismene and the gathering, speaking the traditional words about the courtship and the symbolism of the ring he now held for all to see. This ring, which would stake his claim on her future and bind her to him, was now all the more precious in his hands.

Ismene tried in futility to still her racing heart. She had never enjoyed being the center of attention and here she was, in the midst of all these people, with every eye on her. All too soon she was on the dais, in front of Alistair. His eyes caught hers for a brief moment, his gaze intense. Then he broke it off to step forward to speak.

Ismene didn't understand the words, but Naeemah had already told her what would transpire step by step and was, at that moment, translating behind her.

"Welcome, friends, guests. I am honored by your presence here at this most joyous occasion. I wish to celebrate with you the formalization of my betrothal to the Lady Ismene of Greece. I stand before you with her father's acceptance of my offering of *mahr* and with his consent. It is my wish now to give the Lady Ismene this ring—a gift from the pharaohs to the old and new worlds to represent the immortality of this bond we will make."

Alistair then moved toward Ismene, eyes only on her. They each took the steps necessary to close the gap between them. He said one thing more in Egyptian, but Ismene was now too far away from Naeemah to hear her translation.

Alistair reached for her, taking her hand gently in his. Then he spoke in hushed tones to her in their native tongue.

"I ask your permission, to have you, Ismene, as my wife?" he whispered for her ears alone.

Her eyes locked with his, surprised. This was the traditional Greek request of a father for his daughter's hand in marriage, but he had altered it for her.

He had her hand and the ring poised to slip into place, but he paused, waiting for her response.

"The gods are smiling! I give it."

His eyes glistened as he slipped the ring on her third finger. Before releasing her hand, he squeezed it with gentleness, "The gods are smiling!"

Alistair then turned and beckoned Neterka to come forward and bring him the *shabka*. In that moment, Ismene reeled in the knowledge that she was truly engaged. And not just by some strange ceremony adhered to by some foreign customs, but by her own people's custom. It was all the more real to her, whether she wanted it to be or not.

Moving back toward her, he identified for her and the congregation that it was the *shabka* offering. Then he revealed the most breathtaking, elegant piece of jewelry she had ever seen. It was an Egyptian collar with a gorgeous, skilled layout of beads and gems on an intricate pattern of gold holding them in place.

Ismene felt Naeemah's hands on her neck, removing the simple necklace she now wore so that Alistair could place the *shabka* around her neck. Then his hands were against her skin, clasping the necklace, his face so close to hers. As difficult as it was to meet his eyes, Ismene found herself unable to look away; her eyes were fixed on his. This was the closest they had ever been. She could sense that he was holding his breath and she, too, found herself quite affected by this closeness, fighting the urge to shake her head to clear it.

The moment lasted forever in her mind, yet was over too soon when he broke contact and moved away. She regretted the absence of his hands, but he soon took hold of her hand and, turning back toward the crowd, spoke again, one word. They cheered and applauded in response. Then, from somewhere behind them, she heard music and the crowd shifted as many broke into dancing.

Not everyone cheered or made merry at this most honored celebration. In the darkest corner of the banquet hall, a man fought to contain a snarl that threatened to scramble his features. He knew that he must wait and bide his time—now was not the moment and this was not the place. Soon, he promised himself. Soon.

Ismene was drawn in to the merriment of the people around her. All of the party guests were dancing and singing with a tune that lightened her heart. Glancing around the room, she took notice of the people present. No servants had been invited to join in the festivities, save Neterka, who was serving as Alistair's second hand, and Alonah, who was hers. She was unsure how Naeemah was classified, but she, too, stayed for the celebration. What a gift she had been. Even now, she was by Ismene's side, pointing out things of interest for her.

As Ismene's gaze wandered about the room, her eyes came to rest on Alistair. There he stood, across the room, talking with some of the heads of state. These men, who were rather valued in the kingdom, did not take time out to speak with her, but they were all too happy to monopolize Alistair's time. Seeming to sense Ismene's gaze, Alistair lifted his head from the conversation that was no doubt of great importance and turned to look in her direction. A slow smile spread across his face when his eyes met hers. She offered him a shy smile in return. Then, much to her surprise, he excused himself from the company of those all-important men and made his way over to where she stood.

Naeemah allowed her comment to trail off as she stepped back from Ismene, who paid her little mind. She was concentrating on Alistair's approaching form with great trepidation. Her heart raced. How was she to respond to such a gesture? Why would he abandon such powerful people to seek her out?

At last approaching her, Alistair stretched out his hand toward her. "It is a shame that the most beautiful woman at the party is on the sidelines, gazing at the scenery. You must dance. And I would ask if I might have that honor?"

Her breath caught in her throat and her face felt warm at his compliment.

"Come, milady. Everyone wishes us to make merry together," he said, his voice warm and light. But it deepened as he said, "As do I."

She hesitated. Not because she didn't want to dance, but rather she was attempting to still her breathing.

Alistair took one step closer to her, raising an eyebrow in question. It was a rather attractive expression on him.

Unable to refuse, she slipped her hand into his and allowed him to lead her toward the mass of swaying Egyptians.

Part of her had been afraid that she would feel lost and overwhelmed in a crowd of people so foreign to her. But with Alistair holding her hand and guiding her movements, her anxiety was the last thing on her mind. She was caught up in the shared joy of those around her. They seemed all too thrilled that she would join them as they celebrated her. And for the first time, she could imagine calling this place home and claiming these people as her own. Taken aback, the thought scared her. But why? Shouldn't she want for this to be a good transition? Didn't she want to feel a part of the people she would be spending the rest of her life with? Why did she feel so guilty then? Like a traitor? Still, she wanted to hold back a piece of herself from these people, from this man.

The evening wore on until the earliest hours of the morning. That was when Ismene made her way to her bedchambers. She was relieved that her bed was here in the palace due to the hour in which they retired. This evening had been full of fun and strange new emotions. What was it that she had felt when Alistair stood so close to her, touching her neck to put the *shabka* on her? She touched the necklace even then as she remembered the tingling sensations in her skin responding to his touch. Was it mere physical attraction? Or more than that?

Alonah waltzed into the bedchambers, still dancing. Ismene stifled a laugh at the display. Her handmaiden was perhaps a little too light-hearted from a bit too much wine. But she was still able to help Ismene go through her evening routine of washing off the face paint, dressing for bed, and applying oils to her skin. It was all just a bit sillier than usual. That was fine with Ismene. In the end, she could not stop herself from sharing a laugh with Alonah, and it served to grant her a reprieve from these new emotions for a little while.

It wasn't long, however, before it was time for Alonah to leave for her own quarters and Ismene was left to crawl into bed and face the still, quiet night. As Alonah blew out the last candle and closed the door, Ismene's thoughts were again on Alistair and the days to come.

This would be her last night here in her garden sanctuary. Pharaoh had insisted that he be allowed to throw the bachelor party for Alistair, so they would swap places. Alistair would come to the palace and Ismene would move back into Alistair's grand estate. Starting tomorrow night, the eve of her wedding, she would call the noble mansion her home. That thought overwhelmed her, but not as much as what it would entail. She would be, not only at home with Alistair, but would also be his wife. His *wife*. Her face warmed as the full implication of that filled her. A great fear flooded her mind and body. What was she going to do?

The hour was quite late...or rather, quite early when Alonah walked to her quarters. She sensed that she was, indeed, a little inebriated. It had been a fun party. There had been dancing! And one of the Egyptian soldiers had asked her to dance—twice. He had a handsome face with strong angles and kind, dark eyes. Alonah had blushed when he'd first locked eyes with her as she had found him to be rather good-looking. So caught up in her memories of the earlier encounter, she didn't even realize that she was swaying as if to the music she had just been dancing to.

All of a sudden, two men were on either side of her, steadying her.

"Whoa there, milady, are you all right?" the man on the right said as he gripped her arms. His hands were firm.

She caught herself and attempted to pull her arms free. "Yes, I'm quite fine, thank you. Just caught up in the music, I suppose."

"Oh, we know about getting caught up, don't we?" the man on the left asked, his face was close to hers, uncomfortably close. His voice was husky and she could smell that he'd had too much to drink as well.

"And rhythm." The other laughed.

She struggled to free her arms, but they were being held in viselike grips. "Please let me go," she pleaded. "You are hurting me!"

"Do you suppose it's true what they say about Greek women?" the man on the right stated, moving a hand to wrap around her waist.

Pulling in futility again, she attempted to jerk away from his hand. "Please stop!" Her voice was firm, but she knew it quivered. She was becoming afraid.

"And what's that?" a voice boomed from behind them.

They all twisted their heads around to see who had come. It was the man she had danced with!

"Jabari," one of the men slurred. "Care to join us?"

"You're drunk, Fenyang, and not thinking straight. I suggest you release the lady before you give someone reason to think you are exhibiting conduct unbefitting a military man." Jabari moved closer to them, inserting himself between Alonah and Fenyang, who had loosened his grip on her.

Jabari then placed a hand on the other man's hands. "Sebak, go sleep off the wine."

The man's words seemed to be penetrating the alcohol haze around their brains. The man dropped his hands too. Jabari then moved Alonah away from the men, his movements slow, keeping himself between them and her.

Fenyang and Sebak stood still for a handful of seconds as if trying to decide what to do next.

Jabari placed a hand on his sword. "Go on to the barracks, men."

They seemed a little unsure if that's what they wanted to do, but in the end they sauntered off in that direction.

The handsome soldier then shifted his attention back to Alonah. "Are you all right, milady?"

She nodded, her face warming at his address. "I am but a servant girl," she said, averting her gaze as she rubbed her arms, trying to hide. "So, please, it's just 'Alonah.'"

He glanced down at her arms where the men had held her so tightly. Alonah groaned; there must be red marks. She would have bruises in the morning for sure. But if that was all she had remaining from this late-night encounter, she was lucky. Jabari had come upon them at the right moment. Things could have gotten much worse.

Jabari's eyes sought hers once more. "You are as beautiful as a queen tonight, Alonah. So I will address you as I wish, milady. May I escort you to your quarters?"

Her heart thundered in her chest. She feared he would be able to hear it!

"Please," was all she managed to get out.

He offered her his arm to lean on. She took it gratefully.

A frown was etched into Alistair's features. The sight before him caused his whole body to tense up. It was a sight that had greeted his staff early that morning. Neterka had been the only one brave enough to bring him out there to see it.

"Get it off," he said, each word enunciated and pushed out of his mouth with force. There were plenty of servants gathered around, but he spoke to no one in particular.

On the inner wall of their great garden two symbols, two words, were splayed across the wall in what could only be blood. The thick, red, viscous liquid had dried as it ran, in stripes reaching to the ground.

A din of whispered conversation among the servants could be heard, but only just. No one wanted to speak out for fear of enraging the general further. Many of the servants were unable to read Greek and had no idea what important message was scarred into their master's most prized sanctuary. As if the vandalism alone wasn't enough to evoke a great anger in him, the message itself had pushed him closer to the edge of violence. They had never seen their kind master in such a state.

"What is everybody..." Ismene's voice interrupted their musings. No one, not even Alistair, had even noticed that she had arrived at the grand estate, least of all made it all the way out to the gardens. Her voice, which started light and happy, trailed off as she noticed the source of everyone's fixation.

There were many audible gasps as the servants, like Alistair, turned and saw Ismene's paled face, her mouth moving as if trying to form words, though none came forth.

Alistair rushed over to her, "Ismene, don't look...it's..." he said, trying to turn her away, to go back in direction she had just come.

It was only then that he realized—the message—it was for her. Ismene and Alonah came to the gardens each day to check on her tiger lilies. This wall faced the entrance into the gardens closest to her bedchambers, the entrance she came through every day. How did anyone outside of his house and Pharaoh's know that? His heart sank. There was a leak in one of these houses.

Ismene stood her ground, refusing to let Alistair turn her away. She was shaking.

"Who...what...I don't understand," she managed after several seconds. As she glanced up at him, he could see tears in her dark eyes as she repeated the terrible words that were written there. "Go home?"

His heart ached for her.

"Who wants me to go home?" she asked, voice breaking, clearly injured by the implications.

He pulled her into his firm embrace.

She began to cry.

"Shh, shh." He soothed her, rubbing her shoulders. "It's all right. It doesn't mean anything."

He knew it wasn't all right. She was in a foreign land, a place she was still having great difficulty adjusting to—a place where she was surrounded by people she didn't know and who were so different from her. She was still adapting to these new people, a new culture, a new way of doing things, a new government...a new way of life. This must have been her worst fear confirmed. Not only did she not know these people, not only were they foreign in many ways, they did not want her here.

He kissed the top of her head. "Don't give it any thought, Ismene. Remember last night. Remember how the people cheered for you. They loved you!"

Her crying stilled for a moment.

"This is the work of one person who is dissatisfied with *me* and is doing this to get back at *me*. This is not about you. I promise," he lied. He was quite certain this was at least the truth in part. But he feared that it may be the work of the Alexandrian mob and it may well be aimed at her.

Ismene allowed him to comfort her a little longer, but before he was ready to let go, she started to pull away. With reluctance, he released his hold on her. He then tugged on her arm more firmly until she was facing the direction she had just come, her back to the wall and the horrible message.

"Alonah, please take the Lady Ismene to her bedchambers. I'll have some refreshments brought for her." He made sure that there was no room for argument in his voice.

Alonah took Ismene's arm and led her back inside, away from the small crowd and the offensive markings.

Alistair watched them go. Once they were inside and a safe distance away, he spun back toward the small crowd of servants.

"Get. It. Off." His voice sharp and his words heated; the words penetrated the air, thick with apprehension, before he stormed off.

CHAPTER 4

A Moment of Remembrance

ALL WAS STILL AND SILENT IN THIS PART OF THE GRAND estate. There was no one in sight. Ismene stepped into the shadows, clutching her small box close to herself as she crept down the hallway, moving farther from the sounds of merrymaking and deeper into the quiet darkness in the closed-off recesses of the great house. She had escaped her own bridal party. With any luck, Alonah had been the only one who noticed her slip out.

Even though she was the guest of honor, the women had been so caught up in the merriment of the occasion and the party itself, as it had carried on for a few hours now. Ismene doubted she would be missed for some time. Alonah would answer any questions about her whereabouts with a carefully worded white lie. Her reasons for withdrawing from the party were her own. It was doubtful any of these Egyptian women would understand. She was to be married in the morning and there was something she needed to do.

Moving through the inner courtyard toward her destination, Ismene gazed down at the small box she had borne with her across the desert and into this foreign land. These were some of the most precious things in her life. So much so that much of her loathed what she was about to do. It was but a small comfort that she was keeping a long-held tradition of her people. This would be a chance to feel connected to her homeland and people. But at what cost?

Ismene slipped through the vestibule and out of the house. The wind whipped her in the face. It was a warm breeze that greeted her as she crossed the yard. She fought to keep from being distracted by the stars overhead, instead forcing her attention toward the small private chapel in front of her. Testing the door, she found that it opened without effort. Taking a deep breath to brace herself, she entered the small space.

The one-room chapel was lit by a lone candle in the center of the south wall on a simple wooden stand. There was another candle waiting on a small table in the center of the room. Kneeling down in front of the altar, she set her small box in front of her, but she did not release it. These were things she had kept safe for so many years, for this most specific night. Just as so many other Grecian girls had as they grew up. She remembered coming to this box before, opening it to look upon these things with hopeful anticipation for this day with a little girl's heart full of dreams. Her eyes began to water at the memories of that little girl's fantasies of love and marriage. How young, how ignorant she had been.

Shifting her attention away from the objects, she took the candle from the table and lit it from the eternal flame that now no longer solely lit the room. She brought the candle to light the space around the altar and bowed her head in reverence. Ismene had not believed in any gods or higher deities since she was a child, but this ceremony held meaning for her nonetheless. After several moments of stillness, head bowed so she could center and calm herself while still showing reverence, she lifted her head and moved the box toward herself once again.

Ismene reached into the box and lifted out the first item—her *toga praetexta*, her childhood toga. It was white in the innocence of her childhood, ceremonially clean and pure. She laid it on the altar, smoothing over it with her hand, releasing it from her possession. It amazed her how well kept the piece of clothing had been—first by her mother and then by herself. There was not a blemish on it. Her eyes then skimmed the special toys of her youth that were chosen for this ceremony. Each brought back memories of Greece and of time spent with her family. Once again, her thoughts were filled with memories of the time she had shared with her brothers, stories told by her parents and teachers, and days spent in the sun with no cares or worries in the world.

One by one, she placed them on the altar until only one remained. She lifted it from the box with great care—it was a Pegasus. Ismene remembered the day her mother gave her this statuette of the winged horse of old and how fascinated she had been. Running her hand over the smooth wood, her father's voice floated over her mind, telling her the legend of the magnificent animal once again. She and Thelopolis had been on more searches for the mythical creature than she could count.

Bringing the wooden replica to her chest, she held it to her. Tears brimmed her eyes at the memories. This had been her favorite toy, and she was not surprised that there was so much sentiment attached to it. The things that she had treasured the most about her childhood were wrapped up in this one object. Thoughts of Thelopolis also filled her mind, and, with them, an ache in her heart seemed to throb. It was harder than she had ever imagined it would be to lay aside her childhood and face a future with a man that she had known but two-week's time. Ismene clung to the winged horse and let the emotions pour over her for just a moment, unaware that she had an audience.

Alistair slipped through the entryway without making a sound. Leaving his horse tied outside of the grand entrance lest he risk announcing himself, he stepped onto the grounds of the house that would no longer be his alone. He'd excused himself from a celebration given in his honor at Pharaoh's house, insisting to Ptolemy that there were papers in his office he needed to pass on to his second-in-command before the wedding ceremony.

In all truthfulness, he had been relieved to be able to escape for a minute to clear his mind. So much had happened in his life these last two weeks and it had changed him more than he would have ever expected. Tomorrow would be both the culmination of all the goings-on of these last weeks and the beginning of a whole new life.

When he had first set out to fulfill Ptolemy's wishes that he marry, he had thought it would be as simple as acquiring a new housemate and that his life would continue with little to no alteration. Yet from the moment he had met Ismene, he had known his early assumptions were wrong. Even so, he had still tried to deny that she was having such an effect on him, but just thinking about tomorrow and all that it would bring overwhelmed him. It wasn't just the way things would change that brought a wave of anxiety, he knew, it was also the idea of what she would be to him...she would be his. That thought brought with it a stirring in his heart that he had never known.

Approaching the house, he determined that he would get in and out without notice. It was not his intention or desire to disturb the bridal party. Even now, he could hear the party in the distant corner of the house. Alistair hoped it was everything Ismene could want, and that she was able to make acquaintances with the women who would be her neighbors and, perhaps, her friends.

Stepping closer to the entrance of the house proper, he spotted a light coming from the private sanctuary. This was not odd. The chapel was lit by an eternal flame. But it did not escape his keen notice that the light was brighter than usual, and that was odd. The servants did not use the sanctuary. It was for his use, though he did not use it, and for his guests, whom he expected to all be at the festivities. The military man in him took over, his curiosity got the better of him, and he moved over to the small building to peer through the cracked door. The scene before him caused him to catch his breath.

There she was—Ismene—her form silhouetted by the eternal flame and her features lighted by the candle on the altar. She sat in the midst of a tradition he was quite aware of, but was surprised to see being performed. A Greek bride-to-be would put on the altar the things of her childhood the night before the wedding to symbolize the putting aside of the past in recognition and preparation of the future. It had not occurred to him that she would go through with this ceremony.

Ismene must have saved these things for many years for this, the night before her wedding, hoping and praying for the day this ceremony would come to pass. She had bothered to bring them all the way here to give them up for a man she would have known only a couple of weeks. His heart was moved as he thought about how she was going through this most sacred ceremony alone.

In Greece, she would enjoy the support and company of friends and family. A bride such as she would have been praised for the honor she bestowed on her husband-to-be and it would be an important rite of passage, every bit as much so as the wedding ceremony itself. But here she was, alone. Ismene hadn't made a show about this, hadn't told any of the servants of the house that they may accompany her. Alonah wasn't even here with her. This was a ceremony she was performing for her own sake, so that she would be prepared for her life with him. He knew this symbolic ceremony was more than a tradition to her; it was necessary. She was willing to give up her past for him, for her life with him.

As Alistair looked on, Ismene was holding on to an object he couldn't quite discern. She was hugging it to her chest. Looking at her face in the candlelight, he saw tears in her eyes. The memories flooding her mind, and the realization that what she held was in the past and that she could not return there, were obvious in the pain on her face. It was all he could do to keep from going to her and gathering her in his arms. This was something she had wanted to do alone and without notice. He would let her have that. He watched her movements, transfixed, as she pulled the wooden toy away from herself, ran her hand over its smooth surface once more before laying it on the altar. Tears continued to fall down her face, and she made no move to wipe them away.

Alistair watched from his place of silent vigil as Ismene reached into the box one last time and pulled out her *bulla*, her symbolic knife of protection. Eyes closed, she spoke the words that would seal the ceremony. The ritual was complete: first she had put aside her childhood innocence, then her past, and now she would place her life in the hands of her husband-to-be. She was passing into his protection. As she spoke the last of the ceremonial words, she laid the *bulla* on the altar.

Taking in a slow, deep breath, Alistair was moved with the enormous responsibility he was taking on. He hadn't realized until this moment that another human being was placing her continued existence in his care. In that moment, he also knew that he would never let anything bring harm to her. The rite was complete, and she paused.

All of a sudden, he was aware that he was invading a private moment for her and felt that he should have left long before. With much effort, he shifted his eyes away and, after taking a few more deep breaths to steady his thumping heart, made his way from the sanctuary doorway toward the main house. There was the matter he had to attend to and now another task for him to complete.

Ismene opened her eyes. *Someone was watching her.* She whirled around. There was no one there. *Of course not!* No one but Alonah knew where she was, and her maidservant wouldn't have betrayed her secret. It must be all of the memories, perhaps they created the sense of others surrounding her. Unbidden, another thought crossed her mind. *I wish Thelopolis could be here.*

Shaking her head at that, she let out a long sigh. It was time to let that go, to let him go. Reaching into a fold in her drape, she pulled out the letters Thelopolis had written her. From the first tingling of puppy love to the deeper emotion they now shared, these letters had been so dear to her. These were the things that were closest to her heart—even more so than the Pegasus. Now was the time to give them up. She had to give up the hope of a future with Thelopolis. Her heart belonged with him, it always would, but her future was here with Alistair. She must release to whatever higher power there was her relationship with Thelopolis. Forevermore, it would be in the past. They could never be more than childhood playmates and onetime friends. Ismene was committing her mind and her will to Alistair.

Placing a final kiss for Thelopolis on the letters that she had pored over countless nights, she let the paper linger near her face, feeling the roughness of the parchment. Every word, every pen stroke was etched into her heart, but they would no longer be hers. She placed them on top of the *bulla*, next to the Pegasus, pausing only for a moment before removing her hand. Then she stood up, gazing at the precious things one final time before she blew out the single flame that lit the altar and left them behind forever.

The household servants would come by in the early morning and would do away with these things. She didn't want to think about that, though. It was enough to know that they no longer belonged to her. Stepping out into the darkness of the evening, she made her way back toward the house and to her bridal party. Ismene was determined to put a smile on her face and finish out this evening with as much grace as she could muster.

True to form, the investigator had made himself a nuisance around the house, especially these last few days as everyone was preparing for the wedding and welcoming the lady of the house back in. Pulling aside servants at will and, as Alistair saw it, harassing them did not serve to further those goals, rather it hindered them. But on this of all nights, Neterka had notified Alistair that the investigator wanted to speak with *him*. This was absurd. Pharaoh had insisted on two things to him: one —that he, himself, was not suspect, and two—that he was to cooperate with the investigation. So, he would abide by Pharaoh's command and submit himself to questioning, but he had sent word to Pharaoh that he was being "interviewed," as the investigator preferred to say it. Was this necessary? And on the eve of his wedding no less? No sooner had he arrived at his home from his night at Pharaoh's palace, when Neterka was escorting him to his bedchambers, explaining that the investigator needed to speak with him.

Alistair's thoughts were cut short as Chigaru, special investigator of the secret police, walked into the receiving room as if he were in his own home. This was perhaps the most irritating thing about him—the way he waltzed about Alistair's house as if it were his.

"I see you continue to make yourself comfortable in my home," Alistair said in a gruff voice. He sat on one of the lounges.

"Is that the proper attitude to hold during this important investigation?" It was a snide remark. Chigaru took a seat across from Alistair.

"I have obeyed Pharaoh's orders to the letter. I have commanded my servants to answer questions whenever you pose them. And I have neither barred you from accessing any area nor have I blocked you from doing your duty."

"But your attitude could influence my investigation." Chigaru leaned forward as he said this, with a look of confidence that suggested he was holding all the cards and, in fact, enjoyed holding people under his thumb.

"As I have stated, I have followed Pharaoh's orders to the letter. That doesn't mean I have to be subservient to your paltry hunger for power. If my gestures were not clear enough, then let me put them into words. I find your manner reprehensible and pathetic. If your mission is to intimidate me and have me grovel, then you have sorely failed. If you have actual questions that serve the security of Egypt, then ask them and be done with your 'investigation.'" Alistair was tired of this game Chigaru was playing with him.

Chigaru seemed a little unsure, but continued. "Pharaoh has granted me broad powers to find this traitor, and such resistance is not appreciated." He was espousing a boilerplate statement and Alistair knew it, but his delivery was somewhat timid in comparison to his earlier assertions.

"I'm sure you have said that to many in the past. My loyalty to Pharaoh is not in question. He told me this himself, so if you check your orders, you will find that to be true. Ask your questions." Alistair had gained the upper hand, and he could see it in Chigaru's eyes as the man leaned back with a slightly trembling lip, which stilled soon enough. Chigaru may not be getting anything of value from Alistair, but he was able to mask his dissatisfaction about the turn this interview had taken.

Alistair could see that Chigaru was struggling to keep the conversation going. "Can you confirm the dates when each member of your staff joined your household?"

"Neterka can provide those dates. He is most efficient at managing my home's affairs," Alistair spoke as if bored with the man.

"I see. Has any of them ever expressed discontent with the policies of Pharaoh?" Chigaru licked his lips; his questions were coming out faster.

"Never. They are the most loyal people I have ever had under my care." For his part, Alistair's responses remained even and steady.

"How well do you know the servants that the Lady Ismene brought?"

Alistair started to rise out of his seat when this question was posed. His nostrils flared and he felt heat in his face. In all likelihood, his anger was apparent to everyone in the room. "The lady is not a part of this. We shall not discuss her or her servants."

"My General." Chigaru's face broke out in a smug smile at Alistair's reaction. "Surely *everyone* in this household must be considered? In fact, I doubt you even know the answer to my question, since she has been here less than a month."

Alistair remained silent as he attempted to contain the emotion welling up within himself.

For lack of response from Alistair, Chigaru continued. "You know, that almost sounds like an emotional response from someone who does not *want* to know the answer." At this point, he was looking down, as if he were writing part of a report and speaking off the top of his head.

Alistair felt as if he were going to tear off this man's head and could visualize himself doing it, but his military instincts kicked in. "You are simply trying to goad me into fury. It is your hope that I will become upset and lose myself. But you forget yourself. I happen to know we are looking for a connection to the Alexadrian mob. The lady is Greek and would have no possible connections to the mob. How could she carry any sympathy for their movement?" Alistair eased back into his chair and, realizing the focal point of Chigaru's interviewing tactics, rested in his seat.

He knew then that Chigaru was winging it. He in no way had any substantive questions for Alistair. His attack at the Lady Ismene exposed his inability to uncover a shred of information from any of the staff.

"Are there any more questions?" Alistair asked; it was his turn to give Chigaru a smug look. He crossed his arms and all but sneered at the man who had turned his home upside down.

"Not at this time, but if I have more, I will be in contact." Chigaru wrapped up his interview with Alistair as fast as possible, trying to save what face he could by leaving with the boasting sense of strength that he had arrived with. Only it didn't work; Alistair could see right through it.

CHAPTER 5

A New Dawn

STREAMS OF DAWN PEEKED IN THROUGH THE WINDOW. Ismene stirred as the light grazed her face in the early morning hours. Alonah had parted the curtains so that the sunlight could awaken her ever so gently. But Ismene did *not* welcome the interruption after her sleepless night of tossing and turning. Now that she was awake, her mind once again filled with the struggles that had kept her from sleep the night before. She was dreading what lay ahead of her. She had put aside all things of the past last night; she had only what was to come. So she forced her mind to turn toward the preparations for this day.

After some moments of lying in the bed, staring up at the ceiling, Ismene sat up, pulling her legs over the side and stepping to the window to gaze into the garden in the distance. The gardens would become a place of sanctuary for her. She did feel a sense of peace there among the strange but beautiful buds and blossoms. When everything settled down, she would ask Alistair if she might have a hand in tending more of the garden.

Creak. The sound of her bedchamber door opening distracted Ismene from her musings. She turned toward the intrusion. Alonah led a parade of servants carrying pitchers full of water to her tub. They were followed by others who carried rich perfumes and scents.

Ismene had known that she would be cleansed this morning before her wedding. What was the Egyptian custom like? The Grecian ritual of cleansing involved waters from the Kallirroe Spring. Every bride bathed in these waters on the day of their wedding. Sighing, Ismene felt her heart drop in her chest. Perhaps there was a spring of such significance in Egypt.

Alonah glanced up from her supervision for a moment with a smile for her mistress. It was as if she held a great secret, and it intrigued Ismene.

"Why are you smiling so?" she asked her handmaiden.

Alonah picked up a small pitcher from within the grouping of pitchers being added to the bath water. She looked at the pitcher in her hands and then up at Ismene, her face filled with emotion. Happiness? Yes. But something else was there too.

"Milady, these are waters from the Kallirroe Spring."

Ismene's eyes widened. "The Kallirroe Spring? But how?"

With Ismene watching on, Alonah opened the pitcher with care and poured the precious waters into the tub.

"All I can say, milady," Alonah said, turning back to face her, "is that I have been charged with preparing you for your wedding day. That includes the washing in these sacred waters, does it not?"

Ismene nodded, dumbfounded and filled with amazement. Her eyes watered at the considerate attention bestowed upon her. Who? Her father? Alonah? "They came all the way from Greece? How did you get them here?"

"I cannot disclose that information at my own discretion," Alonah said, smiling. She went back to directing the other maidservants, but Ismene was certain she saw a glittering of moisture in Alonah's eyes as well.

Who could have afforded such an expensive venture? Alistair? But why would he go to all that expense for her? She could not imagine. It would have taken much time and effort to acquire these waters and have them transported. Could he truly have cared about something so...so...and how would she ever thank him?

The wedding chariot kicked up sand as they made their way toward Alistair's estate. Ismene avoided Alistair's eyes as they were driven. She had been doing so since the simple, well-celebrated ceremony. It had been beautiful and planned out perfectly, but there had been so much more going on today. A large part of her wanted to deny that this was happening—not the marriage, but what she was feeling every time their eyes met. There was something different in his gaze today, something she couldn't put her finger on. Alistair had not let her wander from him at all. He had held her hand the entire time, even when not necessary, as if he were afraid to let go, lest she run away.

Ismene was distracted from her thoughts by the loud music and singing that surrounded them—joyful music and joyful people. It was difficult to concentrate on anything. These people seemed to love any reason to celebrate. That thought brought a smile to her face. They were rather thrilled for their general, whom they considered so kindly. This was quite evident to her whenever anyone spoke about or to him. He was well liked by the people of the kingdom.

Such thoughts drew Ismene's eyes to look over at the man who was now her husband, according to Egyptian law. What was he feeling? Not knowing the answer to that question and having the same question posed to herself without an answer scared her. His arm was still around her waist, steadying her as the chariot bobbed and jerked along the pathway that, though smoothed out, was quite bumpy. These roads, after all, were not paved. She couldn't deny that the feeling of his strong arm holding her was pleasant and comforting. Alistair's arm tightened around her, and she prepared herself for a random obstruction in the path or another jolt, but none came. Her attention was drawn forward to find the reason for the change in his posture. The house was now visible in the distance.

Tension was building through the taut muscles in Alistair's arm, and Ismene wondered at the source of it. Ismene knew her own body was feeling flushed with anticipation and anxiety upon seeing the house, nervous about what the next hours would bring. Was that what filled Alistair's mind? Was he nervous, too? The brave general, leader of the great Egyptian army—was it even possible he could harbor any such emotion regarding a lone woman?

This was the part of the day that she dreaded—when everyone would leave and it would be she and Alistair all alone...alone with these confusing looks and gestures. She wasn't even sure what she was feeling toward her new husband. Many emotions played around her heart—anxiety, nostalgia, and sadness dominated. It was true that she was missing her family and felt some level of uneasiness with the faces of all of the strange people around her, but there was more going on in her heart. Something she couldn't identify.

As the chariot slowed, their approach ever nearer, her reflections were swallowed up by a rush of raw emotion. Dwelling on thoughts of him had given her but brief respite from her own trepidations regarding what would be. She was overcome by them now and felt a little light-headed. As if he sensed her weakening state, Alistair tightened his arm to steady her.

Once they stopped, Ismene glanced up into his eyes to thank him and felt her heart beating faster. This did not help her light-headedness. She moved her hands to his arm, hoping to communicate she was fine and ready for him to remove his arm from her waist. A strange cold passed across her body when he did so.

Stepping down out of the chariot, he then reached up to aid her descent. There was no avoiding his eyes as he lifted her with his hands on her waist to set her in front of him. So close. He was so close to her, and she was unable to avoid gazing into his eyes. She remembered the kiss they had shared earlier that day at the ceremony. It had been quick, too quick. But it had caused her heart to beat faster, much like it was now. Was he going to kiss her again?

Alistair's hands moved to clasp hers as the crowd's attention shifted to focus on the house. He led her toward the front door and she took the opportunity to turn her attention downward, making sure she did not step on the hem of the Egyptian wedding dress with its long, cool, soft fabric overlain with a sheer, almost glossy cover. Just as all clothing made for this heated desert environment, even the two layers were light enough to allow her to feel every breeze. Even the bead net, though it lay heavier over the dress, was not too cumbersome.

The crowd parted to permit them a clear path to the doorway. Was it just two weeks ago that Ismene was in this same spot, gazing over this house for the first time? And now here she was, everything was said and done, and she was soon to become a wife in every sense of the word. It frightened her. But she could no more stop time than halt the sun.

At last, they were at the entrance to the house and turned to bid the wedding party good-bye. Alistair's arm slid once again around Ismene's waist. The people cheered for the couple. She stole a glance at Alistair who was nodding and smiling at his neighbors, friends, and townspeople. They were delighted for their general and his new bride. These people meant a lot to him, and she could sense that he was touched by their attentions and well wishes.

As if he felt her gaze upon him, Alistair turned to look into Ismene's eyes. He did not, and could not hide all of the emotions there from her, but so many played across his features that she could no more decipher his feelings than she could her own. Smiling at her, he moved his face toward her to place a kiss on the side of her face and raised her hand to his lips to plant a kiss there as well. She did not have to look too deeply to see that he was proud of his bride and honored to have her at his side. And that pleased her.

Turning back toward the crowd, Alistair spoke to them in their tongue. They cheered again, and he waved at them all one last time. Ismene followed suit, all smiles and waves for these people who found such contentment in wishing the best for them in their new life. Then Alistair spun her toward the entrance to the house and they moved away from the crowd, which continued to applaud and shout after them until they were out of sight.

Once inside and away from the clamor, there was silence as they moved toward Alistair's bedchambers. Anxiety once again filled Ismene, more with each step they took. She had spent a great amount of time preparing herself mentally for this evening and she would not fail herself now. Fighting down the tidal wave of panic, she took a deep breath. When the entrance to the outer bedchambers was in sight, Alistair turned to face her. He almost seemed to be searching for words himself. Perhaps he was just as nervous as she. That calmed her even more.

"Ismene, is there anything you need?" His voice, firm and gentle, betrayed a slight tremble. "Can I get you some refreshment?"

She found a smile for him. "Some fruit?"

He nodded. They had reached the door to his outer bedchambers, and, before turning to get the fruit, he said, "Please make yourself comfortable."

Ismene nodded and watched Alistair walk down the hall until he was out of sight. Then she headed off, almost at a sprint, toward her own bedchambers.

Alistair returned with the fruit and a bowl of lotus blooms. He had instructed the servants to make themselves unseen this evening, more for his sake than Ismene's. Stepping into the outer bedchambers from the hallway, he was surprised that she was not seated on her favorite lounger. Confused, he set the fruit on the stand and glanced about the room.

"Ismene?"

She was not in the outer chambers. Moving toward the inner chamber, he continued to search, growing more and more troubled by the second. Glancing into the room, he saw no one.

"Ismene?" he called again, a bit louder. His heart was sinking. Where had she gone? Had he scared her away?

"I'm here," he heard her voice from behind.

Relieved and confused, he turned around. The sight that greeted him stopped him where he stood and took his breath.

Ismene was at the door to the outer chamber, standing before him. She had abandoned her Egyptian wedding dress for a wedding toga. The bowl of lotus petals slipped from his fingers and crashed to the floor. But he didn't notice, he was so captivated by her. He couldn't deny the growing urgency to make her his wife, but was determined that he would not hurt or scare her.

Ismene stepped toward him. Taking his strong hand in hers, she met his crystal blue eyes full on and spoke to him the words that were as old as Grecian civilization.

"When you are Alistair, I am Ismene."

He stared at her in awe. She never ceased to amaze him. This was the Greek bride's traditional identification with her groom, the crux of the

Greek wedding ceremony. It indicated the bride's willingness to enter her husband's family. But in that moment, it meant so much more to him. Entwining their fingers, he pulled her toward himself. As he lifted his free hand to touch her face, he could feel that she was trembling. The last thing he wanted was for her to be afraid, so he leaned toward her and kissed her. A soft, gentle kiss.

Alistair felt her melt into him as his arms enveloped her. From the moment his lips touched hers, he knew there was no turning back. He attempted to soothe her with his kiss and make his hands work with gentleness, smoothing over her arms, her back such that he might offer her comfort. It took much effort to restrain himself. With slow movements, he pulled her toward the inner bedchambers.

Urging Ismene to sit on the bed for greater comfort, he continued to calm her with his caring hands on her face, shoulders, and arms, neither pushing nor demanding, but patient and kind. The kisses they shared excited him and yet they were not nearly enough. With a boldness that surprised him, she wrapped her arms around his neck and pulled him closer to herself to deepen the kiss. Lifting her, Alistair laid her on the bed and leaned over her, careful not to break contact. He could sense her fear subsiding, but her anxiety remained.

Pulling back to look down at Ismene, Alistair saw the apprehension and reluctance in her eyes, but he could sense her response to his touch. His eyes took in her gaze and drank in her beauty. The features he had come to know so well were stark against the bed of dark curls that surrounded her and framed her face. Something caught his eye—the blunt ends from where a few tresses had been removed by a knife or sword. It caused him to pause for a moment. Then he remembered the offering of hair to signify the passing from virginity to wifehood.

As if noticing Alistair's attention on her hair, Ismene moved a hand to reach up and cover the blunt end of the severed tresses. He halted her hand with one of his. Playing back her ceremony the night before in his mind's eye, a tenderness for her welled up within him and his heart ached for her and what she had given up for him. At the same time, his heart swelled with pride at the dedication of the woman who had chosen to be his wife. Alistair lifted the offended tress and, eyes back on hers, pressed them to his lips.

"Ismene..." he breathed into the hair.

Her eyes questioned him. He let the hair fall and traced the side of her face with his fingers.

"When you are Ismene, I am Alistair."

Ismene's eyes widened as he echoed her earlier declaration. And he knew why. It was not typical for a man to identify with his wife the same way she had done earlier. Women were considered, at least in their culture, to be weaker, lesser somehow. How could he make her see that he did not view her in any such light? He admired and respected her. That's why he was making this statement, this commitment to her. Her sacrifices had touched him.

Without any further prompting, she reached up and cupped the side of his face, reaching around behind his head and gently pulling him back toward herself in a deep kiss. He knew then. Any trace of hesitation that had remained in her was gone.

Nassor paced back and forth at Sefu's house as his thoughts ran rampant. *What was going to happen? Nothing...it had all come to nothing!*

"Calm yourself!" Sefu said from his seat nearby. "You're going to wear a hole in the floor."

Nassor halted before realizing Sefu was teasing him. He grimaced. Nassor was not in the mood to be trifled with.

"What did you think would happen?" Sefu had been on the edge of his seat, disturbed by Nassor's behavior, but he now leaned back, observing, waiting.

"I don't know!" Nassor was annoyed. Sefu was needling him. He had hoped it would all end, but he would not betray his thoughts to Sefu.

"*He* knew it would require more than a simple writing on the wall. Come now, Nassor, we're talking about a general. It's not like we trashed a merchant's fruit stand, or tied up some foreigner outside the city and took his camel. Surely you did not expect it to all end so nicely and expect that soldier to tuck tail and run?"

Nassor heaved a sigh of defeat, at last taking a seat opposite his partner. Sefu was right. He just didn't want to admit it. It wasn't that he thought it would have all ended. He just resented taking further steps.

"What of the others?" Sefu was now showing clear signs of being annoyed. Nassor's mood seemed contagious. "Are they as restless as you?"

"We are *all* prepared to do what we must," Nassor insisted.

"Then why are you here?"

"I just need to double-check the orders." Nassor met Sefu's eyes with more confidence than he felt.

"Nothing has changed. Do I have to hold your hand through every step of this?" Sefu's voice was strained.

"Of course not. I can do this. It is Egypt that I serve," he spoke with a sense of patriotism, meek though it was.

"Then proceed with the next step of the plan," Sefu said, heaving a loud sigh.

And so, in compliance with Sefu's instructions, Nassor left.

Ismene's eyes fluttered open. Dawn streamed into the high window, and she breathed in the fresh smell of morning. Turning in the bed, she gazed at her new husband who was still in dreamland. There was no way to describe what she was feeling—it was different from anything she had ever felt. It was a good feeling, true, but she was still afraid of it.

Her stomach growled louder than she would have thought possible.

"I guess we need to get you something to eat." She heard Alistair's voice.

As she watched, he opened his eyes and fixed them on hers. He reached out to touch her arm, moving as if to pull her to him, but something stopped him.

"Yes. That would be nice," she said, a slight smile on her face as she gathered the bedsheet tighter around herself, oddly modest. "I'll ring for Neterka." She put her bare feet on the tile floor, cool against her skin, pulling the sheets from the bed and around herself as she stood up.

"If you answer the door like that, he'll probably blush brighter than a tomato." Alistair laughed. He pulled on his robe and got to his feet. "I'll take care of getting you something to eat, and I'll see to it that Alonah is called to bring your clothes, if that is your desire."

She nodded, grateful that he had seemed to read her mind.

They stood looking at each other in silence for a handful of moments. Ismene beckoned him to speak, to say something about their new situation, but he did not. Was he waiting for her to start? Ismene, her face warming, turned her head to fix her gaze on the sheets as she readjusted them for yet more coverage.

Alistair broke the now uncomfortable silence by clearing his throat. "Breakfast, then," he said before nodding and moving into the outer bedchambers to call for Neterka.

Alistair pulled the cord that would ring for his trusted valet. Why was it so strange between him and Ismene? Last night had been most amazing. He had never felt anything like that before. But he also knew that his longing for her had not been quenched. That was the oddest thing. He wanted something more and there was more of her...somehow. Shaking his head, he attempted to clear such crazy thoughts. *I'm not making any sense!*

On top of everything going on in his head, Alistair couldn't interpret Ismene's reactions today. Perhaps it was because he was too blinded by his own feelings. What was going through her mind? Was she as confused as he? Was she feeling anything close to the stirrings in his heart?

There was a knock on the door and Alistair opened it to discover Alonah, clothing in hand. Her arrival did not surprise him in the least. Neterka was quite good at his job. He would have known full well that the mistress of the house would be in need of her handmaiden once help was summoned from the master's bedchambers. The only thing that may have surprised Alistair was that Alonah's face was seen before Neterka's. That must mean he was anticipating their needs for food and was seeing to those preparations. Alistair motioned for Alonah to go into the inner bedchambers where Ismene was waiting for her.

He knew he would be waiting for a few moments, so he wandered over to the far end of the room. This was his favorite vantage point from which to gaze out over the grounds. From this particular position, he would have been able to look into the inner bedchambers as well, but out of the corner of his eye he saw the curtains fall over the open doorway, blocking his view and discouraging his reentry.

Was this what marriage was to bring for him? Would he always have this need for something more he couldn't name? How he wished Ismene would talk to him. Maybe she would. Perhaps she just needed time. Last night was new for her in every way. No matter what she was feeling this morning, it was all novel to her. He must give her time to process it for herself before he started expecting her to be ready to share it with him...if she ever would.

Ismene was relieved when Alonah entered the bedchambers with her clothing. She had been sitting on the bed, sheets drawn tightly around herself, afraid that Alistair would come back in expecting...what? What did she think he would expect? A repeat performance? A heart-to-heart? For her to get out? She wasn't sure, but she did know she wanted him to just stay away while she gathered her thoughts. Everything was too topsy-turvy in her heart and in her stomach to be able to converse about anything—even the weather—much less about what happened last night. So what was she going to say to Alonah?

"Please drop the drape," she requested in a quiet voice. The last thing she wanted was Alistair looking in or, heaven forbid, walking in while she was dressing. Again, she was mystified at her odd modesty despite the happenings of the night before.

Alonah, for her part, did as she was told and then came over to her mistress to assist her in dressing. Ismene, deep in her twisting thoughts, allowed herself to be helped. Alonah tried to go about the business of dressing her mistress as quietly as possible, but Ismene wanted for her to ask something, anything, so that she could avoid the issue. Her handmaiden did not, and so Ismene was left to her own thoughts.

The chilled feeling that had come over her when Alistair's body moved away from hers was at long last subsiding as she dressed. For that, she was thankful. It had not mattered how she gathered the sheet around her, the chill had remained and it, too, confused her. Just one more thing she would need time and space to work through.

"Milady, are you well?" Alonah did ask at last, looking Ismene in the eyes for the first time.

Ismene's nod was slow. "Yes, I am fine."

Alonah, still unmarried, did not know what else to say or how else to proceed. She had heard plenty of talk about these things around the servants' quarters, but none seemed like they would be the least bit helpful. Or appropriate. So she remained silent as she continued preparing Ismene.

The silence allowed Alonah's thoughts to drift to the evening before. During the wedding celebration, Jabari had sought her out once again. They had danced together in the crowd of well-wishers. Afterward, they had talked. He seemed to want to know everything about her. She blushed a little even then at the feelings that stirred in her to be pursued by such a handsome man. It was amazing that in one short evening she felt she had come to know him so well. And the more she knew him, the more she liked him.

Jabari was kind, considerate, gentle, and understanding. The man had listened to such boring tales of her childhood with rapt attention. He seemed to have a genuine interest in getting to know her. They had lingered perhaps a little longer than they should have. She was quite tired this morning, but she didn't regret a minute of it. Still, she did find it hard not to sing or at least hum as she went about her work.

"Ow!" Ismene gritted her teeth as Alonah's brush found a nasty tangle in her hair.

That snapped Alonah from her daydreams. "I'm sorry, milady."

"It's all right," Ismene assured her handmaiden.

"Your hair is in such a state today."

"Well, we didn't have a chance to take it down last night..." Ismene's voice trailed off.

Alonah worked the tangle out with more care and pulled the hair back, pinning it into place.

"Shall I go for your face paint?" Alonah asked, already gathering the brush and discarded toga from the night before.

"That will not be necessary for now. We'll leave that until I'm back in my own bedchambers."

Their regiment was complete. Alonah stood back, waiting for Ismene to take the steps necessary to get her to the outer bedchambers where Alistair awaited her. Ismene lingered for a few moments, seeming somewhat reluctant.

"Are you quite sure you are well, milady?" Alonah asked, brows furrowed.

Ismene sighed. "Yes, Alonah, I'm quite all right. Just a little tired."

Only then did Ismene stand and make her way into the outer chambers.

There was a knock at the door and Alistair admitted Neterka with a word. Neterka was but the first in a line of servants bearing bowls with fresh fruits, cheeses, and breads for them. Alistair glanced in the direction of his inner bedchambers in time to see the curtain move. It lifted and his bride made her appearance. She was dressed in one of her simpler togas, one that was quite commonly seen on the streets of Greece. His bedchambers did not afford Alonah the utensils to apply face paint and not much for hair, so the handmaiden had pulled back her mistress's hair with a simple headband and swept back the longer side pieces. Even without fine ornamentation or face paint, Ismene took his breath away. He had to get a hold of himself!

He attempted to speak, but found it difficult. "Please," he managed after what he felt was an embarrassing pause. "Sit and eat."

Ismene nodded and took a seat while a servant girl prepared a plate of fruit and another offered her some bread. She accepted both, thanking them. As she began to eat, she was soon almost shoveling the food into her mouth.

Alistair was a little surprised and somewhat amused by Ismene's hunger.

She peeked up and caught him watching her. "I didn't eat much at the banquet last night," she explained, blushing.

"Why not, milady?"

She offered him a shy look before she was able to manage, "I was...um...too...nervous...to eat."

Smiling as the redness in her face deepened, he found himself a little embarrassed for her and a bit tickled at her innocence.

She shared his smile.

They continued to eat in silence, but more of a comfortable silence. Both wanted to speak, but each wanted the other to start, so neither spoke. They each caught the other stealing glances, which caused an exchange of smiles again before their attention would inevitably return to their plates and meals. The servants in the room exchanged knowing glances and smiles in the midst of their master and mistress's lack of conversation.

As the meal drew to a close, Ismene set her plate down, signaling the completion of her breakfast. Alistair finished his last morsel of bread and placed his plate next to him as well. Their plates were then picked up by the ever-present maidservants.

It was, at last, Ismene who spoke up. "I believe I should be getting back to my bedchambers to prepare for the day."

"I think you look quite lovely," Alistair interjected.

She stared at him, a little wide-eyed at the unexpected compliment. "Thank you, Alistair. I meant that I needed to ready myself for the female neighbors who are to come today."

"Oh, yes, of course." He felt his face warm a little. But why should he be embarrassed for paying his wife a compliment? He didn't like that things were so tense, so...so...he couldn't even find the word. Of course she meant the anticipated visitation from the neighbors. And she was right, they would expect her to look the part.

Ismene was beautiful to him either way, but he understood that she had certain restrictions and requirements placed on her that he could only begin to understand. Perhaps today would not be a total loss. He hoped she might make a good friend from among their neighbors.

"I hope you get some great gifts," he said, standing. "I should ready myself to head out to the palace."

She nodded, standing as well. "Of course. I shall see you when you return, then."

He nodded.

Turning, she slipped out of the room, Alonah close behind her. Then they were off and down the hall toward her bedchambers.

Alistair was a bit disappointed at the abrupt end to the morning. What had he hoped for? A good-bye kiss? Promises of another evening together? Sweet nothings whispered in his ear? Chiding himself for his daydreams and expectations, he moved back toward his inner bedchambers to prepare for the day. He must get some space and explore his thoughts.

Sefu pondered the recent actions at the general's house and the response. In the midst of his thoughts, he found himself reviewing his choice of Nassor as his proxy. He found himself doing that a lot more of late. The man was hesitant, needing reassurance every step of the way. Sometimes that was good, but other times it was irritating. Nassor wouldn't act without direction. That was one of key reasons he had picked him. And Nassor was reliable in carrying out orders, and loyal to the end.

Nassor's second-guessing was becoming a problem. Was it an issue of conscience for the man? No, Sefu decided, it was Nassor's conscience that drove him to follow Sefu, knowing that this was ultimately for Egypt. Remembering that as the wellspring of Nassor's loyalty, Sefu concluded, as he had many times before, that he would just have to put up with all the extra handling this required.

The last visiting neighbor had left and Ismene was spent. She remembered that her mother would entertain guests for hours on end, sometimes for the whole day, and never utter one word of complaint.

Such was the life of a wife in Greek society and even more so as a woman of her mother's station. In Ismene's homeland, women did not leave their houses except to go to weddings, funerals, and special festivals. Her mother had some leeway in that she was also invited to various political dinner parties with her husband. For most Greek women, visiting their female neighbors was the only escape from their homes.

This was something to be grateful for in her transplant to Egypt. As she had come to understand, it was socially acceptable for women to venture out on a regular basis and they had no limitations of where they could journey day to day. In practice, though, women of her station kept to their homes much like the women of Greek society, only leaving their homes to visit their neighbors on the average day.

Ismene had received many nice gifts. The people who had visited her today had been generous and she found, once again, that everyone adored Alistair. He was a hero in their eyes and so they all wanted to be her best friend. They made over her like she was a precious gem. It was a lot for her to take in. Most women would have quite enjoyed all of that attention, but Ismene did not. She tolerated it because it was her place. And she got the feeling that she would be seeing a lot more of it in the future.

Alonah was already putting away some of the gifts, finding places in Ismene's bedchambers, stopping here and there to ask Ismene's advice on the placement of this or that. She had been all smiles and politeness today. A couple of the women, the more wealthy ones, had not been nice to her. They had treated her as if she were nothing more than a common slave, but Alonah had not bent under their rudeness.

"Don't worry so much about it, Alonah, it can wait. I want for you to rest yourself."

"Milady, that is not necessary, I assure you. These are prized possessions, indeed. I must find places for them."

"Yes, yes...regardless, I'm ordering you to take a break," Ismene said, smiling at her handmaiden-become-friend.

Alonah met her smile.

Ismene sank into the chair-pillows in one corner and Alonah gave her a mischievous look.

"What's going on in that mind of yours?" Ismene asked.

"Just a minute." Alonah went to her own bed and pulled out a small board from her clothes chest. It had several holes in it. Alonah also lifted out a small basket. She brought her things over to where Ismene sat and put them down.

Ismene reached into the basket and pulled out one of the small, beautifully carved pieces of wood. It was a jackal's head on a small stick. In the box there were more pieces identical to the one she held and pieces with a dog's head on a stick.

"What in Mount Olympus is this?"

"A board game!"

"A what?"

"A servant girl, Safiya, taught me how to play. It's so much fun! Would you like to learn?"

She watched Alonah's eager face for a minute, gauging her response against her apprehension. Despite how tired she was, she decided to concede. "Sure."

"These jackal pieces are yours and the hounds are mine. The object of the game is..." Alonah's voice droned on in explanation.

Ismene half listened as she just enjoyed the moment's peace with no pressure on her to present herself to neighbors or sort through the myriad of emotions surrounding Alistair and his presence. She just let all of that go and shifted her focus to the game Alonah was introducing her to. *I'm going to enjoy this pastime.*

CHAPTER 6

Uncertainty

It had been one week since their wedding day. That was the last time they had been in each other's presence for any significant amount of time. Since then, they had become nothing more than housemates, seeing each other at meals and passing each other on occasion during the day. This disturbed Alistair. Strange, since when he had first made this arrangement, this is precisely what he had hoped for. But this arrangement no longer suited him. He wanted more from their relationship. He wanted a relationship. He wanted what they had started developing to go somewhere. But they were both so unsure of themselves, and he had been too timid that morning after their wedding night.

There were so many things he should have said, things he wished he had done that could have changed the course that their relationship had taken. Now, they had gotten into this way of life. She went about her day and he went about his. How was he to change that? Would an opportunity present itself? Could he seize it? Would he need to make this opportunity happen? Or could it just be a simple conversation?

Alistair wanted so much more, needed so much more. He shook his head. It was no matter. It would be what it would be. There was no sense in worrying himself over it. Certainly not when he was supposed to be directing troop exercises and maneuvers. He shifted his attention back to the men clashing swords in front of him.

"Jabari is always on offense," he spoke to the man's captain. "Which I like, but he leaves himself open for attack from many angles. See to it that he gets a review of some defensive maneuvers."

The captain nodded.

"Bomani will be a strong soldier." Alistair noticed the young man who was not yet part of the legion, but rather in training on the side-lines. "Captain Ptah, I think it is time you take him on as part of your unit and see to his proper induction."

Ptah nodded. "I have been watching him myself for some time, General. I know he will make you proud."

The rest of the afternoon passed in similar fashion, with Alistair commenting here and there as the soldiers went through their routines. He was well pleased with his unit. They were strong, fit, well trained, and loyal. What more could a leader ask for? As the day wore on, it would become time for them to end the exercises and bring the men together. This was one of the parts of Alistair's day he enjoyed. While the men took their nourishment and water, he would walk among them and compliment them on what he observed that day, conversing with them about their families as he came to know them better. He enjoyed knowing his men well.

After a short time like this, Alistair would speak to the whole group and then release them to return home. He would then have a brief meeting with his captains before dismissing them as well. Alistair had come to look forward to returning to his own home to dine with Ismene. It wasn't much, but he relished every minute he could have with her.

Frowning, Alistair realized he had done it again. He had daydreamed his way to the end of the day. They were but halfway through midday exercises and he had already imagined his way to the end and to home. He chided himself to keep his mind on his work. There was a good chance that Pharaoh and Meleager would come to see the troops in action this afternoon.

It was common for Pharaoh to come to see them at least once a week, and Meleager tagged along, ever ready with his opinions. Alistair had spoken with Pharaoh about these helpful tips that were quite unwelcome. Ptolemy only asked Alistair to humor his brother. Meleager had always dreamed of being a military man, but had not the makings of a commander. So sometimes Alistair would pretend to make note of Meleager's suggestions, other times he would ignore him altogether, but he was always annoyed.

It was all the more reason for Alistair to concentrate on what his men were doing. If Pharaoh came, it would take up part of their regular training time. Alistair took a deep breath and attempted to clear his mind of all traces of Ismene. Then, turning his attention back to his men, he began to walk the line again. But it wasn't long before he was reminiscing...

Ismene and Alonah wandered about the marketplace, checking out the local fare. It had become a custom of theirs to visit this market weekly. Ismene liked to pick up something for herself—a pashmina, a necklace, something—each time they came. She had not found anything that struck her fancy today, so she decided to pick out some fruits she had not yet had the good fortune to try at Alistair's home. Her basket boasted a variety of strange-looking, multicolored, oddly shaped objects that the vendors claimed were edible. Alonah kept pointing to this and that, adding something here and there, but Ismene didn't mind. At least Alonah was enjoying this trip.

Not being so engaged in the purchasing process, Ismene's mind began to wander. Only a handful of days had passed since she had shared Alistair's bed. They'd had little contact since then and neither had broached that rather delicate subject in the least. It had been an amazing experience for her, but she couldn't explain her actions the morning after. She still was unable to sort through her feelings and, to be honest, was avoiding him. It had been all too easy with the nature of his job.

Ismene was jolted out of her thoughts as someone rammed into her, almost knocking her over. Alonah responded quickly, grabbing for her arm to steady her.

"Milady, are you all right?"

Ismene nodded, trying to catch her breath. Whoever it was had just about knocked the wind out of her and had succeeded in upending her basket. Several of her fruits now littered the ground. She turned in the direction of the bump, but it was no use. There were too many people to discern which, if any, of them had been the culprit. It was an accident, she decided, and let the matter go. Alonah was still trying to make certain that Ismene was all right.

"I am fine, I assure you," Ismene insisted.

It was then that Alonah also noticed their wares on the ground. "Oh!"

Both Ismene and Alonah squatted to grab up the fruit before it got trampled. They were fortunate that only a handful had escaped the basket. Ismene found a piece of paper amongst the fallen pieces. Who had dropped this? Paper wasn't all that easy to come by and was not something people wasted.

Was anyone looking for this paper? Ismene confirmed that no one was and decided to open it. She unfolded the papyrus and was surprised to find the words within written in Greek. The message scrawled on the paper, however, caused her heart to jump into her throat:

THIS IS OUR HOME

YOU SHOULD RETURN TO YOURS

THIS IS YOUR LAST WARNING

"Milady!" Alonah's shocked voice sounded over her shoulder.

Ismene again scanned the crowd, trying to find some sinister face sneering at her, taking some sick pleasure in her obvious discomfort. Of course, there was no one to be found that matched that description. No one was watching her or even glancing in her direction. Everyone was busy with their own errands, caught up in their own worlds. There was no way to determine if any of them had left the note and impossible to track the guilty person. But the person could still be lingering, enjoying seeing her twitch. She did not want to give them that satisfaction. At least she could spare herself that.

"We must leave at once," she said to Alonah.

Alonah nodded and paid the vendor for the fruit before following her mistress toward where they had left their chariot and manservant. It was not a long walk back to that rendezvous point, but it carried them several yards. Over the moderate distance, Ismene found herself wanting to glance back for onlookers or for someone following her, but she resisted the temptation. The chance of her catching a glimpse of the culprit was slim to none; the likelihood that the guilty party would make sport of her was better. So she forced herself to keep her eyes forward.

They were back at their chariot in what must have been record time. Ismene made every attempt to be pleasant to the various servants in her employ; however, she was quite short with the manservant at the chariot on this occasion. She communicated that they were prepared to leave and expected to depart forthwith, expressing that he should ready the horse as quickly as possible. It was not a request.

The trip back to the safety of the house was long. Even more so as it was made in complete silence. Neither Alonah nor Ismene knew what to say. Somehow, it seemed as if it hadn't happened as long as they didn't speak of it. But neither could think of anything else to talk about. They rode in silence, both lost in their own thoughts.

When they arrived at the house, Alonah busied herself with her lady's needs, seeing to it that Ismene was settled and resting comfortably in her bedchambers on her favorite lounge. Once Alonah had begun her fussing over her mistress, Ismene broke her silence, insisting over and over that she was fine and did not need any special attentions, but Alonah would not hear it.

"Please rest, milady. I will go and fetch the general."

"No!" Ismene sat bolt upright, nearly causing herself to fall off the settee.

"We must show him this letter," Alonah said.

"We shouldn't," Ismene reasoned. "It will only cause him to worry.

And what can be done? We have no knowledge of who left it. What good can come from telling him?"

Alonah thought about that for a moment and could not come up with a good answer for her mistress. Nothing good would come from telling him. He wasn't going to pack them all up and ship them back to Greece. He wasn't going to repudiate Ismene and send her back alone. It *would* only be a source of worry for him. Still, she thought he needed to know.

"I understand why you want to tell him, Alonah, I do. And I have thought about it the entire ride home. I think this note is more an attempt to scare us all than an actual threat. I do not wish this deviant to succeed. Let us keep it between us...for now. We can save the note and share it with the general if it seems we should."

Alonah, once again, could not find fault with her mistress's reasoning.

"All right," she conceded, "as long as we will share the note should something else happen." Though the plan seemed sound, something about it still nagged at Alonah.

After drilling his men for an intense bout of training exercises, Alistair called his troops to attention. He walked down the ranks and gave them close scrutiny. Not one soldier flinched a muscle. The look of devotion to their general was strong. Alistair then dismissed them, ordering them to report the next day at dawn.

While overseeing his troops during general training was a common task he was often involved in, it wasn't his only one. He often conferred with Pharaoh to stay up to date on war policy and to be sure he was training his men for the right operations. There were some questions about their fast-approaching campaign against Antiochus I, the Seleucid king of Syria who currently had his eye on Palestine, one of Pharaoh's holdings—one that he had made clear was in Egypt's best interests to keep.

After giving final orders to his platoon commanders, he mounted his horse and headed to the palace to consult with Pharaoh. After arriving at the palace and dismounting, he entered the audience chamber with all due haste and bowed before Pharaoh.

"Oh, General, I was hoping you would stop by. There are some last-minute details about our campaign we must go over." As Alistair rose in response to Ptolemy's statement, he took note of the details Pharaoh told him. He would be sure to pass those on to his unit commanders in the morning. Ptolemy must have sensed his uneasiness, because he asked him a strange question.

"Is there something you wish to say?"

"Has the investigator found anything?" Alistair, of course, knew the answer. At least as far as his house was concerned, the man had come up empty.

Ptolemy's eyes leveled on Alistair suspiciously for a moment, then he seemed to remember who it was he was talking to. With hesitation, he offered, "Nothing of significance. Why?"

Alistair's question had a double implication. No doubt, the investigator had caused havoc, interrupting the whole household at the most inopportune times. It was almost as if he picked these moments to catch people off guard, to pose intrusive questions and insinuations. Alistair's question to Pharaoh carried a slight hint of scorn for having to put up with this man digging through his affairs, but Alistair also wanted to know if anything had been uncovered regarding the attacks.

"There is another issue. We have been, shall I say, 'visited.'"

"Visited?" Ptolemy responded with a perplexed look on his face.

Alistair described for Ptolemy what had occurred at his home those days before.

"Do you think it's a random prank or that the mob might be behind this?" Alistair asked. Almost without hesitation, he saw a sense of recognition in Ptolemy's face. He leaned back, almost as if this were expected.

"The Alexandrian mob is made up of those Egyptian men who oppose Greco-Roman rule. This faction exists to take Egypt back into Egyptian hands. They act by subversion and scare tactics." Pharaoh spoke these words in a matter-of-fact way, as if he had mentioned this many times before. Indeed, he needed not retell all of this to Alistair. It was all information he knew.

"It seems they have set their eyes on you, my General."

Pharaoh was confirming Alistair's suspicions. Fear and anger were fighting for dominance within him.

Pharaoh nodded. "The mob would not dare strike the palace, but they would seek to inflict injury on the heart of my rule."

"Why me? Why her?" he clamored in a quick, emotional response. As soon as he had blurted this out, he said in a calmer voice, "Of course they would attack your highest commanders."

"Indeed. You are a great threat to them. The Egyptian army is devoted to you." That had been evident by the incredible progress the army had made since Alistair took command under Ptolemy.

"Have any other members of your council been attacked?" Expecting the answer to be *yes*, since these would be the people closest to Ptolemy, Alistair was surprised when he heard Ptolemy's response.

"No. You are the first of whom I have heard any sort of attack from my inner circle."

This didn't provide the comfort he had sought. Alistair hoped that he could tell Ismene that they weren't alone, and that many similar, harmless pranks were being played on other government officials.

"I'm afraid there is little we will be able to do. The mob has been quite irritating in the past, and they are almost impossible to track down. But they have appeared to be like a small mosquito for the most part—incredibly annoying, but of no real threat." Ptolemy's words further hampered Alistair, though he dared not show it.

"Very well, my liege. If there are no other orders for me..." He bowed before Pharaoh, and was dismissed.

Leaving the palace, he felt as if he had less encouragement than when he had arrived. His dejected gaze fell on the closing of the day, resting on the sun as it met the sand as he rode home.

Ismene heard Alistair in the hall. *He's home late tonight.* She glanced up from her book as he peered around the corner into her bedchambers. It was a bit odd for him to come to her room. Looking up at him, she offered him a genuine smile, inviting him in.

"I'm glad you're home," she offered. "Are you hungry? I'll get something." She was already headed for the door.

"No." He stopped her. "Please, sit. I'm fine." He took her hand. "I just want to sit here with you for a while." Making his way over to the chair next to the one she had just vacated, he sat down, but she did not.

Instead she watched him, having noticed that his features were drawn with the weariness of the day's events. With a boldness she didn't know she possessed, she moved behind him to rub the tension of whatever had transpired that day out of his muscles. He tensed initially under her touch. She sensed that he was surprised and unsure, but he eased as her hands worked. Then she felt the muscles relaxing.

"You are so tense, Alistair. Are you all right?" She didn't make it a practice to ask after his affairs. Most of the things involving his work she would not understand, and a lot of it he would be obligated to not share even with her. It had also been a part of her "let's keep our lives separate" plan, but right now it seemed the most natural thing to say.

"We all underwent some vigorous training today."

"Is that uncommon?"

"Every now and then we go through bouts of this type of training," he explained. "It's more intensive than our usual routines."

"I see." His body was relaxing and her task was complete. She began to draw her hands away.

"Thank you," he said, his voice soft.

She went to move back, but he took her hand and spun her so he could look into her face.

"There is something I must tell you." He tugged on her arm and brought her around to sit next to him. That's when she knew that something was wrong. She saw the weary look in his eyes, and she realized it was more than his physical weariness that put it there.

Drawing in a deep breath, he spoke the words she didn't want to hear. "I have to go away for a while."

He was watching her reaction. Did her features betray the concern she was trying, with great difficulty, to hide?

"We've been called into battle and we must go," he continued, explaining.

"Battle?" Her breath caught.

"I won't lie to you, Ismene, and I won't insult you with half-truths. There is always a chance of defeat or capture or..." He left the sentence hanging. He didn't need to finish. "I think our chances of success in battle are good, but I want only to be honest with you."

Her heart was full of worry; it settled in the pit of her stomach.

"Ismene, this is something I've never had to tell someone. I've always gone and come with no one to concern myself with." His eyes held hers.

All of a sudden, she needed to be doing something with her hands. She pulled her eyes away from his and looked down at her book. Closing it, she tried to be interested in the texture of the scroll. He waited for her to process it, waited for her to speak.

"When will you go?" she asked after some time, eyes still on the book covering.

"Tomorrow."

Her head jerked up. "Tomorrow? So soon?"

"When Pharaoh makes a decision, we proceed at once. And I agree with his desire for immediacy on this matter. The only reason we didn't go today is that the men will need to be rested for what is to come."

Ismene was overwhelmed with her concern for him, but it was more than that. It was something she was getting tired of fighting, but was still afraid to expose.

"What can I do to help you prepare?" She met his eyes, pushing her worries aside. They would do him no good.

There was surprise in his eyes. Surprise to her reaction? And something else. Appreciation? Yes, there it was. A certain respect for her ability to face what must be done. "There are no preparations left to be made for the journey. Everything is ready."

She glanced away, saddened somehow that she was useless to him.

"You could read to me. It would help calm my mind."

She peered at him with a quirked eyebrow for a handful of seconds. Then, resigning herself to his request, she said, "Of course, what would you like for me to read?"

"Read to me of Greece." He leaned back in the lounge chair, glancing at the book she had been reading and smiled. "About Pegasus?"

Her face warmed as she realized he had been looking at her book and noted her interest in something that was a tale for children. When she looked back up at him, there was a question in her eyes, but he gestured that he did, in fact, want her to read from that book.

Ismene settled herself and opened the scroll. "Pegasus is a creature that has made its place among the mythical creatures of old..." She repeated the words she knew almost by heart from her father's stories. Even as an adult, these stories still captivated her—a winged horse! Her imagination carried her away to the skies where Pegasus soared above all the troubles of the world and escaped all manner of tribulation, including war.

A strange sound caused her to glance up from the pages at her husband, only to find him sleeping. How long had she been reading? She looked back down at the book—only a few passages in, not long. He was just that tired.

Setting her scroll down, she moved over to her bed to grab a blanket for him. She returned to where he continued to slumber and laid the blanket over him, adjusting it in hopes of making him as comfortable as possible. It was impossible to tear herself away for some time. So she sat and watched the rise and fall of his chest, watched his face at rest, at peace. Her heart was stirred again with the mixture of emotions she still had not been able to sort through and found herself fearful to surrender to them.

An impulsive idea entered her head and she found cause to give herself over to it. She leaned over and pressed a gentle kiss to his forehead. He stirred in sleep, but did not wake. Their faces so close and, knowing that after tonight she may never see him again, she found the courage to place a kiss on his lips. It had been her intention to kiss him gently and retire to bed, but her kiss caused him to awaken, and he responded, returned her kiss, his hands moving to caress her face.

Pulling back just far enough to look at him, she searched his eyes. There was great affection there and great care. She knew that she cared for him, too. It did hurt her to think that something might happen to him. He sat up and tentatively kissed her again, pulling her into his strong embrace. Her head was swimming. She reveled in the feeling of being secure in his arms. When the kiss broke, she pulled away and stood up. There was a question, and a hurt, in his eyes. Taking his hand without speaking, she bade him get to his feet before pulling him toward her bed. There was no need for words.

When Ismene awoke, she was alone. Alistair had slipped out without waking her. As she rolled that thought around in her mind for a few moments, she was unsure how that made her feel. While she had not wanted to have to see him off this morning, she did want to say good-bye. When she thought about the awkward state between them ever since the morning after their wedding night—the last time they were...together—she realized that his decision had been best.

Ismene watched the sun seeping into the room through the window as she always did in the morning. Beams of light piercing into the darkness never ceased to fascinate her. The sun was a life source. As a child, she always loved to sit under a tree or by a brook, places where she was near those beams, to calm and collect her thoughts.

This morning, she was thinking about Alistair and their marriage. What she had intended and had been determined for their relationship to remain was not the same as it was turning out to be. Her heart was changing, or rather, her determination was starting to bend to her heart. It was time for her to take her place in the household. What better time than now? Alistair was gone and so all the household duties were hers to oversee. Placing a challenge before herself, she sat up to prepare for this day.

As she turned from the bed, she saw her book there on the chest where she had set it the previous night. This morning, a bouquet of lotus flowers covered it with a rolled piece of paper amongst the blooms. She lifted the note from among the beautiful petals and unrolled it.

Beautiful Ismene,

Forgive me, I did not know how to say good-bye to

your lovely face. You know that I will miss you and that I am counting the minutes until I return. This is the price I pay for being a man of my position, but never before has it seemed such a high price to pay.

I have instructed Neterka to attend to your every need and I know that he will serve you well. Please rely on him, he knows the house and staff well and they trust him.

I will think of you fondly as you have captivated my heart with your smile. I have not yet spoken it, but you must know that I love you, my bride. I couldn't leave without letting you know. I am stricken with the thought that I may never return to you, but the image of your face and the sound of your voice are forever with me and they bring me great comfort.

Until our eyes meet again,
All my heart,
Alistair

Reaching up, she felt tears on her face. She had not realized she was crying, but she knew her heart was breaking and soaring at the same time. He loved her. He truly did! Her heart swelled with emotion for him at the realization of how safe she was to feel what she had been hiding. Why had she hidden her feelings for him so deep that she couldn't even recognize, much less express her love for him until it was too late? Longing now for the good-bye she didn't get, she wondered, would she have told him? Ismene wanted to, so much. But wishes of what could have been or would have been were futile and she knew it. She could only move on from here.

The prospect of becoming true mistress of this house filled her with a new purpose. And she was now more eager than ever to take her place as his wife. An idea was sparked. She would surprise him with all that she could do and how well she could handle his household. Then she would tell him that she did it because she wanted to be his wife and because she loved him. Picturing the whole scene before her, she could already see the surprise in those beautiful eyes of his, his eyebrow raised, intrigued. Closing her eyes, she thought on his face for a minute more. Her plan must start today and she must make it happen.

Neterka knocked on the door to the outer bedchambers. He could count on one hand the number of times Ismene had summoned him. It was always a source of much curiosity for him when she did. And all the more so with the general gone—he had expected she would keep to herself these next weeks. Sure, he might pass her in the house, but he thought she would keep to her room or the gardens, or perhaps take a trip to the marketplace. It hadn't crossed into his realm of thinking that she would be summoning for his services already. Was this a foretelling of what was to come? Did she think he was now free to do her bidding? If so, he would have to assign someone to take on that task...perhaps Mesi...or Safiya. No, Rabiah. Yes, Rabiah would do nicely.

"Please, come in," Ismene called out, breaking into his thoughts.

He entered, surprised to find the mistress of the house greeting him at the door.

"Would you wish for me to get your food?" he asked, stumbling over himself.

"I have already eaten, thank you. I would like to do an inventory of the kitchen today," she said as if it were something they did each Tuesday together.

"Milady, I have myself done that inventory just yesterday," he said, his words coming out fast, a bit fumbled. Ismene had never shown any interest in performing any of the household tasks that would have fallen to the mistress of the home.

"Excellent," she said, eyes bright. "I will need some guidance."

"Milady, I mean to say that it is not necessary for you to do it. I can handle that for you," he said in sincerity. Being that the general had been unwed for a matter of time, Neterka had become accustomed to these tasks and it was no trouble for him to continue.

"I do thank you, Neterka, but I know that it's part of my job and I've been neglecting my duties around here." Her features betrayed a slight frown.

"But General Merenre wishes that you not have to do this work that I can take care of," he protested.

"I understand and I do appreciate you and all that you do, Neterka. I will speak with General Merenre when he returns if that is your concern, but I wish to assume the duties of the house that fall on my shoulders. You should not have to do my job and yours. I insist." There it was. Her final word. It left no room for argument unless he wished to disrespect her. Which he did not. Neterka studied her for a minute. Was this a game? Or was she sincere? She certainly seemed so. What had brought about this change? It didn't matter. What truly mattered was her willingness to take her place and be part of the house. This thought pleased him. A smile broke out across his face.

"Of course, milady. Follow me."

He held the door open for her to pass through. Then he came up alongside her and led her toward the kitchen.

It was late at night. Members of the group were wandering into the main room without ceremony, unpronounced. Everyone preferred to discuss business and then get back to wherever they belonged, hopefully before anyone missed them. As the last few people wandered in, Tarik stepped into the center, and called the meeting to order.

"We have recruited several more members. That is good. I told you at the last meeting that more of our countrymen would realize the danger that Greeks taking over would pose, and feel a strong desire to join our ranks." A sense of mutual agreement passed through the room as various members nodded their heads, looking at each other with smiles and increasing confidence.

"But I must also caution you that we are still a small group. Do not leave here with too much pride and do something stupid that would expose us all. Secrecy is critical until we can make our move. If our Greek rulers find out what we are up to before we move, all may be lost. And I'm not just talking about our chance at freedom. We would all be drawn and quartered in the desert."

This tone of voice shocked some of the newer members. Those who had been at previous meetings recognized the familiar words Tarik often used to remind people of the grave consequences.

"Now is there any new business we need to be aware of?"

"Some strange things have happened at General Merenre's home in the last few days." The man reporting this wore a stark blue robe. "I'm sure some of you have heard of this. Several people I have spoken to suspect we are behind it."

Some accusations began to fly back and forth.

"Are we behind this?"

"I didn't know we were making our move."

"We didn't do it."

"It's about time."

Tarik had to stand up and regain control of the meeting.

"We are not a rabble of miscreants! We are proud Egyptians. There will be order!" Tarik silenced everyone. "I, too, am aware of these so-called 'attacks.' None of them have been sanctioned by us." The whole time Tarik spoke, his eyes roamed the room. Nassor noticed this, and couldn't help but notice that Tarik's eyes rested on Sefu a little longer than anyone else.

Why is he staring at Sefu? Does he know about us? Nassor felt rather nervous being unable to decipher what was going on between Sefu and Tarik. He couldn't discern if he saw something between them, or if it was just his imagination. Then a thought flashed across his mind. *Did Tarik hire Sefu?* Nassor had always thought that Sefu was the leader of their faction, but now he realized someone else could be involved. *That is crazy. Sefu could never take orders from someone else.* This "job" they were running was for someone else. That was all. But was that Tarik? Remembering how many times Sefu and Tarik argued at meetings, the thought of those two working together soon vanished.

"As I stated, those attacks are not from us. I hope no one doubts me." As that last comment was made, there was a sinister look in his eyes. Things quieted down rather fast. "The reason I called you all here is due to a serious issue that is culminating as we speak. Several Greek families are relocating to Alexandria. No doubt they are rich families that will bring much influence to the court of Pharaoh. There is already enough of a Greek stench in that palace. The thought of more money and power concentrated in the hands of the Greeks is horrendous."

A huge patriotic surge of shouting broke out, with many people repeating their hatred of the Greeks.

The loudest to shout was Sefu, "The time to act is NOW!"

Everyone heard him, as they often did, and Tarik glared squarely at him.

"At last, Sefu," Tarik said. "You and I agree on something."

As Tarik's eyes swept across the group, he spoke in a rising tone, "Indeed, the time is now. And so we will rise to the occasion. Ready yourselves, men, I am calling you to action."

CHAPTER 7

Attacks

Ismene fell on her bed. She was tired to the bone. Running a house this large was a mountain-sized task! Not to mention she had spent her downtime in the garden pulling weeds. She was dirty and her body ached from the effort. She should bathe before going to bed, but she was just too tired to keep her hold on consciousness. As her eyes fell closed, she noticed there was something strange about her pillows, but that was all the thought she put into it before she let the dark of sleep overtake her.

Alonah slipped into the room not long after Ismene, but found her mistress out cold. How on earth did her mistress sleep, not caring that she was covered in mud from the knee down and from her elbows to her hands? She had worked herself too hard this day. It was one thing to take on the duties of the mistress of the house, another to take them all on at once. Ismene tasked herself almost as if she were punishing herself for something. But what? What could she have done that deserved such penalizing?

There was a chance she would wake, and Alonah wagered Ismene would want to clean herself, so she went about filling Ismene's bedside bowl with water and setting out a clean nightshift. Then she covered her mistress with a thin blanket. If only there was more she could do for Ismene. But she dare not for fear of waking her. Ismene was much in need of her sleep. She let her gaze rest on the peaceful features of her charge for a handful of seconds before exiting the room.

It was hours later into the night when Ismene woke up. Her arm was throbbing painfully, numb from the way she had been sleeping on it. With much effort, she sat up and rubbed life back into the offended limb. Her clothes from the day were no longer comfortable sleepwear or suitable to slip into her bed, caked with dirt as they were. Faster than she thought possible in her sleep-drugged state, she changed out of her filthy linen and discarded the soiled garment for cleaning.

The bowl on her nightstand had been filled with water. She was thankful for Alonah's thoughtfulness. A bath was out of the question, but she felt better washing off the worst of the dirt before getting into the clean nightshift that Alonah had also prepared for her. Then she looked to her nice, fresh bed. Well, it was clean beneath the blanket— the top now had traces of garden dirt where she had been lying. Night had long since fallen and cooled the earth and her bedchambers, and she was eager to crawl between the blanket and sheets.

After several minutes at the bowl, washing and scrubbing her skin, she braided her hair. At last, she felt ready to climb into bed for the rest of the night. Lifting the blanket, she slipped into the warmth it offered. She could detect right away that something wasn't quite right. It felt as if the bed were covered in strips of cloth. Shoving the blanket back with her feet, she sought to reveal what her eyes had not been able to see. In the moonlight, she could see that her sheets had been cut to shreds.

Ismene jumped out of bed and screamed in reaction to what she saw. Who? What? A rush of dread filled her as she realized that some-one...someone with sinister intentions had been in her bedchambers. She couldn't quite get her thoughts straight, much less her voice. So the scream remained the only vocalization she made. Was the person still here? Watching her? Waiting? She jerked her head around, searching in the darkness for any sign of someone else in her bedroom.

In moments, Alonah, whose small chamber was next to Ismene's, rushed into the room with a lit candle, half-asleep.

"Milady, are you well?" She was rubbing her eyes.

Ismene had backed across the room from the offending object and, still unable to find her voice, just pointed in the direction of her bed.

Alonah's gaze followed the invisible line to where she was pointing and saw the sheets. "Milady!" She rushed over close enough to touch Ismene, but kept a breath's distance from her. "Are you injured?"

Ismene shook her head, continuing to back up. Her back hit the door and her shoulder blade smacked something.

She let out a yelp.

Alonah pulled her away from the wall and held up the candle to reveal the handle of a dagger that had been stabbed into the middle of the doorframe.

Ismene fainted.

When Ismene's eyes opened again, it was daylight. She was reclined on a lounge in her chambers. Now conscious, she began to move to sit up.

"The lady is awake!" she heard a voice call out. It was Alonah.

Alonah's face was over her a split second later. "Take it slow, milady, you took quite a bump to your head when you fell last night."

Ismene nodded, the events of last night were jumbled and foggy. She'd had a strange dream, a terribly frightening dream. Maybe that was why she was having a hard time remembering what happened to get her to this point. Alonah helped her get adjusted to a sitting position and propped cushions behind her, so she could still recline.

"I'll send for some tea," Alonah said and disappeared from the room.

What had happened last night? She remembered going to bed early after her long day, waking up, going back to bed. That's when she'd had the strange dream about her sheets being shredded. What a horrible nightmare. How on earth had her mind conjured that up? There was something nagging at the back of her mind. It *was* a dream, right?

Ismene got to her feet, making slow movements. Once upright, her head started pounding. She reached up to brace it somehow and felt the bandaging that someone had done after she'd apparently taken a fall last night. That must have been what was causing her memory problems. After some moments, she made it to one of the columns in her bedchambers. Turning her attention to her bed, she noticed that it had been stripped. Was that because the sheets were being cleaned or because they had been mangled as in her dream? She felt a wave of nausea come over her and she leaned against the column.

"Ow!" she cried as her shoulder protested her weight. It was rather sore. Reaching around, she used her opposite hand to explore the sensitive area. There was a bruise forming on her shoulder blade. Then she remembered. Last night she had backed into, rather smacked into a—no, it couldn't be. Glancing at the door, she sought to confirm with her eyes what her mind was telling her. There it was, a dagger-sized hole. She felt weak-kneed and, despite the tenderness in her shoulder, leaned on the column again for support. Her head was swimming and the room started spinning.

"Milady, no! What are you doing up and about? You are not well enough for this!" Alonah scolded, rushing toward her mistress.

Ismene did not object. She could feel how unwell she was.

Alonah helped her back to the lounge. Ismene leaned on her and didn't care. She was overwhelmed with the realization of what had happened to her the previous evening.

"It wasn't a dream," she managed to say as she was being seated.

"No," Alonah said sadly.

"Who? Why?" she started, stumbling over her words

"You know who. The people who gave us that letter!" Alonah said. "I told Neterka everything."

Ismene nodded; tears brimmed her eyes.

"It will be all right." Alonah squeezed her hands.

"They were in my *room*," Ismene said, louder than she wanted. "*My* room. How...?" The question trailed off and she bit back a sob.

"I don't know, but Neterka will take care of you. We can trust him."

Ismene nodded. She knew Alonah was right. Alistair trusted Neterka with the safety of the whole estate and everyone in it. This was no different.

"And when the general gets back, Neterka will tell him everything."

Ismene nodded again. "It is time."

Alonah watched her mistress's movements carefully. "And it's time you took some tea and got some rest."

Ismene did not argue with her nor refuse her help as she shifted the pillows so that Ismene could drink the tea while stretched out. Ismene drank in silence, her eyes looking off at some distant object, her mind elsewhere. No words were spoken between them as Alonah took the teacup, readjusted the pillows for a more reclined position, and covered her mistress with a thin blanket for sleep. And fall asleep she did—a rather fitful, restless sleep.

Alistair's sleep had been more restless than usual. He never slept deeply when in battle situations, but this was different. His mind was often on Ismene. How did she react to his letter? Should he have waited and said those things to her in person? The unexpected and exhilarating encounter with his precious Ismene that last night before he was to come to this place of war and bloodshed had touched him in more ways than he had ever felt before. If he closed his eyes, he could still remember the fragrance of her hair, the sweet lilt of her voice as she read to him, and imagine the feel of her skin, smooth against his own. It was enough to drive a man crazy.

Alistair only allowed himself to think on Ismene during his bouts of restless sleep. During the day, his mind was committed to the task of war. They had held their ground and held Palestine, if only by a thread some days. Antiochus was ravenous to control Palestine and he came after them day after day. How much longer would it last? Alistair had long since given up trying to guess. By all logical accounts, Antiochus should have given up days ago. One did not have an endless supply of men to die on this front, and in a cause that was so obviously hopeless.

Yet Antiochus continued to come at them, so Pharaoh and his troops continued to defend what was theirs.

This skirmish should have been over weeks ago, and it bothered Alistair that it wasn't. He longed to return home to his Ismene, and this was new territory for him. Built for battle, he had always enjoyed being in the field. Nothing drove him like the pressures of his job, and he never thrived more than when he was in his element.

There had become a routine to his day. He enjoyed being up before dawn to feel the crisp morning air as he walked amongst the ranks of his men preparing for what the day would bring. As they adorned themselves with armor, this camaraderie between soldiers and general boosted the troops' morale and readied them for the challenges of the day. It never failed that Alistair would bolster his troops with rousing words. He was by their side all day, commanding their movements and fighting alongside them as well. Therein is where he earned their respect.

Then, at the end of the day, he refused to eat until all of the troops had been served. That was just his way. After leading his troops to defend the land from another attack, he would retire to his tent and, after reviewing any details with his commanding officers, he would reflect on the day at large. Satisfied with having completed his duties for the day, he would then release his mind to where it had truly wanted to be—on thoughts of Ismene. And the ache in his heart would return.

Morning had come once again. Time for Ismene to rise, eat breakfast, and start her day's routine. Alonah helped her cleanse and dress for the day while another maidservant brought her some bread, cheese, and fruit. Ismene ate in silence, thinking on her day and the things that would fill it. She had her normal morning chores to do, then she would be journeying to the palace for lunch with Queen Arsinoe and many other Greek women recently transplanted to Egypt, followed by some gardening, before her afternoon and evening routines. Her days all began to look much the same, but she threw herself into her work. This kept her mind off of Alistair...somewhat.

It wasn't that she minded thinking of him. The problem was that, while it always started out as a pleasant, sweet thought, it caused an ache to grow in her heart for his absence to be over. She could no more hasten his return home than she could hurry the coming of the moon, but she was unable to keep her thoughts from dwelling on him during the evening when all was quiet and calm. And during the day she did what she could to stay busy, lest she give in to sadness.

Finishing her breakfast, she made her way toward the kitchen. This short trip took her out of the house, through the garden, and to the building behind the house. She couldn't help but stop and check on her flowers. Doing a spot-check on most of them, she took the time to get down on her knees and examine the tiger lilies. Gently touching their petals, she leaned in to enjoy their fragrance yet again.

After several minutes in the garden, it was time to meet Neterka in the kitchen. She moved past the lush greenery and into the building beyond. To her surprise, Neterka was not there waiting on her. Should she wait for him or seize this opportunity to start trying to do the inventory on her own? Ismene opted for the latter. Moving from basket to basket, she made mental notes of their stores of vegetables and grains.

Ismene was about halfway through the bins of grains. She reached for the next lid and pulled it easily off of the bin. Gasping, she jerked back from the sight that greeted her. The bin had been filled with locusts and maggots. It was all she could do to fight the urge to scream as she slammed the lid down. Taking deep breaths, she worked to keep from vomiting or fainting. Moving back out into the garden, she leaned against the outer doorframe as she took in the fresh air. Once she had somewhat regained her composure, she went over to the pool to splash water on her face. It was then that she saw Neterka coming out of the house toward her.

"Milady, I am sorry. I was detained with business of the estate." That's when he took in her condition. "Milady, are you well?"

She peered up at him from her place by the pool on her knees. "There is a bin of grain filled with...with..." She splashed more water on her face. "Locusts and maggots. I don't know how many more are."

Neterka's eyes darkened. "I will see to it, milady. But first, let me send for Alonah."

Ismene flipped around to sit by the pool, propping her knee up and resting her arm on it so that she could hold the back of her hand to her mouth.

It wasn't long before Alonah came from the house. "Milady! Another incident?"

Ismene nodded.

Alonah moved to help her up. Ismene waved her away. "I am capable of getting up. Please make sure Neterka rations bread for the next couple of days." Ismene got to her feet with slow, careful movements.

Alonah seemed to understand then that Ismene wanted to be alone, so she let her move toward the house by herself. Ismene couldn't settle on an emotion—anger or fear. Who was behind these incidents? Why? Why would they single out Alistair? Were they being singled out? There were too many questions and not one answer.

Hours later, Ismene sat in Pharaoh's great dining hall. She picked at the food on her plate, not finding anything appetizing after her encounter that morning. Even now, her stomach turned at the memory of what she had discovered. But it was more than that. Her appetite had not been right for days...weeks, maybe. Not since Alistair had left.

"How are you holding up?" Queen Arsinoe broke into Ismene's thoughts. The queen had seated Ismene in a place of honor to her right.

"I am well," Ismene lied, sighing, part of her wanting to be honest with the queen, and another part not wanting to be so honest in front of these women she had just met. One more glance told her that no one else was listening in.

"I don't believe you, you know," the queen said. "I can see how tired you are."

"You are most discerning, Majesty. I am tired and I miss my husband."

"It is understandable, Ismene. There is nothing wrong with missing your husband. I still miss Ptolemy from time to time, though I am more used to him leaving like this."

"I don't think I could ever get used to this. They have been gone for weeks!"

"And they may be gone for a couple more weeks yet."

"I don't know how I'll manage that."

"You will. And you will be stronger for it." There was kindness and understanding in her eyes.

"Thank you."

Arsinoe nodded to her. "Of course."

After some moments, Ismene found herself interested in the food in front of her and Arsinoe seemed glad to see her eat.

As their conversation came to a break, one of the ladies who had earlier been introduced as Brionna, seated a couple of seats away from the queen, attempted to get her attention. "Excuse me, Your Majesty?"

"Yes?" Queen Arsinoe recognized her to speak.

"I wanted to speak with you about some strange happenings at my home."

"Strange happenings?" Queen Arsinoe picked up her wine glass and took a long sip.

"This morning, and the reason I was delayed—my apologies, Your Majesty—is that a few of our grain bins were full of...well, I don't want to spoil your appetites, but..."

"Mine were too!" a young woman named Nerissa interjected. "And I know what you are about to say." She appeared a bit queasy.

"Anyone else?" Brionna asked.

Ismene and a couple of other ladies nodded.

"Our grain bins were fine this morning, but two nights ago, someone released our horses and it took our servants many hours to collect them." This time it was a middle-aged woman named Irinia who spoke up.

"That has happened to us as well!" Nerissa said.

A couple of other women nodded that they had been victims as well.

Ismene was horrified that these incidents were widespread, but couldn't help being a little bit relieved that she was not the only one.

"We had a message written in...well, written on our garden wall," Ismene spoke up.

No one else affirmed having had anything of the like happen, but they exchanged glances, concerned.

"What did the message say?" Nerissa asked quietly.

Ismene wished she hadn't said anything. She didn't like revisiting these things. But everyone was watching her, expecting her to speak. So she continued, her voice timid, quiet. "Go home."

Nerissa shivered.

"Chilling," Brionna agreed.

"I am glad that you have all brought these things to my attention," the queen said. "There isn't much I can do in Pharaoh's absence, but it will be the first item of business I bring to his attention once he returns home. In the meantime, I will share these concerns with Prince Meleager. If, at any time, any of you feels unsafe in your homes, please know that you are welcome to stay within the walls of the palace."

It was clear from the queen's tone that, while she was sincere, she did not wish to continue this conversation.

Ismene, of course, would concede, grateful to no longer be dwelling on it.

CHAPTER 8

The Hero Returns

Ismene dug her hands into moist soil. Tending the plants on the estate grounds kept her at ease, at peace. It gave her a sense of purpose. Even now she was tending to the plants in the inner court-yard, checking the dirt and seeing to their watering. This was one task she had taken upon herself in its entirety. She now preferred to oversee all of the gardening indoors and out. There were a few servants, including Alonah, who assisted her from time to time, but it was primarily she who tended to the plant life. That was the way she wanted it.

"You want to water it until the soil reaches this consistency." She reached in and felt the dirt, indicating that Alonah should do the same. "This is the right amount. Anything drier is insufficient, anything squishier is too much."

Alonah nodded, but Ismene wasn't sure she was getting it all. Her fear was that when it did come time for Alonah to water the plants, they would get whatever random amount Alonah put on them, that she might assume an overwatering or insufficient watering once or twice wouldn't hurt too much. Ismene was quite particular about her plants. Too particular for this kind of attitude. It had to be done right every time. So at the risk of insulting Alonah, she began the instructions again.

"Lady Ismene!" She heard a servant girl coming through the house, her voice echoing through the halls as she moved toward them. Ismene also heard her sandals slapping against the tile floor as she ran. Whatever was driving her to find her mistress was some manner of emergency in her mind.

Ismene stood to receive her, trying to brush and wipe off some of the dirt with her apron.

"Lady Ismene!" Now that the girl was closer, Ismene could identify her as one of the younger household servants, Mesi. The girl moved into the courtyard and spotted them. She rushed right up to Ismene and halted, attempting to catch her breath.

"Yes?" Ismene asked, unable to hide her amusement.

"Milady," she gasped. "Queen Arsinoe sent word that the soldiers have returned from battle!"

Ismene's jaw dropped and her knees became weak. She felt Alonah's hand on her arm to steady her as much as comfort her. Turning from Mesi, she flew out of the house, out of the entryway, and to the main entry gate. Putting a hand over her eyes to shield them from the harshness of the sunlight, her eyes frantically scanned the horizon, but there was nothing to be seen.

Alonah and Mesi were mere seconds behind her.

"Milady, the messenger also informed me that there is a parade outside of the palace," Mesi continued. "And that the general will march in the parade in victorious celebration. But we can know that he is safe and well."

Ismene continued to stare at the edge of hillside, not turning to look at Mesi or Alonah. *Should I go? Should I stay?* After these many weeks of waiting, she wanted to see him and confirm for herself that he was well. But she didn't want for him to arrive to an empty house while she was away trying to find him. That would not speak well of how she had managed his estate while he was gone.

"Send word to the queen that I have received the message and will wait here for my husband's return."

Mesi nodded and returned to the house to respond to the queen's messenger and send Ismene's reply.

Alonah came up behind Ismene. "We could wait by the window. Neterka can let us know as soon as he spots the general."

Ismene shook her head. "No. He will be here any minute and I want to be here waiting on him."

"As you wish."

"Please, Alonah, I insist you retire yourself to the other room. You need not wait out here."

She seemed almost ready to argue, but it had been a long day for them both and Alonah was grateful for the break. Nodding, she went back into the house.

Now Ismene could focus on the road. In the time that followed, her eyes scanned the extent of their boundaries without fail. Gaze glued to the farthest hill, she waited. She watched the way the reflection of the sun played across the sand as it met the sky and how the breeze blew at the dust. Minutes passed, how many she did not know. The truth was she didn't know how long she waited, watching shadows and studying any movement. It could have been a million years or a millisecond. All she knew was when that lone rider topped that far-off hillside. His form in sight, she could not remain still. Ismene took off after him, running across the warm sand.

Alistair was relieved when he laid eyes on his house, the limestone exterior sparkling in the distance. He was home! After all these weeks of being away, of daydreams of...of *her*. At long last, he would be able to see her, to touch her, to tell her all that was in his heart. As he drew closer to the grand estate, he noticed a form making its way toward him. Was it Neterka? Was something wrong? Squinting in the sunlight, he hoped to gain a clearer image of the runner. That's when he made out the long, lustrous, dark curls bounding behind the figure and he knew it was Ismene running to meet him. He urged his horse to go impossibly faster.

Though it was only a handful of seconds as the gap between them narrowed, to Alistair it felt like an eternity before he halted his horse and dismounted to meet her. She flew into his arms and embraced him fiercely as his arms closed around her. Returning her ferocity in the way he held her, feeling her heart beat against his, he was speechless.

When her breathing slowed to the point where speech was possible, she pulled back from him only enough so she could look at him as she breathed the words she had yearned to say for so long.

"I love you, Alistair." And then she kissed him.

He responded to her at once, drawing her closer still. His need to hold her was so great that he was afraid he would crush her. There were no words that could describe the feeling that washed over him. He felt complete...she loved him. Now he had everything he would ever need. Breaking off only when he became desperate for air, he rested his forehead on the top of her head.

"Ismene." He heaved, wanting to tell her what he was feeling, but was too overwhelmed.

She found her voice quicker than he. "I have wanted to tell you that for so long." Her hands came up to caress his face. "I love you." She rested her head on his chest, loving the closeness and the feel of his heartbeat under her hand. "I was so afraid I would never see you again, would never be able to tell you. Now that you are here, I feel as if I love you even more."

Pulling back so he could look into her face, he saw tears in her eyes, and he could feel them welling up in his own eyes.

"Never before have I felt the way I feel in this moment." He cupped her face. "I never knew that I could feel like this. You have captured my heart and I am hopelessly lost in you. I love you so much." He pressed his lips to hers once more and no more words were needed.

In the darkness, a torch was lit and the light flickered across the faces of the assembled men. Sefu, Nassor, Fadil, and Gahiji were gathered together for the first time in months. The radical faction of the mob seldom met. Since taking on this "extra work," they had not met as a group at all. No one but Sefu knew how many members of the radical faction were involved in this job.

"Brothers," Sefu said, "it has been too long since this many of our number has been together."

Nassor marveled at how Sefu exuded confidence every time he spoke: in the mob chambers, when he was arguing about the necessity of more extreme and direct measures in order for their voice and message to be heard, and in the company of his fellow radicals, who believed the point he was constantly trying to make.

"And will it be longer still until all of our group shall be in attendance?" Fadil asked. He was eager to know who else may have been recruited to their small faction.

"Yes," Sefu said, eyes narrowing, sensing Fadil's ulterior motives, "it is not safe right now for us to meet. We are suspected by many and our best advantage is our anonymity."

"You don't truly think the other members of the mob would betray us to Pharaoh, do you?" Nassor asked, nervous energy causing him to wring his hands. Nassor thought over how the mob reacted to the ideals that were the foundation of this group, how repulsed they were by radicals.

"I cannot be sure of anything if they do not agree with what we are doing." The comment slipped out. It was obvious that Sefu was annoyed with pulling punches for Nassor's sake. Yes, Nassor knew that Sefu was growing tired of reassuring him every step of the way and assuaging his every concern.

"Whatever we are doing is not accomplishing much!" Gahiji spoke up. It was his contact at greatest risk after all.

"Do not be so certain," Sefu countered. "I have it on good authority that we are rattling cages. So now is the time to push them a little further. All the more now that the mob has gotten involved with the other Greek families in the area. This is the perfect time to be bold, to be brazen. We can disguise our efforts as theirs."

"What did you have in mind?" Fadil asked, a crooked smile on his face.

"It needs to be something quite personal to her. Quite *painful* for her," Sefu said, his words deliberate, a slow smile breaking out across his face.

"Painful? Are we going to harm her?" Nassor said, concerned.

Sefu swore. "No, I meant significant. We're not going to kill anyone."

Nassor questioned whether Sefu would cast him in the role of proxy if he had it to do over again. Would he have even recruited him for this sect? His irritation with Nassor seemed to grow with each passing second.

"I think I know of a weakness. Something significant to her," Gahiji said.

Ah, Gahiji, now there was someone who wouldn't let him down.

"I hoped you would." Sefu smiled. "Tell me," he sneered, "what you know."

Alistair and Ismene approached the palace of Pharoah Ptolemy II. Dressed in their best linens, they were to be the honored guests at Queen Arsinoe's banquet to honor the victory of Pharaoh's army. Ismene was thrilled. She couldn't be more pleased with Alistair and his success. She had been coached about this evening's affair. While it was true that they were guests of honor, this evening was meant to honor Pharaoh. This whole thing would be treated as if the victory belonged to Pharaoh only. And, as much as Ismene did not like it, this was the way things were, so she'd had to come to a place of acceptance for Alistair's sake.

The main entrance to the palace was fast approaching. Ismene wrapped an arm around Alistair's. Turning toward her, he offered her a quick smile as he slowed the horses. They dismounted from their chariot at the entrance.

"You seem nervous," Alistair commented, taking Ismene's hand to help her down.

Her eyes met his. "I am...a little," she admitted. "This will be my first political function as your wife and I want to make you proud."

Now that she was down on the ground, he pulled on her hand,

drawing her closer to himself. "Do not worry so. I am well pleased with you. And quite proud to have the most beautiful woman in all of Egypt on my arm tonight."

Ismene felt her face warm at the compliment. She managed a smile for him, though she had no response.

"Ready now?" he asked, their faces so close he needed only to whisper.

"Um-hmm," she muttered, intoxicated by his closeness. She wondered if he would kiss her here in front of all these servants and arriving noblemen and noblewomen, but he did not. After several breaths passed, he pulled away and offered the crook of his arm to her. Turning her body in the direction of the entrance, she slid her hand onto his arm.

They made their way into the palace and then toward the banquet hall. The palace had always been a grand sight to behold, but today it was all the more amazing. The queen had spared no expense in preparing the hall for this party. There were lights, flowers, music, food, and crowds of celebrating people. It reminded Ismene of her engagement party, albeit this was a much grander event. That was the last time she had been in this room. Had it truly been so long ago? So much had changed. Things had seemed so bleak that day. Now her life was full of hope and promise. A life with Alistair.

They were announced as they came into the hall. No sooner had they set foot into the banquet space than they were set upon by hordes of people, or so it seemed to Ismene. Most of the people who came to greet them were the men in the higher military ranks who served with Alistair. She was pleased to meet them, but everyone was all too eager to speak with Alistair about one thing or another. Usually some talk of war.

It wasn't long into the conversations of the evening before she tired of talk of battles and politics. This did not escape Alistair. He could sense in his beloved that she was a sensitive soul and too much of the bragging of bloodshed became offensive to her sensitivities. Alistair excused them from a conversation with one of his captains, a man who was particularly overzealous, when he could see Ismene becoming a little queasy.

"I think it's time we stepped out for some fresh air." He took her arm.

Smiling in gratitude, she allowed him to steer her toward the entrance to the gardens.

At that moment, one of Pharaoh's advisers interrupted their exit.

"Pharaoh is having a discussion with Captain Ptah about a particular maneuver you utilized in battle and wishes you to join them."

Alistair glanced between the adviser and Ismene. "My wife and I were just stepping out for a minute. I'll be back soon."

Ismene sensed that he didn't want to put Pharaoh off, but that he didn't want to be guilty of choosing him over her needs either.

"General, I will be fine. Please, allow me to enjoy the gardens in solitude. These plants and I are old friends."

"Are you certain?" he asked in earnest.

"Of course. Our great Pharaoh calls," she said, smiling.

He pressed a kiss to the side of her face as they parted ways; he moved toward the heat of the party, she moved away from it.

Ismene headed out to the balcony overlooking the gardens she had fallen in love with those months before. If she were able to see through the thick underbrush, she could look into the room she had occupied back then. But it was overgrown in that area to afford those guests privacy from this vantage point. Instead, she gazed up at the stars and enjoyed the feel of the breeze sweeping over the tops of the palms.

"Not much for government and politics, lady?"

She spun around to see Meleager, Pharaoh's brother, watching her from the shadows.

"No, not this evening." She attempted a smile, though she didn't feel cordial toward him. His reputation preceded him. Both Alistair's lack of respect for the man and the general distaste the other noblewomen reported from their encounters with him left her unsure she wanted to encourage further conversation.

Moving out of the shadows, he walked over to where she was by the railing. "I always have mixed feelings about having more Greeks in Egypt."

He watched her. Was he wanting a reaction? She kept her features neutral, unchanging, and shifted her gaze back out over the gardens.

"I am every bit the Greek you are," he continued, "but Egypt is my home and I have always known it to be so. All Greece is to me is a bunch of stories."

She didn't turn back toward him. There was a nervous feeling in the pit of her stomach.

"Do you miss Greece?" he asked.

She thought for a moment. "Yes, Egypt is wild and untamed. Greece is refined and elegant."

"Yes, I can see that." His voice was deeper in that moment. "I regret that Egypt has yet to produce such beauty as we have received from Greece."

That got her attention. She shifted to look up at him. His eyes bore into her. Fighting the shiver that started between her shoulder blades and ran down her spine, she took a step back.

"I thank you for your kind words, but surely you exaggerate..."

He stepped toward her, "Egyptian women are roughened by the sand and sun, but you...your skin is soft and smooth...like silk." He ran the back of his hand down her arm.

She pulled away and backed into a bench, falling to a seated position. "Please, Prince, let me be. You are making me uncomfortable."

He leaned over her as he continued his musings. "Full hair, deep eyes..."

"Please," she repeated as she tried to scoot away, but his body was trapping her. "I should return to my..."

He pressed closer. "I think you should stay right where you are. We are just getting acquainted."

"And I think you should let the lady go before I am forced to remove you myself."

Meleager jerked his head to see behind himself and Ismene peered around him, relieved to see Alistair. He was standing, almost stoic, but his eyes were alive with murderous intent.

Alistair gave him no time to make a decision before he was upon them and Meleager almost didn't have time to move away. He pulled Ismene into his arms and stepped into the newly formed gap between Ismene and the prince.

"Ismene, are you all right? Did he hurt you?" Alistair spoke to her, but his eyes were leveled on Meleager, staring him down.

She shook her head.

Turning his body halfway around toward Meleager, Alistair puffed out his chest. His face was stern. Meleager, for his part, tried to retain some semblance of pride in his stance. He stood firm where he was, but his shoulders, slumped slightly, betrayed his nervousness.

"I suggest you think twice before you approach my wife again for *any* reason."

Meleager just stared back at Alistair. "And might I suggest you watch your words, sir. You are bold to threaten a prince of Egypt."

Alistair met the unspoken challenge with his own. "Don't make this the time and place we do this. I would hate for that display to take the last shred of dignity you have."

Meleager glared at Alistair for only a handful of seconds before he backed down, moving away and slipping back into the house.

Turning back toward his wife, Alistair embraced her fully. Then he pulled back, still gripping her forearms, so he could look her over to confirm that she indeed was untouched. Satisfied that there was no physical injury, his eyes sought and searched hers. He cupped her face with his hand.

"I'm all right, only a little shaken—thanks to you. I'm afraid to think of what might have happened had you not shown up."

He pulled her into his arms again. "Me too, my love. Me too."

They held each other for a time, taking comfort in the stillness of the moment.

"Ismene, I must take better care to protect you. I should have gone with you. I'm sorry."

"No, I told you I would be fine. I never thought there would be so much danger here in Pharaoh's palace."

"I know. Now you know that evil lurks everywhere."

She nodded against his chest.

"Especially when there is such a prize at stake, my love. I have so much to lose if anything happened to you."

"General," a voice called from behind Alistair. It was Captain Ptah. "You have found the Lady Ismene?"

"Yes, thank you. Would you please inform Pharaoh Ptolemy that I will be taking the Lady Ismene home to retire. Tell him that we are quite worn and convey my sincerest apologies."

Captain Ptah nodded and went to his task.

It was late at night, and the members of the mob were filing into the meeting room in silence. Many of them wore hooded robes or other garments to try and hide their features, which was not surprising to anyone. There were many who were happy to see each other because they didn't get to meet at any venue other than this, but the whole atmosphere was dull and subdued. Tarik brought the meeting to order as he stood up at the front of the group and started speaking.

"We have more recruits who have seen the vileness that the Greeks bring to our lands. Our strength grows." The similar sense of agreement at the last meeting was again felt this time. It was always good to hear at each meeting that they were growing, though nobody had actually counted the number who were in the room and compared it to previous meetings.

"We have started our campaign to let these rich Greeks know that they are not wanted here. But don't forget, we are still a small group. Do not do something idiotic that will expose us. If our Greek rulers find out that we are behind these attacks, we would all be drawn and quartered in the desert." Again, Tarik jabbered on with his usual need for secrecy.

"Our attacks?" Sefu shouted out. "You call ruining some of their food and turning their horses out for a run in the fields an attack? What are we going to do next? Dump sand in their beds?" Sefu was exhibiting his usual disgust with this group's lack of true action.

Nassor was chuckling in agreement with Sefu, but when he saw Tarik's reaction, it seemed a little off. He had expected to see the man's anger rise with Sefu's typical insubordination, but their eyes seemed to be clinched together, like they were having a conversation. A slight grin seemed to spread on Tarik's face, and Sefu had a smirk of his own. *What was that?*

"You are out of order," Tarik said. "What would you have us do, Sefu, slit their throats in the night?"

Sefu scowled at that comment. "Come now, that is ridiculous."

They continued this back-and-forth for a short time. Everyone followed the interchange with baited breath, waiting to see who would dominate the exchange and take charge. There were no elected officials here; Tarik's leadership was loosely held. People had accepted him because he had stepped forward when they needed someone most. He had promised them action and shown strength greater than their previous leader. It wasn't long before Tarik took the upper hand in the interchange and insisted they move on to the next item of business.

Nassor agreed that these attacks didn't seem like much of a disruption and felt that his and Sefu's methods were much more effective at sending a signal for the Greeks to get out. But that gaze Tarik held on Sefu...when Nassor had first seen it, he'd thought it was connected to the constant bickering between those two. He had assumed Tarik wanted to toss Sefu out on his ear but couldn't. Tarik's gaze seemed to connote that. But at these latest meetings, since their radical group had started launching real attacks, the connection between Sefu and Tarik seemed a lot more mysterious. Was Tarik the one who had hired Sefu? *Is this the reason the mob's attacks were so pathetic?* He started to wonder if this constant arguing was just an act.

Nassor didn't know how to find an answer to this. *There's no use in asking Sefu. He hasn't told me yet, so why now?* But deep down, Nassor wanted to know who they were working for. His endless sense of uncertainty and need for direction made him nervous, always hoping that more details would give him more confidence.

The meeting broke and everyone parted company, sneaking back to their estates. As Sefu and Nassor left together, Sefu balked out loud, "I can't believe they actually decided to put sand in everyone's beds. This group is going downhill fast."

Nassor let Sefu bluster as he always did after these meetings. He was only listening with one ear as he rolled back and forth his thoughts about Tarik.

Ismene had been bathed at once upon their return home from Pharaoh's party. Alonah was finishing their night routine when there was a knock at the door.

Alonah went to receive the caller, but they both knew who it was. Opening the door confirmed it—the master of the house. He had become a regular fixture around Ismene's bedchambers during the hours he was home.

"Please, come in." She bowed.

He nodded. "Is the Lady Ismene able to receive me?"

"Yes, I shall tell her that you have requested her company," Alonah said before disappearing into the bedchambers. Mere seconds later, Ismene appeared through the door, Alonah close behind her.

Alonah nodded her farewell and took her leave of them.

Once they were alone, Alistair gathered Ismene into his arms. "Love, are you truly all right?"

"I am." She sighed, closing her eyes and just breathing in the scent of him. "Now."

He kissed the top of her head and rubbed her back. When he closed his eyes he could still see the scene that he had come upon when he had found her on the balcony, and his blood ran hot. He forced his mind back to the present.

"I have a surprise for you."

"Truly?"

"I thought I might read to you."

"Oh?" She pulled back to look into his face. "That *is* a pleasant surprise. I think, sir, that you have found my weakness."

"I think you know mine too, milady." He said, drawing her in for an intimate kiss.

When they parted, he moved her farther into her room.

"To bed with you," he commanded, giving her a little push toward the bed.

He tucked her in, letting his hand cup her face and his thumb stroke her cheek before pressing another kiss to her lips.

"Now, lie back and let me pick up where we left off," he said, taking a stool closest to the bed and pulling it over closer to her.

She lay back. "If you can remember where that was. As I recall, you fell asleep the last time we were in this book together."

"Hmm…" he mused. "I'll just pick up…" He opened the book, preparing to select a random chapter to start at, but was startled by what he found and was not able to hide it from Ismene.

As he opened the book, Ismene's tiger lilies, now little more than mulch, had fallen from the pages. And there were gashes in the pages of her book. Her hands flew to her mouth and she let out a loud cry. In one motion, Alistair set the book down and slid onto the bed, gathering Ismene in his arms once again. He held her to himself, soothing her, trying to calm her. She was crying now, sobbing uncontrollably.

"Shh, shh, my love, all is well."

"I can't…it's too much…I…I…"

"I know, I know. Your treasured flowers, your cherished book." Kissing her head, he rocked her. He could not replace these precious things she had just lost—both of them in seconds.

She gazed up at him with red eyes. "This is a great loss to me, but it's all of the other things too—the note, the sheets, the dagger, the food. All of it. It's too much!"

"What is all of this you speak of?" he asked, brows furrowed.

"Did Neterka not tell you?" she spoke, her voice raised, eyes wide.

"None of that sounded familiar."

Ismene, through her tears—some coming fresh as she recalled each event—recounted to him all that had happened, including the note she and Alonah had received and the night she found the sheets shredded and the dagger in the door.

Alistair listened, engrossed in her story, disturbed by all he was hearing.

"Why did you not tell me sooner?" he asked.

"I didn't tell you about the note because I didn't want to worry you. But after the sheets and dagger, I understood that Neterka would be sure you knew of everything that had transpired."

He nodded, not sure what to make of that.

"Who do you think would be doing these awful things?" Ismene sniffled, trying to contain more tears that threatened to overwhelm her.

He paused for a moment. "I am not sure, my love. But we will find out."

She pulled back so she could look up at him. "You know something you're not telling me, don't you?"

His eyes searched hers, not sure if he should tell her what he knew. How much would it worry her? Or was it unfair to keep any information from her? He decided the latter was truer.

"We are not the only ones being harassed by these people."

"Yes, I discovered the same thing at a luncheon the queen held for some of the Greek ladies in the area. The ladies shared some of the things happening on their own estates." Ismene's eyes fell, her face downcast.

Looking at her downturned gaze, he guessed she was feeling guilty about her relief that others were suffering the same things they were. He pulled her face up with a finger under her chin so that he could look her in the eyes.

"I, too, was relieved that it wasn't aimed only at us. We still have a common enemy out there to find, but it means there is not someone out there to get *you* or *me*. It doesn't mean that we are wishing evil on others."

She nodded. "How will we ever discover who is behind all of this?"

"We must examine all of the evidence, piecing everything together. There is an answer there. No crime is perfect. There is going to be some crucial piece of information somewhere along the way and we will find it."

His voice was so confident that she believed him without reservation. She leaned against him, feeling how worn she was from the events of the evening. He pulled the covers up so he could slip underneath and encouraged her to snuggle up to him more securely. Once settled, they both drifted off to sleep.

Alonah found it nearly impossible to sleep. She could not stop thinking about the events of the night before. Not the horrible events that had been transgressed against her mistress, but the wonderful, yet confusing things that had happened to her.

Jabari wanted to marry her. Imagine...she...the wife of a soldier. What would life be like to no longer be a servant, but to be a woman of some standing? Even now, her memory replayed their encounter while her master and mistress were at Pharaoh's party.

"My dear, sweet Alonah, I love you. And when people feel the way we do, they should be married."

"Married? Don't tease me, Jabari!" She turned away from him.

"I would never joke about this, my angel. I want you to be my wife," he said, placing his hands on her shoulders, then wrapping his arms around her.

She paused. "I do love you, Jabari." She shifted to face him, pressing a kiss to his lips. "But can we actually do this? Can we afford it?"

"I can support us with my salary. Many men in the army keep a family on their pay. We may have a small house, but we will have each other."

"I don't need a big house. I just need you."

A broad smile crossed his face then and he took her lips in a kiss that seemed to go on forever. However, as usual, they'd had to part when she'd been summoned that Alistair and Ismene were to return home after Ismene had been assaulted. She'd made her apologies to Jabari and left him there with no real answer.

So, now that she was more separated from the situation, she had some space to think. What kinds of obstacles would they have to overcome? Were there many Greek-Egyptian pairings in Alexandria? Or would they be looked down on, even persecuted for this? Did that matter to her? Would she still work for Ismene? Would it anger Ismene that she would no longer be her lady-in-waiting? If so, that might mean that they would no longer be friends. Alonah counted on Ismene for support in the event she married. Could she do it without Ismene's friendship and support?

In the heat of the moment she had told Jabari all she needed was him, but she was not that naive. She knew that a person needed more than just a spouse in life to get by, especially when one was married to a soldier who was gone all day and absent weeks at a time. No, she dared not burn bridges with Ismene.

CHAPTER 9

Secrets

"CAN YOU PLEASE TAKE THIS BLINDFOLD OFF?" ISMENE loved surprises, but couldn't stand the waiting. Alistair had risen early to prepare a special breakfast for them and served her in bed. Then he had told her that he had something special planned for them today—a special place for them to visit.

"Not yet," Alistair said as he gripped her waist. Their chariot went over a bump which caused him to pull her to him even more tightly. She smiled at the feel of his secure embrace; even after this short time it still caused butterflies in her stomach.

She felt the chariot continue to move down the smooth path with a little rocking here and there as the wheels found imperfections in the road.

"We're almost there, I promise," he assured her. His voice was close to her ear and it gave her warm chills. She thought of the feel of those lips on her neck. There wasn't much time to daydream, though, because, true to his word, it wasn't much longer before she felt him slow the horses and still the chariot.

"Ready for your surprise?" he asked.

"Yes!" She feigned exasperation.

Only then did he reach up, untie her blindfold, and let it fall. "The great Library of Alexandria."

Her breath caught in her throat. She had seen some amazing structures on her journey. Egypt boasted some magnificent buildings, and this was no exception. In fact, it proved to be one of the more breathtaking structures she'd had the chance to behold.

The building was U-shaped and their vantage point at the top of the U gave them the best view of the entire layout. Separating them from the entrance was a massive pool with beautiful gardens lining either side. The surrounding buildings opened to the inner yard with gorgeous columns that seemed to draw the viewer inward toward the main structure. Massive stairs invited Ismene upward into the facility and four large pillars at the entrance gave it ambiance. Potted palm trees livened the journeyer's heart and added to the sheer mass of the entrance.

"Shall we?" Alistair indicated that they should take the path she had just seen and make their way into the library.

All she could manage was a nod, unable to speak, still lost in the splendor of the building.

As they moved closer and closer, she felt smaller and smaller. Stepping inside altered that perception only somewhat as they found themselves standing in a massive lobby. As she gazed around the space, she noted that the floor and walls were covered with beautiful tiles. The floor tiles were dark and patterned, the walls light and clean. Even the lobby had a small, square pool in the center of the room with plants adorning the corners of the room. Ismene could see that the library had three stories as the top two floors had decorative balconies that looked out onto the main lobby and pool. Overlooking the room were two grand pictures of Egyptian rulers. Who they were Ismene could not say and Alistair did not know.

Alistair escorted her into one of the book rooms. Just like the lobby, it was an open room. The tile work on the floor was different, light-colored with a gold-inlaid pattern. Dark-colored pillars dotted and decorated the walls of the room which were lined with bookshelves—diagonally stacked boards that formed diamond-shaped openings for the scrolls that contained each book. There must have been hundreds, thousands even, in this room alone.

"So many books," Ismene said, at last able to find her voice as she reached out to touch one.

"Pharaoh Ptolemy has set a goal of 500,000 scrolls."

She jerked around and met his gaze, wide-eyed. That many books in one place was unimaginable. It was difficult enough to wrap her mind around the number that filled this one room. Having access to books was a rare gift. The fact that she owned her own was rather special. Her book about Pegasus had been a prized gift from her father which he had paid a great amount for.

They continued to move from room to room. She couldn't get enough.

"What a grand library!" Ismene gasped. Did the people of this city know what a rare jewel they had?

"Your love of reading is admirable, so I wanted to share this with you." Alistair smiled at her. "I knew that you could appreciate it."

They came into a room where several men were working at a couple of tables. The men were in deep discussion. Several of the men were impassioned in their speech, others calm but insistent.

"Who are these men?" she said, lowering her voice.

"They are Jews whose land has been conquered. They are attempting to preserve their culture by translating their holy scriptures into Greek. Pharaoh has commissioned them to create this translation so that it is more accessible."

"Oh?" Ismene lit up. She was excited to find such a grouping that spoke her native tongue. Though they were every bit the strangers to her that the Egyptian people were, she felt a camaraderie with them. They were rather intent on their work, a work to preserve a culture. She knew precious little of the Jews and, in truth, what she did know she did not trust to be completely factual.

"Are they holy scriptures about one of the Greek gods?"

"No...they believe in one god."

"Hmm...one god. That sounds different."

One of the men at the table closest to them had overheard and injected. "My lady, if you don't mind my saying, it *is* quite different. We are unique among peoples in that we follow one god."

"And who is the god you follow? Zeus? Ra?"

He shook his head. "Jehovah."

"I've never heard of a god named 'Jehovah.'" Her eyes caught the man's gaze and moved between him and Alistair. For his part, Alistair offered only a slight shrug.

"I am not surprised." The man's tone was gentle, but confident. "He is not a god, He is *the* God."

Ismene was taken aback. "You speak quite brazenly to someone you do not know."

"Forgive me for any offense, but it is because I speak of what I know."

Ismene thought on that for a handful of seconds.

"I would be happy to read you some of our holy scriptures and let you see for yourself," the man offered.

"What are these holy scriptures?" Skeptical, but curious, Ismene couldn't decide what to think.

"They are the history of my people, passed down through the generations."

Ismene pursed her lips. "I admit I know little of your people. I am willing to hear a little perhaps."

"Then I will look for your return," he said before getting back to his work.

Ismene and Alistair moved on, but her mind stayed in that conversation. She had met religious zealots before, but never someone who was calm, collected, sane, and still that confident in what he believed. Perhaps she would at least enjoy hearing the history of his people.

Before she knew it, they had completed their tour of the library. Ismene wanted to take every single book home with her, but knew that they would not allow her to leave with even one. She would have to make this a regular stop. To read, converse with the Greek scholars, and enjoy the solitude.

"This was...amazing. Thank you."

"My pleasure. I had already arranged for Neterka to see that you are able to be brought here as you please, but I sense that you are already making plans for a return trip. And perhaps if I am to be away again, it can be a welcomed diversion."

She nodded, but did not smile. As much as she appreciated his thoughtfulness, she loathed to think of that time of separation or imagine repeating that experience.

While her mistress was on her surprise outing with Alistair, Alonah sneaked out of the house and made her way to the barracks outside of the palace in hopes of seeing Jabari. She took up a spot behind a tree so that she was not easily spotted by the soldiers coming and going. After a couple of hours of waiting, she was rewarded when Jabari came out for a midday stroll.

"Jabari!" she called out, trying to remain hidden.

He twisted around, trying to discern where the sound had come from.

She glanced about and, after a couple of soldiers were back in the barracks, she stepped out from behind the tree. "Jabari!"

He spotted her and jogged over, looking out for others that might spot their rendezvous as well. When he made it over to her, however, all thoughts of onlookers were in the far reaches of his mind. Taking her in his arms, he kissed her deeply.

"I am so glad to see you," he said. "I was a little worried after our last conversation."

She cupped his face. "I know. And I'm sorry. I do love you, Jabari. And I want to marry you. I'm just concerned about all of the obstacles that are in our way."

He rested his forehead on hers as he nodded. "It is selfish of me, I know."

"No. I am so flattered. And you would be rescuing me from a life of servitude. Do not be sorry."

"I should be. For my desire is selfish, Alonah. I fear my thoughts are not for freeing you, but of how much I want to marry you, for you to be mine...forever."

"I want that too."

He pulled her further away from the barracks. "Then why shouldn't we marry? Forget the obstacles. We will overcome them all...together."

"If only we could forget them." Alonah frowned.

"We could." Jabari's eyes lit up. "If we marry in secret."

She looked up at him questioningly, but his eyes were serious.

"We would be bound together forever, but we would have time to take on these obstacles you speak of at our own pace. It's the best of both, Alonah."

"It's crazy, Jabari. You can't be serious."

"But I am...quite serious. Can you not see how perfect it would be?"

She was starting to see how it could be. But there was something in her that hesitated.

"We would get what we want—to be married. But nothing else would change. At least not for now."

Gazing into the eyes of the man she loved, she could not deny him. She loved him too much. "When? How?"

"I know a priest who will do it."

"It will have to be in the middle of the night, I fear." She did not want to get married like this—sneaking away in the dark of night. "I cannot know if or when I can get away like this again."

He nodded. "It will be all right," he said, reading the concern in her eyes. He pressed a long kiss to her lips. "I love you."

She rested her head on his broad chest and savored the feel of his strong arms around her. "And I love you."

The next morning, Ismene woke and reached for her husband. He responded by pulling her into his arms, kissing the top of her head.

"I have to get up soon," he said, regretting every word. They both knew what he was not saying—that he would also need to head out to spend the day with his troops instead of with her.

Ismene groaned in protest and hugged him tighter. She wasn't ready for her husband to be parted from her, but she knew it was inevitable.

They lay in each other's arms for several more minutes before he gave her a warm squeeze and pressed a kiss to her lips. "It is time, my love."

She nodded.

They both moved to their respective edges of the bed, pulling robes on, before moving toward the lounge pieces. Alistair rang for Neterka and sat down next to Ismene to get the last bits of morning snuggling before breakfast.

It wasn't long before Neterka came with their breakfast and they were forced to end their closeness to eat. There wasn't much conversation while they ate. They just enjoyed being together, and Ismene's thoughts kept drifting to the fact that Alistair would be leaving in only a matter of a half hour or so. Ismene had so enjoyed having him to herself the day before. She longed for a time when that would be the norm. But would it ever be? Not realistically. It didn't even matter how much he wanted to be here with her. His first duty was to Pharaoh and the army. That was that. Today she would be throwing herself into her work, trying to will the day to go by faster. No matter what, she knew she would be counting the minutes until his return.

As they finished the last bites on their plates, Alistair pulled Ismene to him again.

"I have to prepare myself and go, love." He embraced her. "Oh, but how I hate leaving you for one second!"

She knew he spoke the truth. "I know. I hate it too."

Ismene had often been thankful she had not been married to a politician or man of government. In that moment, she was jealous of those wives that would have more time with their husbands day to day. But he would not be Alistair if he didn't do what he did. If he were a politician, he would be a different person. She wouldn't change one thing about him. He was perfect.

Alistair released her to stand up. Ismene stood with him, throwing her arms around him, standing on her tiptoes and pulling him to her for a deep farewell kiss. He returned the kiss with his whole heart.

Neterka had not quite figured out what to do with the extra time he had in his day now that the mistress of the house insisted on helping and, in some cases, taking over duties that used to be under his control. It was hard for him to not feel perturbed at the Lady Ismene. He was confused at his own feelings. These were things that shouldn't fall under his purview with a mistress in the house, but they had been part of his day-to-day routine as the house had had no mistress for so long. He should feel nothing but relief that he no longer had anything but his ascribed duties to perform. This was not the case.

On the other hand, he did care for the Lady Ismene. She was kind, caring, and had a desire to do right by Alistair and the staff. They were fortunate to have such a benevolent mistress. She had taken to her duties quite well. It had been clear to him that she had never done anything like this before. Her mother had not properly trained her. Maybe this was not part of Greek culture to train the younger women in the house. Maybe as a daughter of privilege she had been busy with other things. He knew she had been educated. And he discovered that she was a fast learner. That had made his job easy and quick. And soon over, he brooded.

For now, Neterka spent this new free time in his room, where he found himself gazing over the objects that had once belonged to the source of his confused emotional state. It was an evening so long ago when General Merenre had come to him and asked him to save these things from the private chapel. For what purpose, he did not know. It was some kind of Greek ceremony. So Neterka had held on to these things in his quarters. He had, perhaps inappropriately, placed the statue of the horse with wings on a stand in his room. It intrigued him and was, by his definition, very Greek. The statuette seemed so silly to him, something that only the Greeks would come up with. Egyptian figures were strong, heroic, bold. Not what he would call fanciful.

For the first time since he had brought these things into his room, whether out of boldness or boredom, he decided to riffle through the contents of the container. He felt terrible about this, but he had been looking at this box for weeks now and wondering why Merenre had him collect these things in the first place. Perhaps it was so that he would look through and do some checking on Ismene. If so, he had already been negligent in doing his due diligence. Neterka decided it was better to check things out. If nothing was amiss, then he would keep it to himself. If there was something out of place, then he would chance the general's ire for his own sake.

There were pieces of clothing—nothing there. A knife—strange, but nothing too much out of place about that, he figured. Then he rediscovered the letters. He remembered noticing these before and thinking them quite odd. Once again, he had a crisis of conscience. Ismene had placed all of these things in the private chapel and had left them expecting, rightfully so, that they would be disposed of. She would have never imagined that someone would now be in possession of them, wondering if they should be opened and read. Should he read them? There was nothing in Ismene's character that would lead him to suspect her of any malfeasance. Yet, was it his place to make that call? Or was it suspicious enough that she had secret communication that she desired to be disposed of?

Neterka decided that it would be best to read the letters and determine the best course of action afterward. With that in mind, he opened the first letter. As he skimmed the contents, he knew it was going to be a trial—they were in Greek. His lessons in reading Greek were not as far along as his language lessons. What he could pick up made his eyes widen. These were love letters! They were extremely private. He closed the letter at once, and he was no more sure if he should share these with Merenre than he was before.

Ismene stood still as a statue, gazing out across the unforgiving barrenness of the desert. Her eyes were focused, unwavering, on the horizon. Many hours had passed while she maintained her constant vigil, her eyes ever-watchful for Alistair. She sat in his outer bedchambers, that window giving her the best view out of the house in the direction of Pharaoh's palace. Alistair was late in returning home. Her mind, of course, dwelt on the last time his return had been delayed and what he had said to her that night.

"When Pharaoh makes a decision, we go..."

Had they been called away into battle? So abruptly that they were unable to send word? Perhaps there was an attack that had led to defeat? Such thoughts plagued her mind and made her restless. All she knew for certain was that her heart ached for him to be home and it scared her to think that she would be lost without him. That's just how she felt at that moment—lost and helpless.

A noise from behind her startled her from her daze. Her head jerked to the direction of the disturbance and her eyes met Neterka's. There was both concern and understanding written on his face.

"Pardon my interruption, milady," he started.

She nodded. "Of course. Has there been word?" She knew from his expression that there hadn't, but she asked for good measure.

He shook his head.

She turned back to face the window, glaring out into the night and willing his figure to appear over that farthest hill. However, nothing materialized, least of all Alistair. It was no use. Wishing him to be there would not conjure him up.

"Milady, you must rest," Neterka insisted.

She did not respond or even turn to face him. Stubbornness had never been one of her more prominent character traits, but on this night, it was the one that showed through.

"This is not the first time the general's arrival has been delayed without word." Neterka tried to reason with her. "We have come to accept it and expect that we will receive word if something has happened to him. Pharaoh's house would have sent a messenger if they had been attacked or sent to battle. They would not leave us to wonder."

She nodded, turning back to look at him. "I know that you are right..."

He offered her a small smile, relieved that she was listening to reason. Raising his arm, he waved his candle to light her way to her room.

"But I cannot shake this restlessness. I prefer to await his return right here," she said, leaving no room for argument. There was going to be no convincing her otherwise. Rational or not, this was her decision. It made no sense, in her opinion, to retire to her suite to sit up and worry after her husband when she could do the same here, but know that much sooner when he was returning.

Neterka's expression was hard to decipher. Disappointment? A sad understanding? Either way, he had no choice but to concede.

"Thank you for your concern," she added.

He was ready to protest, but thought better of it and nodded instead. "If you need anything, I will be listening for you."

She nodded and returned to her vigil at the window, eagerly gazing at the hilltop in the direction of Pharaoh's palace. Neterka excused himself and moved back out of the room.

Slipping through the front door, Alistair was careful not to make too much noise. He was well practiced at these late-night returns. Now that he was home, his mind returned to what it had been dwelling on all evening—his regret at not being home to spend the evening with Ismene. Alistair missed her smile and her comforting presence, but duty called. As much as he wanted to, he would not even entertain the possibility of waking her for his own selfish reasons.

As soon as he was in the house, Neterka was in front of him, startling Alistair. It had been a while since Neterka had greeted him on one of his late-night returns. Over their time as master and valet, it had taken many scoldings on his part to convince Neterka that there was no need for him to wait up for Alistair or wait on him when he did get home. Alistair assured Neterka that he was capable of finding food for himself. He knew that his faithful servant still always waited up for him, but at least Neterka had stopped insisting that he serve Alistair at such an awful hour.

At this unexpected welcome, Alistair's question was written all over his face before he spoke it. "Has something happened?" His thoughts were immediately on Ismene.

"No, General, everything is fine," Neterka replied, trying to assure his master that there were no dire circumstances.

Alistair allowed Neterka to take his cloak.

"I am pleased you are well and home," Neterka said.

"Thank you." Alistair did not appreciate the pleasantries, so he got to the point. "You know that I am not pleased to see you up and about." They began making their way down the hall.

"Do you require food?" Neterka continued to attempt to wait on Alistair.

"No, thank you." Alistair was becoming irritated with Neterka's manner. Why was he still up? Had they not had this discussion multiple times? "Pharaoh's house sent food for the soldiers, but I would like to know what has kept you up. Not me, I hope." There was an edge to his voice.

Neterka nodded. Now that they had arrived at Alistair's private receiving room, he seemed prepared to share why he had been waiting up. "I have not been the only one awaiting you."

Opening the door to Alistair's outer bedchambers, Neterka indicated that Alistair should enter. He didn't have to. Through the open doorway, Alistair could see the light cast from a candle within and the scene that greeted him warmed his heart. Ismene had pulled a chair over to the window to sit and watch for his return. Her body leaned toward the window in her watchful vigil, but her form was still and quiet. Exhaustion had overcome her.

"How long has she been like this?"

"I insisted that she retire for sleep, assuring her that had something happened to you, we would have received word. Still, she insisted on watching for you. Since your lateness was notable, she has been here...perhaps four hours or so. She passed to sleep only within the hour."

"Thank you for your diligence, Neterka." Alistair regretted his earlier annoyance with him. He was only doing as Alistair would have wished—waiting up to keep an eye on the mistress of the house.

"Of course, General. Do you require any other assistance?"

"No, please retire yourself for the night." Alistair hoped that his voice and eyes communicated his apologies.

Neterka nodded and moved to leave.

Alistair watched his wife's fitful sleep and felt guilty. Chiding himself, he realized that he was still conducting his life as if it were his own. She was not one of his servants who would have to learn to abide by some arbitrary rules he set up; she was his wife and her concern for him touched him. He remembered another night quite some time ago when he had arrived home late to find her waiting up for him. That night his news had disturbed her and the month that followed, not knowing what was happening to him, had affected her.

A couple of months ago, he would have expected her to not worry after him, but things were different now. He scolded himself for his thoughtlessness.

Alistair continued to watch Ismene in the candlelight. He had thought that it was not possible to love her any more than he already did, yet here he was, his love for her swelling within him even now.

He crept to where she sat and touched her face. After a moment, he leaned in to kiss the woman who overwhelmed him with her devotion. She stirred and returned his kiss, leaning into his embrace as if by instinct. The moment was all too brief before she pulled back. Her deep eyes gazed up at him and he saw the worry there.

"I feared I'd never see you again," she said, choking back tears.

"Ismene, I..." he started, but he couldn't find the words to excuse himself.

"Why did you not send word?" Anger born from loving concern was present in her voice. "I thought of all the things that could have happened to you. They all had the same terrible ending."

"Ismene, my love, I am so sorry. I was wrong. It never occurred to me that you would be so concerned at my lateness. It was thoughtless and stupid."

"Yes it was. I was so worried and distressed that, had I not lost my hold on consciousness, I was forming a plan to go in search for you myself."

Alistair's eyes widened at the thought of her going out alone at this dark hour. He realized then the full measure of her concern. His eyes searched hers in silence. He was unable to voice the rush of emotion in him—relief that she had not gone out and regret for her distress. The only response he had was to take her into his embrace and hold her firmly. She held on to him as well.

"I am so sorry, my love," he whispered into her ear. "So sorry."

She nodded against his chest. "It is so hard to wait for you here. If Pharaoh calls for battle, you must go."

There was no answer for her, no reassurances he could give. She was right. His duties called for him to be subservient to the Pharaoh in such a way. If his men went to battle, so did he. It had always been that way and it had never been a question in his mind. To lead his men, he had to be the first one to sacrifice, the first one to give, but he had never had to give up so much, risk so much as this last ride into war.

Loving her meant hurting for her as well. He had never known such empathy before. He ached for her. This was a challenge he had underestimated in his decision to marry. Then again, he had never dreamed he would have fallen so completely in love with his wife.

"Come with me?" he pulled back to look at her.

She nodded.

Alistair stood, taking her hand in his and leading her out into the dark hallway. They walked in silence through the maze-like corridors until they reached the garden outside.

He stopped just outside of the house and turned to her. "Wait here."

She was only alone for a few minutes before he returned with a ladder. He leaned it against the wall and urged her to go up ahead of him.

Coming up behind her, he helped her up the ladder as he went. It wasn't long before they reached the top. She stepped onto the roof of their house. She had never been up here before. A quick scan told her that the rest of the household frequented this spot. There were mats in one corner made of straw, pitchers in another, and leafy branches in bundles in several places. As big as the house was, the roof didn't look so big, but it was staggered.

Alistair walked up behind her. "The roofs of Egyptian houses are used as open bedchambers during hot nights," he explained. "These mats and branches provide soft beds for the household servants as they choose."

She gazed out over the garden and closed her eyes as a gentle breeze sweeping over the tan earth reached her and lifted her hair from her shoulders. In that moment, she felt the peaceful stillness of the vast desert around her.

Alistair was watching her thoughtfully. Shifting toward him, she opened her eyes; they were bright and ever so deep in the moonlight. She was even more breathtaking in this light.

"There's more," he managed when he found his voice.

She raised an eyebrow and reached for his hand, curiosity and excitement in her eyes. He led her across the area set up for the house servants to a small ledge. Jumping down with ease, he held his arms up to swing her down. Obliging, she relished the feeling of any chance to be close to him.

As she gazed over the roof, she tried to map out the house in her mind. The spaces were not easy to correlate, but there wasn't much time for her to dwell on these things as Alistair soon drew her attention to where he was leading her. They moved toward a far corner of the roof. A portion was raised quite a bit higher, set apart from the rest of the building. It was a strange structure and she was amazed that she had not noticed it before from the outside of the house. When they reached it, he paused for a moment.

Turning toward her, he placed both hands on her arms. "Please wait here."

She nodded, then watched his silhouetted figure as it moved around the large structure and disappeared behind it.

It was only then she realized how tired she was. The day had dragged on for too long and the last few hours had been emotionally draining. In order to keep her mind active, she busied herself studying the layout of the building. If the gardens were back there, the servants' rooftop area must be above the dining chamber. That gave way to the great hallway and major guest arena. That would mean that the ledge they had dropped down from must be the division between the dining and sitting room areas. She was able to identify the kitchen and servant quarters before she heard movement. Spinning around, she saw Alistair approaching her.

Ismene was all too ready for Alistair when he reached for her. He led her behind the structure. As she moved around it, she saw that it only appeared to be on the corner of the building. It was just far enough away from the outer wall that it would not be visible to those on the ground. There was a ladder woven from rope hanging down from the roof of the structure. Only it did not look as weathered as the straw mats. Alistair must have had a hiding place for it.

"Can you make the climb or would you rather I pull you up?" he asked, his voice soft.

"I can climb it."

She took the farthest rung she could reach and started to pull herself up, using the loopholes for her feet. Alistair came up behind her. His arms were on either side of her and he was almost holding her as they climbed, supporting her as they went. Could it be that his nearness still distracted her this much? The feel of his arms around her and his breath on her hair made her head spin.

They reached the top faster than she expected. He helped her onto the top of the structure, onto her knees with her legs underneath her. Pulling himself up, he pulled her to her feet. She was not prepared for the scene before her. It was difficult to decide what was more surprising —the view from this point or the setting prepared for her. Before her on the roof was a large pallet topped by silken cloth and an array of pillows. The pallet was surrounded by burning incense and candles. A beautiful scene indeed.

Beyond that the landscape spread out before her. Mountains peaked in the distance, the sand stretched out as smooth as silken rivulets. The moon was bright and full, and the stars twinkled like jewels in the sky. From the top of this outpost, it felt like she was in the sky, swept up in the wind. She didn't know if she swooned, but she felt Alistair come up behind her and put his arms around her, holding her to him and anchoring her to the ground.

"It is the most beautiful..." She had no words to describe it.

"I had this structure built so I could have this private place that was my own on hot summer nights—a place to go and think and be alone. But I no longer want it to be my own, I want it to be ours." He kissed her hair and then her neck.

She turned in his arms. "Thank you for sharing this with me. It is incredible."

He led her to the pallet he had made for them and he pulled her to sit next to him. They leaned back to lie down, reclining on pillows. Her breath caught as she lost herself in the sea of stars above her, all around her.

They lay in silence for several moments, enjoying the peace of their solitude in the presence of each other.

"Did you learn about the stars in your studies?" Alistair asked.

She nodded and pointed out to him the great bear and the hunter and the few star shapes she knew.

He pointed out a few more and told her the stories behind each shape. One particular picture he took extra care to tell her about. The shape was built around six stars forming a torso of a person.

"This is one that my grandfather showed me. It is Diana. Diana was a beautiful Grecian maiden. I'm sure she had long, dark, flowing hair, deep fathomless eyes, and skin as smooth and fine as porcelain." He smiled down at her. "Sound familiar?"

She realized he was describing her and gave him a silly look. "Sounds like my mother," she shot back at him.

He raised an eyebrow. "Oh? Well, then, I must make sure to meet this Grecian beauty. Certainly if she's half as lovely as her daughter."

"Um-hmm." She smiled at him. "So, Diana was a beautiful Grecian maiden..."

"Yes, and she fell deeply in love with Achius, a man who served the great army of Greece. There was a particular battle that he went off to fight and when the men returned, he was not with them. Her heart was heavy with grief, not able to imagine living another day without him. She pled with the gods to allow her to join her love, to be with him again. So sincere was her plea and so pure her heart and her love for him that the gods took pity on her and honored her request. They placed her in the heavens." He drew the outline of the figure in the sky. "She is with her Achius and the gods saw fit to allow her to shine down on lovers who are separated by distance and circumstance."

"That is a wonderful story." She put her free hand over their intertwined fingers.

Alistair rolled over onto his side, leaning over her with his arm on the pillows behind her head and his other hand lacing fingers with her hand resting on her stomach. He glanced down at his wife, so moved by the night sky above her. She shifted to look at him.

"Ismene, my love," he started.

"Yes?" She breathed the word.

"You know that I love you more than I have ever loved anything or anyone."

Smiling at him as a tear fell from her eyes, she said, "And I love you, Alistair."

He loved the way his name sounded, spilling like precious jewels from those sweet lips. "You can't even imagine how much I wish that I could give you some assurance that there will never be a night like this or a time when we are parted. You are right—it is a reality of my station before Pharaoh. I am at his mercy and at the command of his will."

She nodded in sad understanding.

He lifted her hands up to his mouth to plant a firm kiss on each of them. "But I can assure you, my love, that when we are apart, I will be looking up at Diana in the stars, knowing that she is looking down on you and hoping that you are looking up at her as well."

She offered him a slow smile. That thought comforted her. Though they may be separated by distance, they would be able to find each other in the stars. Pulling his hand down, she mirrored his gesture by pressing a kiss to his palm.

He moved his hand to cup her face and brushed her lips with his before wrapping his arms around her. She found rest there, in the refuge of her husband's embrace. And she slept, releasing all of the worry and concern of her day, exchanging it for the security of his love for her.

CHAPTER 10

A Moment of Truth

THEIR CHARIOT ONCE AGAIN BORE ALISTAIR AND ISMENE toward Pharaoh Ptolemy's palace. Ismene could not contain herself. The long awaited welcoming celebration had come. It was here at long last! Pharaoh had announced a banquet to welcome the Greek families that had moved to Alexandria a couple of weeks ago. The party would include all of the new Greek families, of course, as well as the Egyptian nobility. Ismene had been excited to be among such a contingency of her countrymen and, as always, looked forward to hearing her native tongue spoken fluently for an evening. Her studies in Egyptian language were going well, but it was always a pleasure to have interactions with multiple people who did not require her to rely on her new, still-limited skills.

Alistair had told her about this banquet too far in advance, she had decided. She had counted the days and waited with much anticipation for far too long. To what Ismene owed this privilege, she didn't know. Why these politicians had decided to make such a long trip to Egypt, uprooting their families and transplanting them, was unclear to her. Alistair had been quiet on the subject, and Ismene didn't spend much time concerning herself with it. She had been far too excited.

They arrived early and in style. Ismene hadn't let Alonah paint her with *kohl* this evening. No, she would be going as the Greek she was. Oh, she was still in the more practical Egyptian clothing, but that was all that spoke of her new life. Her hair, her face, everything else read Greek. Ismene soon discovered that she was in good company. Most of the Greek women were similarly attired as she, but lacked the painted face.

The party started off well enough. Ismene made small talk with the women she had met at the luncheon held by the queen and introduced them to Alistair. In turn, she enjoyed being introduced to their husbands.

As the evening dragged on and she became party to more conversations with these men and women, new arrivals to Egypt, her excitement faded to disillusionment. She had never realized how prejudiced her countrymen could be. The harsher comments, she noted, came from the men for the most part. These men were rather similar to her father's friends and acquaintances in his work, as well as in his day-to-day life. Did her father share these opinions?

Often in these conversations, she would steal a glance at her husband to catch his reaction. He remained quite distracted by the duty of entertaining and translating for both sides. They had escaped into many Greek conversations only to be confronted with stereotypes and ethnocentrism.

Alistair had long since noticed Ismene's uneasiness as she shifted beside him. Turning, he watched her features. She was attempting to mask her disgruntled feelings and appear to be interested in whatever was being said. How had she not been more prepared for these politicians? Was she so naive about her countrymen? She had been only a child when she frequented these types of functions in their homeland, ignorant of these opinions and people that were being degraded. Had she, too, at one time held to this same way of thinking to some extent?

Feeling Alistair's eyes on her, she turned her attention toward him.

"Are you all right?" he asked, taking her hand.

"Yes," she replied, not in Greek but in Egyptian.

That seemed to surprise him. They had been using their native tongue as they were, at the moment, surrounded by Greeks. She most often spoke her own tongue any and every chance she got, for certain with him. Her experience with the Egyptian language was still quite limited.

"I need some fresh air," she continued, still in Egyptian. "I'm feeling a little closed in."

He nodded, squeezing her hand as he stood. She followed suit.

"Gentlemen, if you will excuse us. I would like to take my wife for a walk among the gardens. She admires them so."

He set her hand on his arm, but she pressed into it to halt him.

"I do not wish to pull you away. Please stay, I'll find Alonah or Neterka to walk with me," she insisted.

"Are you certain?" His eyes searched hers to ensure that she was fine.

"Yes," she said, offering him a smile she didn't quite feel. She knew what he was concerned about—her fearfulness of a recurrence of what happened before. However, he had been sure to check on Meleager's whereabouts. The prince was halfway across Egypt and, therefore, neither at this party nor in the palace. Alistair had since communicated that Meleager had apologized at Pharaoh's behest. Apparently, Pharaoh believed, or wanted to believe, that the whole matter was a terrible mistake born of too much wine, and that his brother was mortified at what he had done. Alistair still did not trust the man.

"I shall check on you later." He kissed the side of her face and she took her leave of the group.

Glancing around for Alonah and Neterka in the servant's area, she saw neither. Rather than return to the party, she decided to venture out to the balcony on her own.

She stood on the terrace overlooking the gardens for a few moments, taking in some deep breaths. The responses of her countrymen confused her and she sensed that they aggravated her husband. Alistair had a great deal of respect for Ptolemy and his ideals. She knew that Egypt had staked its claim on Alistair's heart.

To her dismay, she realized that these ignorant statements came from an attitude that she had, in fact, at one time shared—an attitude of superiority. It had taken her time to discover that Egypt and its people were beautiful and wondrous in their own way. Difference did not equate inferiority. Why would these men refuse to see that?

She should seek out Neterka or Alonah rather than venture outside of the palace alone, but the thought of someone trailing her did not appeal to her. The quiet, thoughtful solitude that a stroll alone in the gardens would offer was what she truly wanted. And, she reasoned, the only real threat to her was miles away.

Her mind made up, she slipped down the stairs, finding her way out into the lush gardens. The path gave way to a somewhat winding maze that showcased many types of plant life, from flowers to hanging trees. She enjoyed the stillness of these living things in the night, moved only by the wind. A light breeze seemed to sing to her and carry away all of the serious and heavy thoughts of the conversations she had just witnessed. Instead, she concentrated on how bright the moon and stars shone through the clear night sky. Scanning the starry blanket, she spotted Diana.

Sighing deeply, she took in another breath, allowing the aroma of the flowers around her to intoxicate her senses. She continued her wanderings. As she passed a taller hedge, rough hands reached out and grabbed her, forcing her back against the bushes, arms pinned.

In the moonlight, she attempted to make out the features of her attacker. She found herself staring into two familiar brown eyes. Her mouth opened, unable even to form his name. Thinking it an invitation, his mouth covered hers.

Ismene's immediate reaction was to melt to him as she had so many times before. That comfort only lasted mere seconds before her mind overcame her senses. Alistair's face was in her mind's eye and that image made these rather familiar arms seem foreign.

She pulled back from his kiss.

"Thelopolis." She breathed, gasping for air.

"Yes, my love, 'tis I!"

"What? How?" she stammered for some grasp on reality. This was all a dream!

His hand reached out to caress her face. "Ismene, I have missed you terribly."

She gazed up into his caramel-colored eyes that had always held such comfort, such stability for her. "I have missed you, too."

He tried to pull her into his arms again. "How I have longed to hold you again. Only you make me whole, my love, my Ismene."

To her credit, she maintained her wits enough to resist him, placing a hand on his chest to keep him from pulling her against him again for another kiss.

"Thelopolis, you know that I am married, that I belong to another."

"You are wrong, Ismene. You are wed to another, but you love me. You belong to me. That's why I have come all this way. Forgive me, my love, I was so stupid. I never should have allowed you to be taken away from me. We should have run away. I didn't fight hard enough. But I am here now and we're together. Don't you see? I *couldn't* stay away, no matter how hard I tried. I moved heaven and earth to come for you. I had to come for you. We are soul mates."

She was moved by his words, pulled back into the past, into a place where she truly believed that, so she forgot the present for one moment and allowed him to pull her close and press his lips to hers.

Alistair's eyes darkened before he turned away, unable to endure any more. True to his word, he had left the party to come and check on his wife. Not finding her on the balcony, he had started to worry, but thought he spotted her in the gardens below. The sight that greeted him caught him completely off guard. Anger and hurt fought for dominance and his eyes stung with tears that would never be permitted as he retreated.

Ismene pulled away from Thelopolis. How had she let this go so far? She found herself perplexed. She had felt nothing in that kiss—no reaffirmation of love, no fulfillment of longing—the things she always feared she would feel if faced with this situation. The only thing she felt was a strong sense of betrayal to Alistair and an ache for *his* embrace. That's when she knew without a doubt that her romance with Thelopolis had been adolescent love and was nothing compared to what she shared with Alistair.

Thelopolis was looking at her with a question in his eyes.

"No, Thelopolis, we are not soul mates. And I no longer belong to you. I belong to my husband. Please understand that a part of me will always love you. But Alistair is my true love, my future."

There was hurt and disbelief in his eyes. "What has he done to you, my Ismene?" He reached out to touch her hair.

"No!" She pulled away. "This cannot be! Never again. I am sorry that you have come all this way. And I am sorry I cannot give you the answer you want."

Thelopolis's arms fell by his side. "So am I."

"You will always be a part of me," she said with tenderness in her voice.

He nodded, his eyes sad as he turned his face toward the ground.

"But this is where our paths must diverge." She attempted to be firm, though she knew her voice was shaking.

He nodded again. But did he truly understand?

She wanted to lean into his embrace once more, to press a platonic kiss on the side of his face. However, that would not serve either of them. While she would miss her friend, she had to do what was right for them both. A thick silence hung between them.

"I must get back to my husband," she said at last, needing to walk away, but hating the pain she saw in his eyes. Part of her wanted to stay, to find some way to make things better for him, but she knew that nothing but time would heal it. They were at an impasse. She was set on her path toward Alistair, and Thelopolis would struggle through the many emotions she could see in his face: rejection, hurt, emptiness, some anger, and uncertainty, his plans for his future ruined.

He opened his mouth to speak, but closed it again. There was nothing more to say. She turned and moved away from him, knowing all he could do was watch her walk out of his life for the second time.

When Ismene returned to the palace, she felt numb. She had a difficult time getting a grasp on what had just happened. And the implications. What was she going to tell Alistair? He needed to know. Now was not the time. Pushing her thoughts of Thelopolis to the side, she set about trying to find her husband.

She had a difficult time tracking down Alistair. When at last she did spot him, he seemed to be avoiding eye contact with her. Or was he just that deep in conversation with Dmitri? Deciding the latter must be true, she went over to join in.

"...of course the chariot racing may be conducted in a different way here, it is a nice sport to view," Alistair was finishing his sentence as Ismene entered their sphere.

"Ah, Lady Ismene, my wife is hoping you will escort her around the marketplace, show her the best places to buy the best things," Dmitri said.

"It would be my pleasure." She smiled, linking arms with Alistair, wanting to take what strength she could from him. "It won't take long before she is navigating the market quite easily herself, I assure you."

"Should I be worried, General?" he joked.

Alistair's eyes were on Ismene, but they seemed to be looking through her, not at her. "Hm? Oh, no. Ismene will be an excellent guide, I am sure. If you'll excuse me, there is something I needed to speak with Captain Ptah about." He extricated himself from Ismene and moved off.

"Of course," Dmitri said, seeming a bit confused by Alistair's response and behavior. "Is he well?" he asked Ismene.

"He gets so distracted by the affairs of his station. Something is on his mind and he is off to tend to it. I have gotten used to it," she lied.

"Ah! Well, now, I understand that you, yourself, are a new transplant to Egypt..."

The remainder of the evening went like that. If Ismene did catch up to Alistair and his current conversation, he would soon excuse himself. It was not like him and she was becoming concerned that something was wrong. He seemed to be avoiding her, practically running away from her. Had she said something wrong? Or was there that much of a guilty look on her face?

She put off the issue. The night was coming to a close and she would have ample time to speak with him about it once they were alone. Then she would be able to share with him what had occurred this evening with Thelopolis and tell him everything. But she was nervous to proceed with such a sensitive subject if things were already amiss between them.

It wasn't long before Pharaoh was giving his farewells, signaling to the whole party that it was time for the festivities to come to a close. Ismene was relieved. She didn't know how much longer she could stand this cat-and-mouse game she and her husband were engaged in.

For the last time, Ismene once again attempted to seek out her elusive husband. She didn't have to go far—he found her. All but knocking her over, she was so startled with how quickly he came up behind her. Perhaps she was most surprised that he came up to her at all.

"I regret that I must stay for a while longer. Pharaoh needs to speak with me."

"Perhaps I can wait for you..." she started.

"I would rather you be on your way home," he interrupted. "I do not know how long I will be and do not wish to keep you out late." His tone was not harsh, but it did not leave room for discussion.

"Oh," she said, stunned into silence. "Well, when you do get home," she said as she smiled and whispered playfully, "don't hesitate to come to my bedchambers." She wanted to talk, but more than that, she wanted to keep things lighthearted in the event he was just distracted by whatever was weighing on his mind.

"Don't wait up," was his only response. And then he was gone.

No farewell, no kiss, nothing. She felt as if she'd been slapped in the face. It was obvious he intended for her to make her way home alone. That would be something new...and scary with all that had been going on of late. Still, she made her way toward the door, but hadn't made it too far before Captain Ptah came up behind her.

"Lady Ismene," he called after her.

"Yes?" She spun around to see who was calling for her.

"General Merenre requested that I see to your safe return home."

"Thank you," she said, managing a slight smile. At least he was concerned for her safety. Perhaps he was just distracted with the affairs of the state. Maybe something had come up while she was out in the gardens and it had taken his mind captive. That's what she kept telling herself as the chariot brought her closer to home.

Once they were at the entry to the grand estate, she thanked the captain for escorting her home. Her mind was still solidly on Alistair and his behavior that evening. She was only half aware of her actions as she went through her night routine: undressing, nightshift, hair down, face washed, and oils. Before she knew it, she was sitting on the edge of her bed, all preparations complete.

This night she had allowed Alonah to do everything. All that was left was for her to go to bed, but her mind was spinning with her confusion over the evening. Not to mention she was still reeling from Thelopolis's sudden appearance. How she wanted to tell Alistair and get rid of her guilty conscience! Yes, she was all too ready to beg his forgiveness for what she had allowed to happen, albeit briefly, but betrayal it was.

Ismene reached up to move her hair out of her face and felt wetness on her cheeks. Only then did she realized that she was crying. That was all that was needed for the floodgates to open. She lay down and cried. She cried over the awkwardness with Alistair when she needed him most, over her betrayal, over her lost first love, over hurting Thelopolis —all of it. How long she lay there, tears flowing, she didn't know. At some point, she slipped into a restless sleep.

The next morning, Ismene awoke to find herself alone in her bedchambers. A little surprised, she hurried to dress so that she might call on Alistair in his bedchambers. She didn't bother with face paint and pulled her hair back and pinned it. After donning one of her simple, but appropriate clean, fine linen wraps, she made her way through the house. Nearing Alistair's rooms, she bumped into Neterka.

"I seek an audience with the general," she explained.

"Milady, I apologize, but the general has already left for the day."

"Already left?"

This concerned Ismene. How could he have already left? He didn't come to her last night and then he left without speaking with her this morning? And there was his strange behavior at the party last night. She was worried about what might be going on in his mind. But there was nothing she could do about it right now, not until he got home that night.

Ismene spent the day in solitude, thinking on the mystery that was before her and of all that had occurred the night before. She kept to her rooms for the most part and did not receive anyone.

Neterka took care of the household duties himself that day, just like it had been before. Ismene regretted that this was the case, but she could not bring herself to get back out of her room for her chores. There was no motivation in her. By afternoon, Alonah was able to convince her to take a stroll through the gardens, and that the tiger lilies, just trans-planted a few days ago, needed to be checked on by her, if nothing else. Not even the gardens could lighten her spirits from the momentary depression she found herself in.

Alistair crept into his home. He was very tired. The day had stretched out long before him with his troops, but he had lengthened it for himself as well to delay his homecoming. The house was quiet and dark. His plan had worked. Making his way down the hall to his rooms, he took off his armbands as he went. Then he walked straight through his outer chambers and into his bedchamber, setting down the armbands and taking off the bands on his legs.

"You are out late," he heard a voice say from the chambers he had just passed through. His heart dropped at the sound of the voice that, in normal circumstances, would cause it to leap for joy.

Alistair dropped his shin bands and walked back out to the receiving room.

"I did not expect anyone to be awake at this hour," he said, his voice flat, even.

"I gathered as much. But I think we need to have a conversation."

"All right," he said, sitting down. "I'm listening."

"Why didn't you come to me last night?"

"It was late and I was tired. Rather much like tonight. Is that all?" He started to rise, sounding bored.

"No. Is something wrong, Alistair?" She hadn't meant to allow her exasperation to come across in her voice, but it had.

"Ismene," he said, his voice was clipped. "I don't have the time or the patience to answer a lot of questions. And I didn't want to get into this, but apparently you won't be satisfied until we do, so I'll get right to it. I'm not so happy to find that my wife is involved with another man."

She recoiled as if he had backhanded her. "What?"

"Don't insult me with denials, *dearest*." The word was spoken in sarcasm. "I saw you with him last night." For a moment, Alistair couldn't believe his behavior, but he ignored that small voice which told him to stop, to think about what he was doing—he was hurting too much.

"Oh, Alistair, I was hoping to speak with you about that. It's not what you think! That was a friend of mine from back in Greece. He came to Egypt thinking I was unhappy and tried to comfort me and offer to help me if I was miserable. I told him I was quite happy with you and we said our good-byes."

Listen to her, the voice said, but Alistair couldn't hear it above his anger and wounded heart.

"I don't kiss my friends farewell like that," he challenged her.

"Perhaps I let myself get carried away, but only for a moment, I promise. That was all there was to it, my love. It was nothing."

"And the love notes? Are they nothing too?" he asked.

"The love notes?" She was puzzled by this.

Alistair went into his inner bedchambers to gather the notes and returned to throw them down on the table in front of her.

"Where did you get these?" Her voice took on a dark quality.

"Does it matter? They say plenty to me, Ismene!"

"You *read* them?" she said, incredulous.

"You are continuing to see a man you had a relationship with since before we were married, which you never disclosed, and you are concerned about whether or not I read the notes?" He couldn't believe the audacity of her reaction.

As she glared at him, he could see naked anger in her eyes, but he could also see the betrayal and the hurt that she felt from the violation of her privacy. He didn't care. As his wife, she didn't have a right to this kind of privacy. She had wronged him.

"This isn't what you think," she insisted, her eyes watering.

"No? Then tell me how it is, Ismene."

"It's...it's..." She couldn't finish her sentence.

"That's what I thought," he said curtly, taking up her letters.

"You don't understand," she pleaded, now crying. It was obvious that she was dealing with overwhelming emotions.

He didn't care. "Well, I'm waiting for you to *explain it*."

Alistair watched as she waged a battle to get control over her emotions. At long last, she seemed to give up. She leapt up, running from the room.

"Exactly," he harrumphed to himself.

Everything in Ismene's world was whirling. She refused to let him see her cry anymore. How did he get those letters? How could he have read them? He had read those private words between her and Thelopolis. She felt angry, hurt, embarrassed, and betrayed by the man she had trusted with her whole heart.

How could he not have trusted her? How could he not have seen those letters for what they were? How could he have jumped to such conclusions about whatever he saw last night and not let her explain? Was he not the man she had thought he was? No, she couldn't entertain *those* thoughts. Surely he was just reeling from hurt and a feeling of betrayal himself. They were both so clouded by emotion. Too clouded.

Running into her room, she threw herself onto her bed and allowed the sobs to rack her body. How would this ever be made right? She wished she could have been strong enough to stay, to explain. Why had she run? Because she had been too angry and, in the moment, too proud to let him see her break down like this. But if she trusted him to see the truth, to see *her*, then she should have trusted him with her breakdown.

She had been a coward, an overemotional coward. Now it was worse. Looking over her shoulder, she longed for him to stroll through the door and gather her in his arms and tell her that everything was all right, that they would work it all out. But that was not to be. Her door remained quiet and she was the sole occupant of her room.

Sefu knocked on Nassor's door. The night air was cool and he pulled his cloak around himself a little tighter while he waited. It was some time before his associate answered the door, wearing a robe and rubbing his eyes. It was clear Sefu had gotten him out of bed. Yawning, Nassor opened the door wider to admit Sefu into his home.

"To what do I owe this late-night visit?" Nassor asked, leading the way to the main living space of his home.

"*He* paid *me* a late night visit. We need to ramp up the progression of his plan," Sefu said, taking a seat. Sefu was referring to the man behind this job that their faction had been hired to do.

"What?" One didn't have to be a mind reader to see that Nassor was a little uncomfortable with the way things were going as it was.

"He is not pleased with the way the general is taking the message, so we need to send a stronger message. The next step will be bigger. Poison." He regretted telling Nassor this and could anticipate his reaction.

"Poison? But you said we weren't going to kill anyone." Nassor protested.

"Don't worry yourself." Sefu pulled a small package out of his pocket. He unrolled it and exposed some green root to Nassor. "It's not that kind of poison. This is a special kind of root," he explained, rubbing his fingers over it. "She will become rather sick, but it won't kill her."

"I don't know, Sefu. That sounds like a bit much."

"Exactly. What are we always saying? That we need to make bigger moves, that sitting around and hoping things will change is not the answer. They never will. And now, *Pharaoh*," he spit out the word, "is inviting more of these Greek scum into our home. We cannot let these things go unchallenged. Think, Nassor, this may be the last step we need to get our point across."

Nassor peered at the root, then back at his friend. Sefu knew that he was quite uncomfortable with this kind of thing. He had made it clear that it had been his hope they wouldn't have to hurt anyone. And while they weren't being called upon to kill anyone, this took him into territory he wasn't sure he was ready to go into. But Sefu's message was the same it had always been and Nassor had signed up to support that.

Sefu was able to read the thoughts displayed on his features. "Don't give up on me now, friend, I know the end is near. Just pass the root along to your contact inside the house and your part will be done. It's not as if you will be giving her the tea yourself."

He knew Sefu was speaking the truth, but he also knew that in essence he *was* giving her the tea if he was a link in the chain. His guilt was not absolved just because he didn't actually hand the poison to her, but he was already in this far and he had committed himself to see this through. And he needed to hang in there. It may be that, down the line, if he stayed with this, he could keep them from harming her if this didn't work.

After several seconds, he nodded. "I will pass it along."

Sefu clapped him on the shoulder and gave him a broad smile. "Your countrymen owe you a debt."

The more this continued, the more he doubted Sefu's claim that this was for Egypt. The deeper they got, the more it seemed they were serving the personal agenda of whomever Sefu was taking orders from and that it rather loosely served their own purposes. Maybe Tarik was right about radical factions—they ended up doing more harm than good and their leadership ended up serving personal agendas instead of their ideals.

Maybe Nassor should have remained with the Alexandrian mob and not joined this faction, but he had believed in Sefu and his words. He believed that more needed to be done. But now he worried that they were giving up too much of their humanity to accomplish their ends.

Alistair rose early and dressed with all due haste. He hoped he would be able to get out of the house before anyone else was up and about. By "anyone," he meant to avoid Ismene. Their conversation the previous evening had not ended well and he was not ready for an encore. His sleep had been restless. That small voice had gotten louder when he wasn't defending his position. But he had drawn a line in the sand and he decided that he would not back down. Part of him regretted that he was hurting her, but another part of him wanted her to experience the pain that he felt. Moving into his outer bedchambers, he went to ring for Neterka.

"You're up early," he heard behind him.

He spun around to see the outline of his wife in the small bits of early morning light that seeped into the room through the drapes.

"We have maneuvers early this morning," he lied. In truth, he had vague plans to ride around the countryside. Anything to get him out of the house and away from her.

"Ah. I was...hoping we could finish our conversation from last night." She shifted uncomfortably, hesitating so as to keep her emotions in check.

"I didn't know there was more to say."

Neterka entered the room and Ismene moved over to look out of a window so that he wouldn't see her cried-out face. He had a breakfast of meat, bread, and fruit for Alistair.

"Milady!" He was startled to see her there. "I did not know you were here. Shall I bring you some breakfast?"

Alistair and Ismene spoke at the same time.

"Yes."

"No."

"No, thank you," Ismene reiterated. "I'm not hungry."

"As you wish," Neterka said, bowing and taking his leave.

Alistair took a seat next to his food. "It feels a little awkward to eat in front of you if you are not going to eat," he said, his voice harsh.

"Please." She shifted to face him. "I assure you, I am simply not hungry."

As she turned, standing next to the window, with more light on her face, he could see the effects of both crying all night and the lack of sleep. It tugged at his heart, but he was too hardened by the events of the last thirty-six hours to be softened so easily.

They remained in silence for a few minutes. Alistair started his breakfast and Ismene stood looking out the window, arms crossed over her chest, unsure how to start.

"How could you read those personal letters?" she started at last, her words spoken in a soft tone. Whether it was from the sleepless night of the crying or something else, she didn't know, but she was rather queasy this morning. Her stomach was doing flip-flops. In fact, her whole body seemed topsy-turvy.

"Believe me, at the time, I did not relish reading them. The person who brought them to me insisted that I would want to know what was in them. I knew the letters were personal and I did not want to read them. I felt guilty, but now I see it was better I knew. How could you not tell me about such an important relationship?"

"Did you tell me of all of your relationships?" she challenged.

"It's not the same." His voice was raised. "Any relationship I had was in the past. Can you honestly tell me this relationship with Thelopolis was over?"

She could not, so she remained silent. Putting her hand to her head, she began to feel light-headed.

"That's what I thought. And even knowing this, you agreed to be my wife without sharing this piece of information with me, even though I gave you every opportunity to opt out."

"I didn't *truly* have that option, Alistair. I couldn't return home an unwanted bride," she explained

"So you married me against your will."

"That's not what I meant. I appreciated that you gave me that option. But you were a stranger to me when we married. What can you expect with an arranged marriage?"

"That's all this is to you? An arranged marriage?"

"No. Well, it was when we were first married. Our marriage is so much more now. I am so glad I married you. You can't imagine how glad."

"Then why all the secrecy and sneaking around with Thelopolis?"

"There was no sneaking around!" She was exasperated with this and she wasn't feeling well. The emotional night was catching up with her.

"Then what did I see the other night? It wasn't a handshake."

"That was...that was..." Ismene doubled over as she was overcome with nausea. Her body was twisted in as much turmoil as her heart over the things he was saying to her.

His face changed in that instant, concern covering his features. It was brief, though, before he managed to return into a stature of offense.

"Are you well?" he said, his voice steady lest he betray his fleeting moments of tenderness.

"Yes," she tossed back just as firmly and stood up. What she didn't want was his pity. She would be strong...she would. The world began to move around her, and her head swirled. Losing hold of her balance, the sensation of falling was the last thing she knew before all was dark.

"Ismene!" He was only just able to catch her as she fell toward the floor. He shook her gently, dropping his iron exterior. "Ismene!"

He felt along her neck for the pulse of life to assure him that she was not in imminent danger. His fingers did find the soft, gentle rushing movement. Lifting her in his arms, he rushed into the inner courtyard, seeking anyone who could assist him. He cursed the early hour of the morning. At this hour, any servants in the house steered clear of the bedchambers lest they wake the master and mistress of the house. It seemed like forever before he came across a servant girl carrying linens.

"Send for a doctor!" he called to her, not caring that he all but yelled at the young girl as he shoved past her in the hallway on his way Ismene's room. He didn't even wait to see her nod and run to fulfill that charge.

Pacing, Alonah wondered if or when she should go to her mistress. Or should she wait until Ismene returned? Would her mistress need a shoulder and a listening ear? Or space? She knew that her mistress had waited up for Alistair, that they had fought, that Ismene had not slept, and that she went to speak with him again this morning.

Alonah wished it was in the scope of her job that she be allowed to ask what was going on. Alas, that was not permitted. So she was left guessing what had disturbed her mistress so. How she hoped Ismene would talk about it. She was certain it would help Ismene feel better.

Just then there was a pounding on the door. She didn't have time to think on it before Alistair was there, having kicked the door open, with her mistress in his arms. Ismene's body was limp, almost lifeless, and Alistair held her to himself with tenderness. Maybe that meant that they were past whatever had gone awry. But her first duty was to Ismene's current condition.

"She fainted," he explained, moving toward the bed. He was beside himself.

Alonah scrambled ahead of Alistair to ready the bed for Ismene. She made it there only a millisecond before him. He rested Ismene on the bed and backed away. Then he didn't seem to know what to do with himself. Alonah paid him little mind; her attention was on Ismene in that moment, shifting pillows and her limbs. Reaching out, she felt Ismene's face—it was cold and clammy. Unsure what to do for her mistress, she did the only thing she could—tried to keep her comfortable.

Only then did she turn to look upon the master of the house. She had never seen the great general lose his composure, but there he was, pacing, shaking his head, burying his face in his hands. Every few minutes, he would sit, then after a few moments, he would get up and pace some more. He didn't seem to notice that Alonah was there; he was too overwhelmed with what was going on with Ismene. They remained much like that until the doctor came.

It seemed to take forever for the doctor to arrive, but once he did, he dismissed Alistair out of the bedchambers so that he could examine Ismene. His time with Ismene dragged on, and with each minute Alistair became more nervous at the prospect of what was going on with her. A few maidservants moved in and out of the inner chambers, which did nothing to ease his tortured mind. A million scenarios ran through his brain and none of them were pleasant.

Alistair's thoughts were broken as the doctor opened the door to Ismene's chamber. Before he was out of the room, Alistair was almost on top of him.

"She is ready to be seen now. But only for a few moments," he warned. "She needs her rest."

"Did she ask for me?" There was a glimmer of hope in him. Maybe this would be enough to soothe his wounded pride.

"I think it best to keep the visits short," the doctor reiterated the instruction before taking his leave.

Alistair nodded, supposing that was answer enough. She must be upset with him. Maybe she didn't want to see him at all. Part of him wanted to turn and leave, but he decided that he would not run like a schoolboy. He would see her whether she wanted him to or not. After all, he was the master of this house.

Alistair stepped into the room, now darkened as the curtains were pulled over the windows. Alonah was settling Ismene in the bed, and a few other maidens were cleaning up after the doctor, carrying off Ismene's clothes, lighting candles. Ismene had been dressed in a night-shift. As much as Alistair's heart melted at the sight of her, knowing she was truly all right allowed him to fall back into the emotions that had fueled the fire of his anger earlier. He didn't know what to say, what to do.

"Thank you, Alonah," Ismene said, her voice too quiet. "Ladies, a moment, please."

The girls all bowed to their mistress and to Alistair as they exited.

Part of him wanted to pick up where they had left off, but he also wanted to speak of his relief for her returned health and take his leave. He was unsure where they stood.

There were several moments of silence after the handmaidens had departed before she started, "Did you speak with the doctor?"

"Only for a few moments. He insisted that you get plenty of rest."

Her face was difficult to read. As much as he despised the way they had faced off earlier, he wasn't sure he liked this—them regarding each other as strangers almost. He felt that she needed to make the first move. It was she who had wounded him, after all.

She nodded. "He didn't say anything further?"

"He suggested I come in to see you."

She nodded again. Her face was drawn. It seemed as if she had something to say, but she hesitated.

"I am...relieved you are well," he said after some moments of silence. *Why* was he behaving this way? One of them had to break this stalemate! It should be him, but he felt justified in thinking it should be her.

It was clear that she was deep in thought. How long should he wait for her to say something? Should he just leave her be?

"I should leave you to your rest," he said, moving to leave. He could no longer bear to look at her and not pull her into an embrace. But there were doubts, serious doubts still about Thelopolis and her feelings for him. The thought that she never loved him, that he was her second choice, still stabbed at his heart. So his protective shell was still up. As much as he wanted to speak tender things to her, there was still that part of him that wanted her to hurt the way that he did.

"Alistair, don't go," she spoke up.

He paused, his back still to her. "It doesn't seem as if we have anything to say to each other," he said, his voice tight.

"I have something to say," came from her in a rather harsh tone.

Her tone only put him back on the defense. "Well, say it."

She closed her eyes and took a deep breath. "I'm pregnant."

He spun and stared at her. The words weren't registering with him in his current state of mind. Those huge brown eyes peered up at him—those eyes that had seemed so vulnerable, so innocent. Had it been a charade all along? He would not, could not pretend. Not even for those eyes that he had so loved falling into. Angry, hurt, jealous, torn, emotionally hardened, he was unable to stop his response. "And who is the father?"

She glared up at him, shock showing on her face just as if he had slapped her. And the hurt...he could read her hurt so well in those deep brown eyes. There were tears welling up in response. He regretted it in that instant, regretted letting his hurt and wounded pride push him to say something he hadn't meant.

Ismene seemed to struggle to respond as a tear slid down her face, but she managed to form two words. "Please leave." Her voice was hard, even.

Alistair knew then. He could have ripped out his tongue and eyes for his stupid mistake born from selfish, pitiful jealousy. He should have known, *did* know all along.

"Ismene, I..." he started, unsure himself what he was about to say.

She cut him off. "Please *leave*!"

There was a fury in her voice that he had never known. Relenting, he removed himself from her bedchambers. He was thankful no servants were in the hallway just outside at that moment as he sagged against the door, racked with a thousand emotions. Her sobbing behind him was audible through the door. There was a war within him—to go to her and beg forgiveness or to give her space, knowing she was getting a taste of the hurt she had inflicted on him?

He would always look back on this moment as one of most cowardly in his life. Hearing Alonah approaching the outer chambers, he regained his composure and walked off.

CHAPTER 11

The Fallout

ISMENE REFUSED TO BE SEEN FOR THE NEXT THREE WEEKS, IN which she kept to her rooms for the most part. Alistair made a few attempts to see her, but she turned him away each time. Alonah was forever fearful for her mistress's health, which rather annoyed Ismene. A gloom seemed to have settled over Ismene. Nothing made her happy. There were days that she did not get out of her bed at all. But other days, she would visit the marketplace. She had taken up visits to the great library as well.

True to his word, the Jewish scholar would sit and talk to her of his God. Ismene liked sitting and hearing the history of the Israelites and what their people had been through. It was an amazing history of survival if it were, in fact, all true. There was a part of their history that took place here in Egypt that told of them being enslaved by a pharaoh and forced to build bricks without straw, and of all sorts of atrocities that were committed against them.

She wished she could ask Alistair about these things. Although she doubted he would know the truth himself. As she listened to the stories, she imagined it could be true. If a pharaoh so desired to enslave a people living under his rule, he would be capable of doing so. But why would

God allow His people to endure such hardships? Many times she left her sessions with the scribe while pondering such heavy questions.

Mostly she left thinking of how powerful this man's God must be. The tales of what He could do were truly amazing. She marveled at how personally He seemed to care for those who followed Him, like Abraham. Abraham talked with God...they had conversations! Could a god as mighty as this one care so for individuals? It seemed impossible. But she was left with this—she must decide if she believed this history or not. She knew she could not pick and choose what to give credence to. It was all true or it wasn't true at all.

Today was one such day in which she had finished her session with the scribe. Alonah had stayed home, so Ismene took advantage of the time to wander around the beautiful building and let her thoughts dwell on this God and the things He had done in the stories the scribe had told her that day. How nice would it be to have a god who hears as Jehovah did when Hagar was all alone in the desert? Oh, how she needed to be heard, to be seen right now. She felt as if she were invisible. Surrounded by a darkness that seemed to go on forever...could He pull her out of this darkness?

Ismene found a quiet spot in one of the library rooms to sit and think on what she had heard. She was so deep in thought that she didn't notice the dark figure approaching her until he was almost on top of her.

Once she did catch sight of the aggressor coming upon her, she opened her mouth to scream, but the man threw back his hood and placed a finger on his lips and hers to silence her. It was Thelopolis! She jumped up and glanced around to see if anyone had noticed. They were alone. Still, thinking better of the close proximity of their bodies, she backed away a few steps.

"What are you doing here?" she hissed.

"I watch you often at the library," he confessed in a quiet voice. "I can't stay away, Ismene. I tried, I truly did," he said in earnest.

"You must try harder, Thelopolis. We cannot see each other."

He took a deep breath. "What if I understand and accept that we cannot be to one another what we once were or what I had hoped we could be again? Can we not then be friends? We were once good friends."

She stepped closer and seethed, "What you speak of is quite dangerous."

"Can you tell me, in all honesty, that you have not missed our friendship?" He also took a step forward.

"No," she conceded.

He walked around her. "Do you remember the day you told me you were to marry another? You wanted me to tell you that we were going to be all right. That power is in your hands. Can you tell my heart to continue beating if I can never see you again?"

She closed her eyes. "You do not know what you ask." Why was it so hard to say no to him? Had she not put this behind her? Her hands fell to her abdomen—her child. She had to make things right for her child.

Perhaps Thelopolis believed what he was saying, that they could have a platonic relationship, but she knew otherwise. Ismene knew that he cared for her and that he just wanted her in his life. She did wish she could give him that, but her choice was clear here: a hope for reconciliation with Alistair or a relationship with Thelopolis. But she couldn't hold up much longer to his persuasion; he knew her too well and could see straight through her.

Ismene looked at him, stopping him in his tracks. "I can't, I'm sorry."

She pulled her arms to herself and rushed from the room. He called after her, but she didn't look back until she was outside being loaded in her chariot.

In the days that followed, Ismene became rather ill. At first she assumed it was morning sickness, but she became sicker as the days wore on. As time passed, she was unable to move between her bed and the chamber bucket. She had to be lifted back into bed. Her body retched and seized with pain as she lay curled up on the sheets.

Alonah begged her to call for a physician. This could not be normal, she insisted. Worrying after her baby, Ismene had the doctor summoned. That's when Alonah discovered a new symptom.

"Milady, you are burning up!" Alonah said. "Please, lie down."

Ismene was not about to argue with her. "I may need your help."

Alonah was able, with much effort and help from Fenuku, one of the home's manservants who had helped them throughout the day, move Ismene as needed, to get her to her bed where she collapsed once again into a heap.

"Milady!" Alonah cried out, shaking her.

She was still.

"Ismene!" Alonah moved her to prop her up on pillows while calling for help. Mesi and Safiya rushed into the room.

"The Lady Ismene is unwell. Get some cold water, Mesi. Safiya, help me check her. Fenuku, notify Neterka."

They did what they could to cool down her fevered body. Fenuku excused himself as they began stripping her of her nightdress to lay cold cloths over her body. Safiya brought in two young girls with large fans to help cool off their mistress, while the three women attempted to settle her in the bed and continued to apply fresh cold cloths until the doctor arrived.

Alistair sat deep in thought over his papers when he heard a knock at his door.

"Yes?" he called. He stacked up the confidential papyruses before admitting Neterka. Alistair was no longer trusting anyone in his house after these recent incidents, not even Neterka.

"Sir, I thought I would let you know that a doctor was sent for. The Lady Ismene is unwell," he spoke in a calm voice.

"Unwell? What has happened?" Alistair was already on his feet.

"I do not know. The doctor arrived just minutes ago."

Alistair was out the door, headed for Ismene's bedchambers. Her room seemed too far away in the state he was in. Upon entering the hallway outside of her chambers, he found that the door was shut for the doctor to do his work. He had no choice but to wait while the doctor finished. Trying to be calm, he leaned against the wall outside of the door. But he found that he just couldn't make himself be still. He was too worried...and too confused.

Ismene had refused to see him countless times, but he had required regular reports from Alonah and she had been doing fine. The report yesterday was that her morning sickness carried throughout the day, but that was not too uncommon. What had happened between yesterday and today? He felt as if he were going to crawl out of his skin. He found himself pacing.

Several minutes went by before he heard movement at the door.

"How is she?" He nearly caused the doctor to stumble over him the way he rushed up to the man.

"The Lady Ismene has taken ill, but she will recover." The doctor went about straightening his garb after his near miss. "It may be some time yet, so she will need lots of rest, and plenty of cleansing teas to get the poison out of her system."

"Poison?" His eyes widened. Who would poison his beloved? But he knew. He and Ismene must both have tasters from now on.

"I suspect some mild poison meant to make her gravely ill. Since she is not dead, I doubt that was the intent."

"And the baby? How is the baby?" Alistair's heart froze in his chest.

"I cannot be certain. Concentrate on the lady's health and the child's condition should remain stable."

Alistair nodded. Never had he been so scared in his whole life. He'd rather face down several battalions of soldiers than face the prospect of losing Ismene or the baby.

"May I see her?" he asked.

"Of course, but don't linger. Remember, she needs her rest," the doctor insisted.

Alistair didn't wait to see the doctor out, but rushed into Ismene's bedchambers. There she was, lying as if lifeless on the bed. If he didn't know any better, he would think it was the sleep of death. But as he watched, he could see the gentle rise and fall of her chest.

Alonah moved around the bed to speak with him. "She is well, General," she whispered. "As you see, she is resting now. Please do not trouble yourself like this. I will come and get you if anything changes."

"I can't leave just yet. May I find a chair and just sit by her bed? I won't disturb her." There was no further compromise in his voice. He was staying.

Alonah hesitated, but nodded.

Alistair pulled a stool closer to the bed and took a seat to keep watch over Ismene. He was determined to maintain a vigil over his beloved for as long as it took. How he had let his emotions carry this so far, he did not know. He had to make it right, and this was a first step.

Alonah watched the master of the house, broken with grief, at her mistress's side. She wished he would leave her in peace. Perhaps it wouldn't be so bad for him to stay for a few minutes. If it would make him feel better. It would be fine, Alonah reasoned. He would soon tire and make his way to his own bedchambers. Alonah took her leave of the room, closing the door behind her.

She busied herself with her evening routine: cleaning the area around the chambers, communicating with the staff as to her mistress's more immediate needs, and returning to her own small chambers for a moment of peace. When Alonah checked on Ismene later that night, Alistair still sat in vigil over her, much to Alonah's surprise.

The general had dozed off, though. He had laid his head down on the bed and put a hand on Ismene's. Alonah knew that Alistair would follow the doctor's orders to the letter and not do anything that might disturb Ismene. He must have leaned over and reached for her in his sleep.

Alonah shook his shoulder gently to rouse him.

He awoke with a start. Ready for attack.

"Shhh, shhh!" She put her hands up in defense. "You must retire to your bedchambers, General. You are not doing the lady any good wearing yourself out like this."

"I am fine." He rubbed his eyes. "I don't need rest as much as I need to be with her."

"I was being kind, sir. The lady needs her undisturbed rest. With all due respect, I must insist upon the doctor's orders."

Alistair knew she was speaking wisely. He gathered himself up and headed out of the inner chambers, turning for a brief moment. "You will come and get me if anything changes? If she stirs, if she calls out, if her fever breaks, anything?"

"Yes, sir, *any* change," she promised.

Once the general was gone, Alonah went about with her checks on her mistress. She was burning up! There had been no improvement since the doctor's visit a few hours ago. How long would it be before she awoke so they could start the tea treatments?

Alonah patted down Ismene's face, arms, hands, and chest with a cloth wet with cold water to soothe her fevered skin. She reached up to move a stray hair out of her face and discovered that there was a tear in her eye. Wiping it away, she replaced her brief sadness with determination. This illness would not overcome her mistress if she could help it.

Picking up the water and cloth, Alonah moved out of the chamber to dump the water. That's when she found Alistair, still in the hall just outside of the room, pacing.

"General?" She was startled by his presence.

"I couldn't go any farther," he said in an almost apologetic voice.

"Sir, I fear for your own health. You will make yourself sick with worry." Alonah's voice was stern.

"I must be near her." His eyes were pleading.

Alonah opened her mouth to continue, but they were interrupted.

"Alistair!" It was Ismene's voice.

They looked at each other, eyes wide. The general rushed into Ismene's bedchamber, Alonah a step behind him. Ismene was tossing and turning in the bed, calling for him. He fell to his knees by her bed, taking her hand.

"I'm here, Ismene." He brushed her hair from her forehead with his free hand.

She opened her eyes slightly to look at him. "Alistair," she murmured. Pressing his arm with her hand. Then she stilled.

"I'm right here," he assured her, his voice tender and soft.

Ismene closed her eyes and went back to sleep.

Alistair watched her, stroking her face, lost in thought.

Alonah could not bring herself to make him leave. Neither did she think she would meet with success if she tried. So, nodding to Alistair, an understanding passed between them. She turned and slipped out of the room.

Alonah continued to check on Ismene throughout the rest of the night, pressing cold cloths to her face, neck, and chest. Upon further visits, she would find Alistair tending to her in the same fashion. But she never caught him sleeping again. It was almost as if he feared Ismene would reach out for him again and he wouldn't be awake to hear her.

Just before dawn, her fever broke. Alonah and Alistair rejoiced together.

Not long after Alonah had left to gather foodstuffs for her and Alistair, he noticed some movement in Ismene's hand. Leaning forward, he clasped her hand. Her eyes fluttered open.

"Hey," he said, rubbing her forehead with his free hand.

Ismene met his eyes, but she was clearly not as pleased to see him as he was to see her awake. She shifted her face away from him, hurt still evident in her eyes.

"Ismene..." He wanted to tell her how sorry he was, how it was all a big mistake, how he wished he could take it all back.

"Please go," she said once she found her voice.

He could hear in her voice that she was fighting tears.

The sound of the door opening alerted him to Alonah's return. He heard the sound of a tray being laid on a table and footsteps approaching the bed.

"Milady, you're awake!"

Alonah looked between her master and mistress, seeming to realize that she had interrupted something. An awkward silence fell in the room. It was Alonah that broke it.

"How are you feeling?" she asked Ismene, a little hesitantly.

"I am tired and confused," was her lady's response.

"I will go gather some of your tea." Alonah bowed her head and moved to take her leave.

"No, please stay. Alistair was just leaving," she insisted.

Alonah glanced from Alistair to Ismene again.

"Ismene..." he started again.

Turning then to look at him, he could see the tears in her eyes, though she was trying to hide them behind a firm expression. "Please leave."

Another silence. This one thick with emotion. Alistair wanted desperately to explain, to apologize, but she had shut him out. And her pain was evident.

It was Alonah who spoke into the silence again. "I'm certain that the lady would enjoy a bath and something to eat. I will attend to her and send word when she is again resting."

Alistair nodded, dejected. He stood, his movements slow. There was great hesitation in him as he turned. But what could he do? What could he say? It was obvious she was not ready to hear anything from him. He moved toward the door and relieved her of his presence.

"None of it!" Nassor said. "None of it has come to anything! The general is still here and has no plans to leave Egypt."

"I have a plan," a dark voice said from the shadows.

Nassor's eyes widened. He had thought that he and Sefu were alone. His attention was drawn to the shadows where a man stepped forward. Nassor couldn't believe his eyes. *This* was the man who had been giving their orders? Their benefactor? He could scarcely believe it was real!

He looked to Sefu. "Is this some kind of trick?"

"No." Sefu was expressionless.

"Then I am mistaken as to why we are doing what we are doing."

"No, believe me," Sefu said. "Our goals are the same, though our reasons may be different."

"Let's not waste time with these things," the man said. "I'd rather discuss the details of the next phase of our plan."

Sefu nodded. "Nassor, we can talk about your concerns later. Right now, you must trust me and listen to his plan."

Nassor was quite nervous with this whole setup, but he did trust Sefu. He fought down the wave of uneasiness and listened.

"Are you well, Lady Ismene?" The Jewish scribe paused in his reading.

Her gaze had drifted and she drew her attention back to the man in front of her. He was staring at her.

"Hmm? Oh, yes, I am well," she said. "I have been deep in thought over many things that you have read to me."

"Yes?" he prodded for her to continue.

"I wonder about this God who speaks to men. He spoke to Abraham, to Moses...He cares about people as individuals. Even for one such as Hagar, a maidservant who is carrying an unwanted child. Your holy text says that God heard her. There was even a special name for God there."

"*El Roi*, the God Who Sees?"

"Yes. Do you think He sees me?"

"Of course."

"Even though I'm not sure that I'm ready to believe in everything you have said?"

"Yes. He still sees you. He still hears you."

Ismene thought on that for a time. "Because," she started slowly, "there are times I feel that I am alone." She had come to trust this man, but how much, she wasn't sure.

"You are never alone. And you can always call out to Jehovah and know that He will hear you. He will help you. I know you will come to believe in time."

There was that confidence again that this man always seemed to have in his God. If it were true that his God had done all of these things that he claimed, she didn't doubt there should be every confidence in Him.

But did she believe these things were true? They didn't seem like stories to her. What people would write for themselves such stories about their own misdeeds and mistrust? No, this was a story of a god who kept reaching out to people who made mistakes, who were imperfect, but who were loved by their Creator. Could she truly have that?

Alonah arrived at the scribe's house quite breathless. She didn't know how long she would have before Ismene would return home and find her missing, but this day was worth the risk. It was her wedding day. She bore two bags with her. One held Ismene's wedding clothes, which she would borrow, and the second held some of her possessions.

The Egyptian marriage ceremony for the most part consisted of a contract and for her possessions to be moved to Jabari's home. Jabari did not have a home for her to move into, and, as they were keeping their marriage a secret, that was a step they would not yet take. But it was important for them to perform this step. So she had brought some of her possessions for him to keep with him as a sign that she was now his wife.

Jabari greeted her with a huge embrace and a sweet kiss. She could tell that he was excited about today. She sensed no trepidation in him about the secrecy of what they were doing, that they would have to hide, and the risk of it all.

"Are you certain?" he asked.

She nodded, letting her forehead rest against his. "I've never been more sure."

Hand in hand, they knocked on the scribe's door. An older man answered and recognized Jabari at once.

"Is this lovely woman the one who agreed to be your bride, Jabari?"

"Yes!"

Jabari had told Alonah that the scribe was an old friend to his family and had agreed to write up the contract and share in their secrecy.

"Excuse me," Alonah spoke up. "Do you have some place I might change?" She indicated the bag she had brought with her.

"Of course." The scribe ushered her to a back bedroom, closing the door behind her.

She changed into one of Ismene's simple linen dresses and pulled her bride bead over her head. The bead net was heavier than she expected, covering her head to toe with a netting of beautiful beadwork. Alonah was certain she didn't appear nearly as grand as Ismene had on her wedding day, but she wanted to look special for this occasion.

When she stepped out of the room, Jabari's eyes caught hers. His eyes were wide and his mouth parted. It must have been the bride bead.

Perhaps it was all the more real to him that this was his wedding day to see the woman he loved dressed in bride bead.

"Alonah, you are stunning, I..." He moved to gather her into his embrace again.

"Now, now," the scribe said. "There will be time for that! Let's get this contract signed."

Alonah and Jabari looked over the paper while the scribe read it to them. It listed their names, the date, their parents, Jabari's profession, the scribe's wife as witness, and had a place for each of them to make their mark.

Jabari seemed all too eager to make his mark on the paper, grabbing the writing utensil and marking on the paper in one quick motion. Then he handed the pen to Alonah. She had never been party to a contract before. This was monumental for her. Lifting the pen with a sense of respect for the act she was performing, she made a mark on the paper similar to Jabari's.

The scribe rolled up the paper and took the pen from Alonah. "It is done. Congratulations!"

Jabari took Alonah in his arms then and kissed her deeply. She only wished that they were moving into his home and that they would be able to celebrate their union the way all husbands and wives around the world and across time had.

Then the scribe cleared his throat.

"Thank you," Jabari said, still holding Alonah, not quite ready to let go of his new wife. "You said we must get this to the temple?" He reached out for the paper.

The scribe looked at his wife. "We have decided to take this to the temple and then to take a walk through the market. The back bedroom is made up."

Alonah was shocked. This was an unexpected kindness.

"No," Jabari said. "We couldn't."

"We insist," the scribe said. "I know it's not ideal, but it's your wedding day."

There was no further argument from Jabari, just silence as he and Alonah watched the scribe and his wife gather a few things and take their leave of the house for the rest of the afternoon.

Alonah could not help the tears that came down her face as she thought of the kindness of the gesture being bestowed upon them. As the door closed behind the scribe and his wife, Jabari turned to his new bride, only then seeing her tears.

"Alonah, it's all right. We don't have to..."

He misunderstood.

"No, that's not it. I'm just so overwhelmed at their kindness. This is a big day for me, Jabari. Don't you see? I am a maidservant. People don't give up their homes for a maidservant. Servants don't sign contracts. No one marries a servant but another servant. And these people who care for you didn't look down on me. They accepted me because you accepted me. I don't know what the general and Ismene will do when they find out, but thank you."

She kissed him and all thoughts of her world outside of this house vanished. For the next couple of hours, this man was her whole world.

Thelopolis paced in the small space that was his rented room. It had not been as difficult as he had feared to navigate the marketplace or even rent a room knowing no Egyptian because, as it turned out, everyone spoke money. As he bit into an apple he had purchased earlier from the marketplace, he wondered, not for the first time, why he didn't just pack up his things and catch the next boat back to Greece.

For whatever reason, he still couldn't tear himself away from Ismene. While it was true that he had believed her when she told him she was happy with Alistair before, the events of the last weeks told him a different story. He had been following her to the library and on her trips to the market. She could not hide her downcast demeanor from him. No, he knew her too well. What had happened to her?

At the library, she seemed to be receiving lessons from a Jewish scribe about their history. He dare not linger closer to her than he already had, but the snippets he could catch from his distance told him as much. It puzzled him. What did Jewish history have to do with Egypt or Greece? Had she taken up a new hobby to keep her out of the house and away from her husband?

Unfortunately, he did not know much about what was going on inside the house. Oh, he had tried a couple of times to get close enough to see in or even sneak in, but security was pretty tight. Alistair had even posted military men to guard all the entrances to his estate. That was a bit extreme, Thelopolis thought. But it did prevent him from getting in. His heart longed to approach Ismene again as he had in the library. He needed to ask her what had her so dismayed. No one could read her or lift her spirits like he could.

Thelopolis rubbed his eyes. Perhaps tomorrow he would be able to see her. Tomorrow was market day for Ismene and Alonah. The library had been a safer place to approach because Alonah did not often go with her, but perhaps he could grab a few minutes at the market if they split up.

Ismene and Alonah made their weekly trip to the market with protection in tow—one of Alistair's trusted guards, Nkuku. Since the beginning of all of these incidents, Alistair had insisted that whenever Ismene traveled out of the home to the market, she had to take protection. Even though they weren't on speaking terms, she still honored his word on this. In truth, it did not make her feel squelched, it made her feel cared for. The things that had happened to them over the last couple of months worried her just as much, even more so now that there was a baby on the way. So she was grateful for that extra measure of protection.

"I meant to ask after your health." Ismene stopped to look at some cloths one of the merchants had on display.

"My health?" Alonah was confused.

"Yes, when I returned from the library, Safiya told me you were unwell."

Alonah remembered. She had asked Safiya to cover for her in the event Ismene got back before she did. Here she had been so lost in thoughts and daydreams of Jabari that she had all but forgotten. Yesterday, after their afternoon together, she came home to find that her mistress had retired early for the evening. And so she did, too, but found herself unable to sleep for quite some time, so captivated by thoughts of the events of that day.

"Thank you, milady. I am well, as you see."

"Yes. I'm glad." Ismene shifted her attention back to where they were going.

They had already purchased several fine linens for Ismene's expanding figure and some fruits that looked good to her. Her appetite of late had become voracious. They were now looking to pick out some jewelry pieces to go with her new linens.

Making their way toward their favorite jewelry stand, Alonah could not help but notice that Ismene's gait had changed. It was becoming more akin to a waddle. Her hand covered her mouth lest she let a laugh escape. Ismene would not appreciate that.

Ismene greeted the store owner, a woman named Lapis, who ran the store with her husband. Lapis created all of the jewelry herself, and Ismene thought her pieces were the best on the strip. Alistair thought them to be the most expensive. Ismene always liked that there was a great variety in the store, and every bit of it was unique and beautiful. Alonah couldn't agree more. She only wished that she had the money to adorn herself thusly.

Moving in toward the more interior parts of the store, they were ooh-ing and aah-ing over the new creations they hadn't seen the previous week. All of a sudden, Nkuku tensed beside them, on alert. So caught up in their shopping was she that Alonah hadn't noticed Lapis ushering the other couple of clients out of the store and shutting the doors behind her. Now they were alone in the shop.

Nkuku grabbed Ismene and backed up toward the door. Alonah scooted along with them. He checked the latch. Locked.

Alonah's heart pounded. What were they going to do? She spun around, looking for any manner of escape. None appeared for her. Gripping Ismene's arm, she dug her nails into it, fear arresting her, but Ismene ignored the pain.

Moments later, men filed in from the back of the store. More came down the stairs. They bore sticks and knives. Their faces were etched with snarls and menacing glares. This was not going to end well.

Nkuku drew his sword and moved Ismene and Alonah behind

himself. He pushed them along the wall and to a corner where he could best protect them. Alonah knew it was hopeless. There was no escape.

"General Merenre!" Alistair heard his name as it was called from the corridor outside of his war room.

"Excuse me." He pardoned himself to step to the doorway.

One of his most trusted household servants, Fenuku, was running down the hall, tailed by Pharaoh's servant, no doubt trying to precede the unannounced intrusion.

"Fenuku, what is it?" Alistair was concerned about Fenuku's breach in protocol.

Pharaoh's servant interjected as Fenuku was catching a breath. "General, my sincerest apologies. He wouldn't wait to be announced. He—"

Alistair held up his hand. "It's all right."

Pharaoh's servant bowed, tossed Fenuku a frustrated glare, and took his leave.

"General Merenre, something terrible has happened. It is the Lady Ismene. Someone has taken her."

"What?" Alistair was on edge, ready to leap into action.

"She was in the market with her handmaiden and Nkuku. They were attacked. Nkuku was sacrificed fighting off their attackers. The handmaiden Alonah was injured, and the Lady Ismene was taken."

"Gentlemen," was all Alistair said to his captains as he excused himself, exiting the room and rushing out into the corridor. Fenuku followed him, attempting to share what scant details he had. But Alistair was focused on getting back home to speak with the one person who could give him more answers—Alonah.

As they exited the palace, Alistair noted that Fenuku's horse was already saddled and present, so he mounted the waiting horse as he waved off Fenuku.

"Thank you. Please make certain my horse is returned to the stables of my estate."

Not waiting for Fenuku's response, he dug his heels into the horse's flanks, urging him into action.

Nassor moved through the compound, desperately seeking some answers. At last, he found Sefu.

"That was not how this was supposed to be! This is not right!"

"Old friend, all is well. We are near the end. This is the time we need to stick together," Sefu reasoned.

"I can't believe you are so calm! What makes you think they won't be led right back to your shop?"

"You worry too much. It's all been taken care of."

Nassor thought for a moment. "I don't think I want to be a part of this anymore."

"If that is your choice, I cannot stop you. But I warn you, once you leave, there is no coming back."

Nassor took a long, tortured breath. In the span of those moments, he came to his decision. "I want out."

Sefu nodded. "Good-bye then, old friend. I trust you will keep our confidence."

"Of course." Nassor spun on his heel and walked away. Sefu did feel sympathy for his friend. The man behind their movements had foreseen this. And he had a plan for Nassor.

CHAPTER 12

Dashed Hopes

A SERVANT MUST HAVE WARNED NETERKA THAT ALISTAIR had been spotted on the horizon. As he approached the door to the house, his faithful valet was awaiting for him, along with a servant boy prepared to take the horse to the stables.

Alistair did not have to ask to be escorted to Alonah. He was catching his breath as Neterka proceeded.

"This way, General." Neterka stepped into the house, through the courtyard and into Ismene's chambers. The household servants had made a pallet on the floor for Alonah. It was thoughtful of Neterka to do so. They had not wanted to put her in her mistress's bed, but they wanted her to have more space than her small servant's quarters afforded.

Alistair leaned over her. "Has someone sent for the doctor?"

The maidservant Rabiah, who had been tending to Alonah, was confused by this. Alistair understood. It would be highly irregular to pay an expensive doctor's fee for a servant.

"No, General. Do you not wish I tend to her myself?"

"Don't question the general," Neterka interjected. "The doctor!"

Rabiah exited, thoroughly scolded, not even raising her eyes to meet Neterka's.

Alistair's attention returned to Alonah. She stirred, moaning as her return to consciousness brought with it a return to pain. Her face was already bruised, there was a deep cut on her forehead, and her lips were swollen and bleeding. In their cleaning, the servants had reopened fresh wounds there. *What had these animals done to her? Had they done worse to his Ismene?* Alonah's arm was in a makeshift sling and the rest of her was covered. The wheezing of her breathing indicated that there were cracked ribs.

Heavy eyelids opened with much effort to see the master of the house leaning over her. Alonah seemed startled, and the sharp intake of breath was a mistake. Her eyes glazed over from the pain.

"General," she whispered. "General, I am so sorry. I tried, I tried to..." Tears were flowing as she gazed off in the distance. Was she reliving the attack even then?

"Shh," he soothed, pushing his urgency for answers to the side. "Be still, Alonah. No one is here to harm you now. The doctor will be here soon. Try not to move too much."

She tilted her head in acknowledgment of his words. "Please, I want to tell you what I know."

His eagerness drove him to push her, but he knew she needed to rest. He also knew that they had waited long enough to begin the manhunt, that for every minute that passed the trail became colder and harder to follow.

"Only as long as you can stand it," he replied.

Her eyes refocused and she seemed to look through him as her mind returned to the past, recalling those memories. Once those relevant bits of information were retrieved, her gaze refocused on him.

"It was a trip to the market. We did not even suspect...Ismene just wanted to get out into the marketplace. Nkuku came with us." She paused, swallowing a lump in her throat at what Alistair was certain were images of the soldier's sacrifice. Her eyes shifted toward the ceiling.

Alistair took her hand. "Alonah, what happened?"

"We were in our favorite jewelry store. The one on the corner. She—the owner—locked the door and the men...they came from everywhere and surrounded us. I was so afraid, but Ismene showed no fear. And Nkuku...he..." She began losing her grasp on her emotions.

"It's all right. I know," he reassured her. "What happened next?"

"After Nkuku fell, I don't remember much—darkness and pain. And then I was here again."

"These people—do you remember who they were?"

"No, General, they didn't say much. They came for Ismene and that was all we knew."

"Do you remember what they looked like?"

She closed her eyes. "They were Egyptians...and gypsies." She was remembering more as she concentrated. Her eyes flew open. "Gypsies, General! There were gypsies!"

Fighting down his own disgust, he calmly led her on. "The Egyptian men, what do you remember about them?"

"They were not dressed as slaves, and I don't think they were merchants."

"Nobility?"

She looked up at the ceiling again, thinking. "No...yes...maybe."

He let her think.

Turning back to face him, there were tears in her eyes again. "General, I can't remember anything else. I'm sorry."

He gently squeezed her hand. "No, Alonah, you have been most helpful. Now rest. The doctor will be here to help you and I want you to rest. I am relieved you are safe."

Releasing her hand, he stood up. Nodding to the servants who had brought in warm water and cloths to clean her wounds again, he began to move toward the door to the hallway.

He stopped one of the servants on his way out. "Bring her some vinegar water. The doctor will not be able to be as gentle with her."

The servant nodded her understanding, and Alistair passed out of the chambers with Neterka not far behind.

"The doctor will be here soon, General. I will inform you when he arrives," the servant woman called after him.

"That is not necessary," he said, turning. "I will only need to speak with him when he is done." He moved to continue on his way.

They walked in silence until they reached the safe confines of the general's chambers. Neterka stood nearby and waited for his master's instructions. Alistair planted himself by his window, gazing out across the sand dunes. He remained still and quiet, allowing his thoughts and emotions to absorb him for a few moments.

After some time passed, he faced his valet. "I don't know what to do, Neterka."

Neterka remained as he was.

"I mean…" His voice was softer. He began to pace, wringing his hands. "I've never felt quite so…out of control before." His eyes met those of his closest confidant. "Every fiber of my being tells me to tear this country apart to bring her back to me—to turn this world upside down if I must."

"But this is not what the general in you says?"

He shook his head, turning away from Neterka and gazing at the wall. "I need a plan. And to formulate a plan, I need more facts. Before I go chasing down my enemy, I need to know what their motives and intentions are. And I need to have at least *some* idea what they want."

"You do know *who* is responsible?"

"I have no doubt this is the work of the Alexandrian mob." There was disgust in his voice.

He caught Neterka's eyes, and for the first time in all the time he had known this man, there was a dark mystery within those pools. It gave him pause. But he didn't have time to ponder this too. No, Ismene was out there. Somewhere. Enduring who knew what.

Stopping and setting his eyes on the door, he made his decision. "I'm going after her. I can't wait here any longer. There is one good lead and I'm going to follow it."

Ismene stirred and made her slow return to consciousness. Her head ached, and, touching her fingertips to her forehead, she discovered that the pain was internal and external. As if by instinct, she called for Alistair, mumbling his name.

When her eyes opened at last, she discovered that she was in a strange place. A rather cold, damp, and dark strange place. Pulling herself into a sitting position on the dirt floor, she remembered her earlier struggles. She was sore and bruised in many places, mostly on her arms and torso where they had restrained her while she fought for her freedom.

That brought back the memories of the attack. Nkuku had fought valiantly and sacrificed himself in her protection and then Alonah...she, too, had fought so hard. They had restrained Ismene, but had toyed with Alonah, letting her resist them only to beat her as she struggled. And then that one final blow...Ismene could still hear the sickening smack as Alonah's defenseless body hit the wall. Tears streamed down Ismene's face as she realized that she had lost her best friend. Alonah was gone.

She longed for Alistair's strong embrace that could protect her against the harshness of reality and his gentle voice that could soothe her aching heart. But she had been robbed of that as well. Here she was, alone in this dungeon.

You must stop feeling sorry for yourself! If she was going to get out of here, get back to Alistair, she would have to pull herself together. She could do nothing about what had happened to her. All the regret in the world wouldn't undo it. Closing her eyes, she attempted to focus her mind.

Who had abducted her? Why had they taken her? Two questions she wished she could answer. They had never made any demands. There wasn't any hesitation in their actions, only determination and coldness. *What were they going to do with her?*

Ismene couldn't help but think on what her fate may be. This caused her to regret some of the decisions she had made. Why hadn't she tried to make things right with Alistair? It wasn't that she didn't fear her own demise, but more than that, she feared that it would all end with things between her and Alistair still at odds. She felt remorse for so many things. She knew that he regretted some of the things he had said. Why had she been so stubborn? Because she was hurting; she had let her pain rule her actions.

Her face dropped into her hands. She allowed herself a few moments of grief for what was and what should have been. Then her thoughts drifted to Jehovah. Was He watching her even now? Did He truly care of her sadness? Of her situation? If Jehovah was indeed listening, she prayed that He would keep her safe until she could make things right.

Shuffles nearby caused Ismene to break off her prayer. Her eyes searched in futility to discover the source of the sound. Everything was too dark and her eyes were having a hard time adjusting to the lack of light. There was definitely movement within the confines of the walls around her. The sound of her heart thundered in her ears, cutting off her ability to hear anything else. Whoever it was drew near her.

"Who?" She tried to form the word with dry, parched lips, but it just wouldn't come.

The intruder knelt over her. The voice that spoke was not much more than a whisper. "Don't worry, it's me, Thelopolis."

"Thelo...po...lis..." she managed. "What?"

"Shh, don't try to speak." His hands were checking out her injuries. "You took quite a beating." She could hear the anger in his voice. Had Thelopolis seen the whole thing?

"How?" she managed, resisting his hands. She needed answers.

Thelopolis sighed. Then he began to recount to her what had happened that day from his perspective.

"I was following you," he confessed. Her eyes were starting to adjust to the darkness. She could make out his downcast face. Then he lifted his face to meet her eyes again. "It was my hope to catch you alone. And I was trying to find a way into the store when I saw that an attack was imminent. So I thought it was best to lay low and then to follow these men to wherever they would take you.

"I assumed they intended to abduct you. It did worry me when your guard was killed, and I again tried to find a way in, but it came to nothing. My first guess was right—you were the target and their purpose was to kidnap you. So I did follow them to this place.

"And I have been waiting, watching for an opportunity to make a move. Sneaking past the entry guards during a change in shift was easier than I thought. This cavernous structure is inside a mountain out in the desert. Perhaps their seclusion makes them a little lax on security. Since then, I've been wandering the tunnels, looking for you."

Her eyes searched his in the dimness, wondering at the truth of his words. She believed him, but she was still trying to absorb it all.

"We must go," he insisted, slipping an arm under her shoulders and one under her legs to attempt to lift her. As he did so, she cried out in pain. She hurt everywhere. She tried to stifle further reactive utterances as he stood, shifting her even more.

"Don't worry, Ismene, this will all be over soon. I'll get you home, I promise." His voice held such tenderness for her. It tugged at her heart, but not enough that she forgot Alistair.

Thelopolis moved through the dark tunnels. Some were barely lit, though from what light source Ismene was not able to discern. It was, as Thelopolis suggested, a series of tunnels and caves. They could hear voices in places along the way. In those spaces, Thelopolis would press against the wall in a crevice until he could make out where the voices were coming from. His heavy breathing was steady in her ear. Unlike Alistair, this kind of thing was not something he was used to. She knew that his worry was getting the best of him.

Moments later, as they continued to navigate the tunnels, Ismene's absence must have been discovered. There were loud voices that seemed to come from all around them. Thelopolis spun around, moving first this way and then that. There did not seem to be a safe route any longer. *What were they going to do?* Leaning against the side of the tunnel, he took several deep breaths. Was he contemplating his next move? Uncertain of their ability to fight their way out, Ismene became fearful.

"What's this?" he said, turning toward the cave wall, eyeing the spot where his shoulder had been.

Ismene's eyes scrutinized the rock and saw what Thelopolis must have felt with his shoulder—a sizeable gap in the stone wall.

Shifting Ismene, he was able to set her in the gap. "Don't make a sound. I'll be back for you."

She nodded, even knowing he couldn't see it.

Alistair had sent for a handful of his most well-regarded soldiers to come to his home. He planned to send them out in different directions, hoping to seek out the hiding place of the mob and, thus cover more ground. Captain Ptah and some of his men—Gyasi, Bomani, Jabari,

Ubaid, and Ottah—had arrived at his estate. They were each, in turn, ushered into his receiving room and briefed on the situation. As they were given their assignments, Alistair warned them not to proceed into any location they suspected to house members of the mob without him. It was to be clear that he would be the one seeking out contact with the mob.

As they were being dismissed, Jabari came up to Alistair with some hesitation.

"Yes, Jabari, did you have a question?" Alistair was already somewhat distracted with the next thing: his own assignment.

Jabari paused before continuing. "I wanted to inquire after Alonah. Is she all right?"

Alistair was confused by the question, but decided to answer anyway. "She is healing. The doctor says she will make it through and be just fine." Why would he care to inquire after Alonah?

Jabari breathed a sigh of relief and whispered a prayer of thanks. When he spoke again, he fairly stumbled over himself. "Might I...may I...is it possible for me to see her?"

By this time, Alistair had reached the end of his patience. "See her? I don't understand. What possible reason could there be for me to concern her with one of my soldiers?"

Jabari's eyes met Alistair's. He seemed to be struggling with the answer to that question, but he didn't apologize or move off to complete his assigned task. At last, he did speak, his voice rather timid. "General Merenre, I hope you can understand my predicament. I know this will not be easy to hear. But Alonah and I, we...we are married."

"Married?" There were many things Alistair wanted to say. How could Jabari marry a servant in his household without consulting him? Why had they done this in secret? When had this occurred? His anger flared. At the same time, he knew that nothing could undo what had been done, and he could see in this man's eyes the same ache he felt. He could not deny Jabari a few minutes with his wife.

The soldier before him looked as if he expected a tongue-lashing, and he should give him one. He had every right to be angry, every right to demand that the man march out on his given orders and never return to Alistair's home. But Alistair felt his features soften. How could he not take pity on a man separated from the woman he loved? No matter what their circumstances, they needed each other just as he needed Ismene.

Alistair sighed. "Let me take you to her."

They walked the short distance to Ismene's suite. As Alistair knocked on the door, he fought down a wave of emotion that threatened to overtake him. When he came to this door, it was to see his wife. And, on any other day, he would be greeted by Alonah's smiling face. But not today.

When the door opened, it was the face of Rabiah, who had taken charge of tending to Alonah, that greeted him. Smiling up at her master, she opened the door wide for him to enter at will. Jabari was shifting behind him, trying to look around Alistair and Rabiah to catch a glimpse of Alonah. He and Alonah caught sight of each other at the same time. She was awake, propped up on pillows.

"Jabari!" she cried out.

He rushed to her, falling on his knees next to the pallet on the floor.

Alistair had wanted to iterate to Jabari that this discussion about his deception was not over, but he did not have it in him to interrupt his and Alonah's reunion. So Alistair indicated to Rabiah that they should give the two a moment alone. The two of them stepped out into the hall.

Once outside, Alistair knew there was no more time to delay. He took his leave, heading off to follow his first lead.

Thelopolis moved down the tunnel, hugging the wall, lest he make himself too much of a target. It was of no consequence, however, for when the men came down the tunnel with torches, he was easy to spot. They took him without effort. He didn't even bother to fight them off. It would do Ismene no good for him to be killed in a scuffle.

The group of men moved him farther back into the cave, all the while searching out where he might have left the wounded prisoner they knew he must have been carrying. They stopped when they reached another search party.

"Sefu!" The leader of the group holding Thelopolis called to another man and jerked on Thelopolis's arm. "Sefu! We found this one in the tunnels."

A man came up to Thelopolis, stopping just inches away from his nose, sizing him up.

"I haven't had the misfortune to run across this Greek scum yet. They are bringing them over by the boatloads by now, I suppose."

Thelopolis met his gaze.

"Where is the Lady Ismene?" came the man's harsh question.

Thelopolis's mouth became a thin line.

"I know she didn't walk out of her quarters herself. You must have carried her and hid her somewhere. Now tell me where she is."

Thelopolis continued to stare at the man without uttering a sound.

"I warn you, my associates here can be terribly impatient," the man said, wandering over to where one of the torches was affixed to the wall. He handed it to one of his men.

"Now," he said, still facing away from Thelopolis. "I will give you one more chance. Where is the Lady Ismene?"

Thelopolis clenched his jaw. The man's associate moved the torch to sear his skin.

Back in Ismene's chambers, Jabari stroked Alonah's hair and gently pressed a kiss to her face. Tears slipped down her cheeks.

"Oh, my angel, look what they've done to you!" Tears brimmed in his eyes.

"It looks worse than it is, love. I am well." She ran a hand over the side of his face, enjoying the feel of him being here with her.

They stayed like that for several minutes, enjoying one another's presence.

"Nothing would make me happier than to remain here with you," Jabari said, kissing her hands one at a time. "But I must do my part to seek out who is behind this plot and bring your mistress home."

"I know," she whispered, mimicking his gesture and kissing his hands. "Go. Go with great speed, love. And then come back to me."

Alistair's credentials at meting out swift justice on the battlefield to the enemies of Pharaoh were well known. It was one of the reasons the Egyptian army was so powerfully devoted to him. This penchant bore the same fast reaction as Alonah gave him the description to the jewelry shop where she and Ismene had been attacked.

Mounting his steed without further ado, he galloped into town. It didn't take long to track down the store. After he dismounted, he entered the shop. No one seemed to be there. He wasn't surprised. There were whispers from others outside the store. In all likelihood because they had heard some version of the events from earlier.

Alistair didn't stop just because the shopkeeper wasn't present. He found the steps in the back leading upstairs. Bounding up the stairs, his eyes swept the residence until they landed on Lapis. He closed the distance before she could move. Just as she was turning around at the realization that another had entered her home, he was in her face.

"What are you doing in my home?" came her shocked, innocent reaction.

"Don't play games with me, woman. Tell me who you work for, and your life may be spared," he said with a cold voice, as he clutched her by the shoulder. Alistair had a menacing look in his eyes as he glared at her.

"I...I..." she creaked. She was speechless, obviously fearing for her life.

As his eyes continued to scan in a more subtle fashion, he noticed a couple of knapsacks that appeared to be full. "Hmm...going on a trip?"

Her eyes shifted to the bags, and then in the other direction.

"Taking something else?" As he released Lapis, he looked over to where she had. He walked toward that part of the room, scanning everything he could see.

There was a side table that had some vases filled with freshly purchased flowers. In the center was a small box with a lid and a drawer. He rummaged through it, and at first found some keepsakes, but underneath that was a sizable amount of money.

"Tell me who hired you, and I might talk Pharaoh out of having you chained to a rock in the desert." He said this without even looking back at her, but he knew the shocked reaction that was on her face. As he moved toward her again, she began sobbing.

"Sefu...my husband's name is Sefu. He is the one that got us in with the Alexandrian mob. I told him we could make enough, but he wouldn't listen to me!" She was falling to pieces.

"I didn't know the Alexandrian mob paid big money."

"Sefu told me we could make some more on the side."

"This," he shoved the money into her face, "is blood money." He got in her face again, searching her eyes. She was afraid of him...terrified. It was clear that she would answer his questions.

"Where is your husband?"

"I swear I don't know." Her voice broke as tears started forming. "He told me to pack our things and prepare to leave town. That's it. Not a word about where he was going."

To his dismay, Alistair could sense that there was no lie in her. It was then that he heard some of his soldiers coming up the stairs. As they topped the stairs, he backed away from her.

"Place this woman under military arrest and place two men at the house to wait for her husband to return. He is to be taken into custody if and when he returns."

Alistair didn't wait to watch them put Lapis under arrest. As he made his way down the stairs and out of the building, he felt the tension of the last several minutes release...somewhat. Where was he going from here? This lead had gone cold. He could not imagine that Sefu was ever coming back here. Something had kept him from returning for his wife and, if he was half as intelligent as he would have to be to plan the things he'd put into play, he would know not to return home.

Alistair moved toward his horse, still considering where to go next, what his next move should be. He felt the pressure of time slipping away. Then it hit him.

"Ubaid, I have an errand for you..."

CHAPTER 13

Great Haste

ALISTAIR MADE HIS WAY TO PHARAOH'S RECEIVING ROOM and, for once in the entire time he had been coming here, there was no aide to greet him. He opened the door with hesitation.

"General, please come in." Ptolemy motioned him in.

Alistair obeyed. "Did you send for him?"

Pharaoh nodded. "I was most disturbed to hear of the events of the last few hours, General. I will do everything in my power to help you find your wife and bring those responsible to justice." He sat and invited Alistair to sit as well.

Alistair managed a half smile for him. "Of course, my liege."

"I requested Chigaru's presence forthwith, so he should be coming with all due haste."

"I do thank you." Alistair was not much for conversation right now; his mind was clouded by images of what may be happening to Ismene, what questions to ask Chigaru to get the information he needed, and what step to take next. But that was the problem. There was no next step. That was why he was having that snake Chigaru summoned; he was Alistair's last resort.

Alistair had long since suspected that the mole was, in fact, in his house or in Pharaoh's. The mob knew too much about Ismene, about her comings and goings, and her interests. He wished now that he had paid more heed to the investigation and given it more credence. He hoped Chigaru could give him some kind of lead, *something*, no matter how small, to go on.

The door opened and Paki announced the investigator's presence.

As Chigaru entered, confusion and then surprise registered on his face. Truth be told, Alistair had not expected to cross paths with him again. Perhaps Chigaru had felt the same.

"My liege," Chigaru said as he bowed before Pharaoh. It was obvious to Alistair that the man was uneasy. He wasn't sure what to expect. No results in a critical investigation could have a rather terminal effect on one's career. And that might have been his suspicion about why he was summoned.

Ptolemy waved his hand, and Chigaru rose. "I'm sure you remember the general." This was Ptolemy's way of indicating who actually wanted to see this investigator.

Chigaru's attention shifted to Alistair.

"I am here to ask *you* some questions," Alistair said, giving an indication that Chigaru's life wasn't on the tip of a sword.

The investigator eased a bit, but still seemed as mystified as when he had entered.

"I'm not sure you have heard, but the Lady Ismene has been abducted."

"I'm aware of it. It is my job to stay informed of such critical developments." Chigaru was shifting out of his mode of self-preservation into his more common role of detective. "Why? Do you know something new?"

"Indeed. The mistress of the shop was packing to leave, and had a considerable amount of money." Alistair pulled out the money he had seized, showing it to Chigaru. "She said that her husband, Sefu, is the one that got them into the mob, and that they were hired to seize the lady."

Chigaru looked closer at the money as Alistair handed it to him. Then, looking up, he asked, "Did you arrest her?"

"Of course. She has been detained by my men. Did you run across anyone who knew Sefu as you queried my staff?"

"No, that name never came up. Why do you believe this to be the case?"

"It is too coincidental that the mob would know so much about the lady's movements and not have a contact inside my household. I thought maybe you had heard names, but did not know the significance of the name *Sefu*."

"Unfortunately, what I did uncover doesn't quite line up with that." Chigaru looked back towards Ptolemy.

"What you uncovered?" Ptolemy was rising out of his chair with a growing sense of vehemence.

"My liege, I found some suspicious things, but nothing I could act on, let alone build a case around." The words rushed out of Chigaru. Now he *was* defending his life. "It seemed that two of the general's staff could not account for their whereabouts on one evening in particular: Neterka and Akil. I had hoped that questioning other members of the staff would cause their names to come up again and point me in a direction, but nothing else surfaced regarding those two."

"Neterka? You must be mistaken. He is the person I trust most in my entire household. The man runs the whole estate and often must be in many places at once. I'm not surprised you couldn't place him on one particular evening." Alistair's eyebrows were knit together as he thought about what Chigaru was saying.

"That was my conclusion after speaking with much of the staff. Several of them confirmed for me that he often must go into town to handle your affairs. With nothing more than that, I couldn't go and investigate all of Alexandria."

"But you also mentioned Akil," Alistair prompted.

"Yes. As a porter and common manservant, his duties didn't seem as widespread as Neterka's. So I tried to cross-reference his activities with others, and..." Chigaru paused at this point.

Alistair was confused by Chigaru's hesitation. "Well, you cross-checked, and what?"

"It seems he was seeing someone outside the household. The maids knew about this, and tried to cover for him, but I was able to break them into telling me this. On one evening in particular, none of the maids saw him leave. They only remember his return. I'm sorry,

General. Her name is Habibah. She swore to being with him and wouldn't back down when I pressed her on this point. I didn't believe her, but couldn't get any further."

How many people in my household are out on romantic quests? Alistair wondered as he reflected on Alonah.

"And this is all you know? Akil has only been a member of my household for about six months. This woman, Habibah, you think she was lying?"

"That was my gut instinct when I spoke to her. But when it comes to being romantically involved with a household servant, it is hard to discern what she was lying about. I didn't think this was enough to take back to Pharaoh. If this was a real lead, there would be more connections to your household. Connections that never materialized. All of this is being written in my report." He became somewhat defensive.

Alistair bit back the comment that almost escaped his lips. "Thank you," he said instead. "You have been most helpful."

Chigaru nodded.

"If I may." Alistair stood up. "I would like to keep my men informed of every lead I get, so we can follow up on them."

"Do you not think it best to turn this investigation over to the secret police?" Chigaru spoke up, his eyes hopeful.

Alistair opened his mouth to answer, fearing he would not be able to keep his thoughts or comments to himself this time, but Pharaoh spoke up first.

"I do not think that is necessary. I am deeming this a military matter and the secret police will assist the military as needed."

Chigaru nodded, disappointed.

Pharaoh looked back over to Alistair. "If that is all, General, you have your leave. May the gods watch your steps."

That was all Alistair needed. He turned his back on Ptolemy and Chigaru and made his way out of the palace and to his horse.

Jabari had loathed to part from his Alonah. She had been so badly beaten. The only thing that gave him some reprieve was knowing that when he found the men who did this, he would be able to delve out justice as he saw fit. If only he could find them first.

They had left Alonah for dead, but they never imagined that she would survive and live to give the general the lead she gave him. That made her too dangerous. He wanted to stay with her, but he knew that no one would risk walking into the general's home right now.

He could not help but wonder what would happen to him and Alonah now that the general knew the truth. Would he be discharged for lying? Would she be released from service for the same reason? Where would they live? How would they live? *Don't think like that!* The general was a reasonable man who seemed to understand their plight. Or was that wishful thinking on his part? He would just have to wait for things to unfold.

Jabari was so deep in thought that he almost didn't see the man stumbling toward him until he was quite nearly upon him. The man was clutching at his chest and having a hard time staying upright.

Jabari caught him.

The man pressed something into Jabari's hand.

"Please..." Nassor pleaded. "I'm...sorry. Never...meant to...hurt..."

With that, the man started gasping for breath. He convulsed a few times and was still.

Jabari knew he was dead.

Ismene could hear Thelopolis's screams. Holding her knees to herself, she bit her lip to keep from crying out. They had been torturing him for some time now. Tears squeezed out of her closed lids. It was too much! And then it stopped, just as suddenly as it had begun. What had happened? Had he passed out? Had they killed him? What would become of her?

She could hear movement again in the tunnels around her and a voice calling out. They were too far away for her to make out. As they got closer, she could piece together what they were saying.

"Show yourself or your would-be savior will be sliced from navel to nose," came the menacing voices of the men in the tunnels.

No! She could not allow that to happen! The thought occurred to her that they might be bluffing, but she dare not take that chance.

"Stop!" she screamed.

There was a flurry of movement out in the tunnels as they attempted to discern where the sound came from.

She used the cave walls to pull herself out of the crevice. "Stop! Don't hurt him! I'm here!" she continued to say as pain tore through her body with every movement.

It wasn't long before she was surrounded by men. Two men dragging Thelopolis came into view, and she couldn't bear the sight of his burned and bloodied face and limbs.

They tossed him down next to her. Dragging herself over to him, she pulled his torso into her lap as much as she could.

"We are not without mercy," the man whom the others called Sefu said. "You may have a moment to say farewell."

Ismene looked up through narrowed eyes at the man who had tortured Thelopolis. How dared he speak of mercy! She held her tongue and focused her attention on Thelopolis.

"Look at what they've done to you!" she cried.

"It will be all right." He fought to get the words out.

As he breathed, something in his chest rattled. Ismene knew he must have sustained serious internal injuries. One look into his eyes told her that he knew as well.

Lifting a hand, he cupped her face. "Tell me that you love me, that this is breaking your heart, that we'll be all right."

She cried as he echoed their farewell words from so long ago—a lifetime ago when nothing mattered but the two of them. So much had changed, but some things had not.

"I do love you, Thelopolis. A part of me always will. My heart is broken for you. We will be all right." She leaned down and pressed a kiss to his lips. Somehow she knew that this was the last time she would see his face in this life.

"And this is breaking my heart!" Sefu said, his voice dripping with sarcasm. "Enough."

Men grabbed at Thelopolis, pulling him away from her while another man jerked her to her feet. They were marched toward the opening of the cave, then around the side toward the back side of the mountain pass.

"Let's help the man down the mountain at least. Give him a good start to his journey," Sefu said.

Ismene was confused. Were they letting him go? For certain, they would not. Did they expect him to succumb to his injuries in the desert? If so, there was a chance for him! She watched as the two men who held Thelopolis walked him down the hillside and let him go there.

Despite his injuries, he was able to stand and walk with some stability on his own. He began to move away from the caves, and Ismene saw a glint of something off to her left. Turning, her heart dropped. It was an archer!

"No!" she screamed. "You can't!"

Her captors started pulling her back toward the cave mouth, but she was still able to see when the archer released his arrow. She watched in horror as it struck Thelopolis squarely between his shoulder blades, and then she watched him fall.

Ismene fell over, screaming, crying out at the atrocity that had just been committed, but it was useless. One of the men picked her up, carried her inside through the twisting tunnels, and deposited her right back in her chamber onto the thin blanket she had been sleeping on earlier.

She didn't know how long she cried. It seemed like hours. She couldn't believe that Thelopolis was dead. He was dead. Dead. It didn't seem right.

After a while, she couldn't cry anymore. She wanted to give up, to die, too. But she knew she had to be strong for Alistair, for their child. Her eyes had adjusted better to the dark as she had been crying. Taking in her surroundings a bit more, she could feel that the blanket underneath her was on top of some straw. The room also had a bucket, some water in a jar, and a narrow opening to the sky. The air was damp and dank; it caused her to cough, though her lungs already felt tight from her physical expression of grief.

Shifting her attention to the piece of the sky she could see, she gazed up at the stars, searching. At last, she found Diana, the woman no longer separated from her love, now together for all eternity. Once her eyes found the familiar constellation, all awareness of her current circumstances faded and her mind rested on Alistair and the night he had showed her Diana. Then she closed her eyes, remembering the safety of his arms and the comfort he provided for her. How she longed for that feeling now! She had longed for that comfort often these last weeks, but dared not allow herself to reach out for it. The wounds were too deep. But her love for him was deep, too.

Ismene opened her eyes. Was he thinking of her? Loving her? Her thoughts continued to drift to their more recent exchanges full of anger, jealousy, and, most of all, hurt. Did he still love her? How could he if he couldn't trust her? For that matter, did he ever truly love her? Was she now being punished for her betrayal? For her stubbornness?

Shaking her head, Ismene attempted to clear those thoughts. No, he *was* coming for her. And he *did* love her. These things she knew. She was also certain that he was, in fact, gazing at these same stars, longing for her forgiveness.

She closed her eyes and concentrated on her love for him, *I forgive you, Alistair. And I love you. Jehovah, if You are out there, please let him know I love him. Please help him find me.*

A sense of relief washed over Alistair. He felt the same way he felt when he and Ismene were together in the best of times, almost as if she were reaching out to him. Looking up at the stars as he was riding, he knew they gazed at the same sky, and he tried to return that feeling of love to her.

Before Alistair knew it, he was at his house, dismounting and turning his horse over to the stable boy.

"You did not see me," he told the young lad.

The boy nodded his understanding.

Alistair slipped into the house and made his way to Ismene's rooms without notice. Alonah was still there on her pallet on the floor. The doctor had seen to her wounds and they were now cleaned, covered, wrapped, and her arm cast. She seemed to be sleeping comfortably.

"General!" Rabiah said, seeing him. "Allow me to see to your needs."

"No, I thank you. But I do have a request. Do not tell anyone that you have seen me."

"I don't understand, you…"

He shook his head. "Just…don't tell anyone."

She nodded, though still not understanding his intentions. She simply accepted that it was what he wanted.

"I need to know the whereabouts of Akil and Neterka. Go find this information for me and return here. But remember…"

"Yes, General, I have not seen you. I know not where you are."

He smiled. "Thank you."

She slipped out of the room, and he went over to look closer at Alonah, who lay in peaceful slumber on the mat. He wished that she could have been more helpful for her sake. She would be devastated to find that her information came to nothing, but he couldn't concern himself with that now. He had to find Ismene before the trail became cold.

Alistair looked over her chambers; it seemed unreal that Ismene, too, was not resting in the bed as she had been these last weeks, unreachable by him. Their fight had been so senseless. His anger had come from hurt and a wounded pride more than actual suspicion of wrongdoing on her part. Why couldn't he have seen through the pain sooner? They might have avoided all of this.

In the process, he had delivered a greater wound, a blow to her heart that was unforgivable. He wouldn't blame her if she was never able to forgive him for what he said, for what his statement had implied about her. But he could handle life the way it was, with her refusing to see or talk to him, as long as he knew she was safe.

His thoughts were interrupted as Rabiah came back into the bedchambers.

He was upon her in a moment. "What have you discovered?"

"No one seems to know where Akil has vanished to. His absence was not noticed until I started inquiring about his whereabouts. Neterka is readying himself for a trip into the city."

Alistair looked at the door as if he could see through the walls to where Neterka was.

"Thank you," he said. "You have been most helpful." He moved toward the door before turning. "How is she?" He indicated Alonah.

"She is well, General. The doctor says she will recover."

He nodded and moved out of the door and into the corridor beyond. Though he had serious doubts about everything Chigaru said about Neterka, he needed to follow every lead. At least he would be able to clear his faithful valet's name, if nothing else.

Alistair moved toward the stables, but placed himself in a quiet, dark part of the corridor just inside of the building so he would be able to see the stables, but would be well hidden from passersby.

He didn't have to wait long before he saw Neterka stroll through the gardens from the main exit of the house and head straight to the stables. He spoke to the stable boy, who went to fetch him a horse. When the boy returned with a horse, he said something to Neterka, who frowned. Had the boy just given him away? Neterka spoke to him one last time before urging the horse forward.

Hurrying to the stables, Alistair demanded a horse. The boy stumbled back into the barn to ready a horse with all due haste for his master. He returned quicker than Alistair thought possible.

As Alistair was mounting, he asked the boy, "What were you and Neterka speaking about?"

The boy looked as if he didn't want to tell Alistair.

"It will be all right, boy, but you must tell me," he insisted.

"One of the manservants, Akil, has gone missing," the boy said.

Alistair almost laughed, but held his face firm. "I'm sure Neterka will see to it that he is found."

It took some carefully timed maneuvering to stay far enough behind Neterka to not be noticed, yet close enough to not lose him. Alistair leaned on his skills of stealth used in combat. Neterka, for his part, seemed oblivious to the fact that anyone could be tailing him. Alistair was able to follow him right to a nobleman's estate.

Alistair found a tree several yards away to tie up his horse. He would make the rest of the journey on foot, so as to not be spotted. His heart sank as his suspicions grew. What business could Neterka have at an estate like this so late in the evening?

As he approached the estate proper, Alistair noticed that there were several lights on in the barn in the back while the house remained dark. Moving toward the back corner of the house, he made his way toward the barn. But...this house had *two* barns. He saw that one was for the animals and the other structure, the one that had lights near the entrance, seemed not to have any entrance large enough for livestock. He moved toward it.

Alistair attempted to grab the ledge of a window and lift himself up, but it was too dark inside to see anything. Looking in, he thought he saw movement, but he couldn't be sure. It was certain—he would need to go in, but there was just the one entrance as far as he could discern.

This might give him away, but he had to do something. Pulling his sword, he laid his hand on the door's latch and pushed. He stepped into the darkness. There was a place in the center of the room, a circle, lit from a skylight illuminated by the moon. As he moved farther into the space, he could sense, rather than see, the presence of other bodies in the building.

He was not afraid. "Show yourselves!"

Nothing. There was nothing.

"I am not afraid of you. Perhaps you are afraid of me, cowards!"

Then he was attacked from several different directions at once. Using all of his skill, he was able to take down a few men, but there were just too many. It wasn't long before his sword clanged to the ground and he was overtaken. Alistair struggled helplessly against the men who held him. They readied him to deliver a couple of direct punches to his face— payback for the good ones he had gotten in. He smiled and faced them.

"Hold!" a booming voice called out.

All of the men holding him froze. Alistair, for his part, took the opportunity to separate himself from the men who held him, but they encircled him.

"So, the great General Merenre has found us at last." A hooded figure stepped out from the shadows. Alistair could make out his nose and mouth, but nothing else. He would be almost impossible to identify even if Alistair was having a face-to-face conversation with him again.

"I had no choice," Alistair said. "You have something that belongs to me."

"I *think*, dear General, that you have something that belongs to *us*." His voice tightened. "You Greek *fakirs* hold Egypt as if it were nothing more than your playground."

"Do you not see that we seek only to prosper Egypt? To fight for Egypt? To protect Egypt?" Alistair was almost pleading.

"For your precious Greek Empire!" The hidden man spat.

"For Egypt—our home!" Alistair shouted back.

"Egypt is *our* home. You may occupy the land, but know this, General. Your days of occupancy are numbered."

Alistair glared at the shadows and the movement there, biting back his reckless comments.

"I know what you seek," the man continued.

Alistair fought his overwhelming rage. "Please," he said through gritted teeth. "You have no quarrel with my wife and now you have me. Let her go."

The man watched Alistair for a moment and then made a motion toward another figure still hidden in the shadows. As this figure moved into the light, Alistair saw that he was also clad in a hood, a dark blue one.

"Your wife is not here," the man spoke.

"You cannot expect me to believe that!"

"You have no choice but to believe it," the odd voice said. There was something about that voice.

"You expect me to believe that we experienced all of this harassment at your hands, except this? That now, all of a sudden, there is someone else in the picture?"

"We have not been responsible for any harm done to anyone in your house," continued the man in the blue robe.

"I had hoped we could do this peaceably. You cannot think that I would come here without notifying Pharaoh's guard to follow. They will be here soon, and if I am still here and have not been released with my wife, woe be unto your mob."

A look was exchanged between the two hooded figures.

The second man stepped closer to Alistair and started to pull his blue hood down.

"General, you must believe me," Neterka started.

Alistair's eyes widened. "Never in all my wildest imagining could I conceive that the closest to me was my vilest enemy!" He pulled against his captors and was struck from behind with such force that it drove him to his knees, the wind knocked out of him.

"Why? Why would you betray me so?" Alistair gasped out.

"It has nothing to do with you...and yet everything. My service is first to Egypt. And Egypt belongs in the hands of *Egyptians*, not your kind." Thinly veiled disdain played on Neterka's face. "You may change your names and take on our customs, but you cannot change the fact that you are all fair-skinned *fakirs*!"

Alistair's anger fueled his response. "*We* are not going anywhere."

He was hit again from behind.

"Please, just tell me where she is!" he managed to say, exasperated.

"General, we do not have the Lady Ismene," Neterka said.

Alistair's look was confused and skeptical.

"Sir, I know you're not inclined to trust me at this moment, but I tell you I speak the truth. Regardless of my feelings on the rule of Egypt, you must know that I could never have been a willing part of harming the Lady Ismene. Do you want to stand here, wasting time accusing us, or do you want to go out there and continue looking for who might have done this thing?"

CHAPTER 14

To the Death

ISMENE EYED HER CAPTOR AS HE ENTERED THE ROOM AND took a seat across from her. It was difficult to hide her shock and revulsion. She fought off another coughing fit, but it was useless; her body was racked with coughs.

"Well, Lady Ismene, I trust you find your accommodations acceptable?" the man started.

She looked away, not wanting to offer him the pleasure of a response, even as much as she wanted to snap back at his words in anger.

"Come now. I hope our relationship is not to be full of hate and silence." His voice was smooth, but snake-like in her ears.

She shifted to meet his eyes. "Why have you done this, *Prince* Meleager?" Her words didn't have the edge she wanted them to as her voice had gotten weak.

"My dear lady, I do not want to weigh down your female mind with such heavy thoughts," Meleager jeered.

"Prince Meleager, as a daughter of privilege, I was trained in academics and logic along with my brothers, who were provided with the finest of Grecian scholars. Humor me," she retorted.

His eyebrows rose.

She could have kicked herself for allowing herself to be irritated by him.

He continued to eye her as if she were his next meal.

"Why? Why would you do this? Is your life not satisfactory to you?" The bitterness was evident in her voice, now knowing he intended to betray his own brother.

"Not when I could have *everything*! And who does *Pharaoh* love? On whom does his favor rest? His general...over his own brother."

"Is that why you've taken me? To hurt Alistair?"

"You know, I didn't expect him to run just because some animal blood was used to write an inflammatory statement on his house. No, that was just to kick things off. Shredding the sheets of your bed and destroying your precious flowers should have made it clear that you were the means to strike fear into his heart." The prince was gloating with a diabolic tone of voice. It was as if he wanted this all captured for posterity.

Ismene started remembering the stories of the pharaoh of ancient times told by the Jewish scholars. She was visualizing the prince as this exact kind of man: evil, brutal, and with a heart as cold as stone. She had debated so many times in her own mind whether these stories were true or not. For the first time, she felt an undeniable belief that they were.

The prince continued his self-aggrandizing rant. "Making you sick almost to the point of death should have done the trick. And by the way, I believe congratulations are in order. I couldn't have asked for a more fortuitous circumstance. Morning sickness combined with the poison should have been enough to scare any sane man to run away with his bride. But no, it seems he was willing to gamble with your *life*."

As Meleager uttered these last words, he turned to walk out of the small cell. Ismene realized that this was not part of his original plan. She feared what his mad thirst for power would lead him to do. It seemed it wasn't his intention to kill her at first, but now that his plan had gone awry, there was no predicting where things would go.

"Jehovah!" Ismene prayed silently, hoping Alistair would find her before it was too late.

"Huh?" The prince spun around.

Ismene hadn't realized that her utterance of the Jewish God's name was audible.

"There was once a pharaoh of ancient times who was merciless against the slaves of this land. Do you know what happened to him? His firstborn child was slain. His entire army drowned in the sea. His cruel desires reaped nothing but death and destruction for him. Perhaps your fate shall be the same," Ismene said with bold confidence.

Prince Meleager backhanded Ismene with a force he had never shown before. She fell back, knocked out cold. The rage that welled up within him was stronger than he had ever felt. How dare this *woman* threaten him. He was a prince of Egypt and she was but the wife of an overrated, puffed-up military commander who was in need of being taken down a peg or two. *And I'm the man to do it*, he thought. *And I'm going to enjoy it.*

The members of the mob had released Alistair only after blindfolding him and leading him out into the desert. At least they had left him his horse. He returned to his home, dejected and discouraged. *Two* leads had come to nothing today. Night had fallen and Ismene was out there somewhere probably suffering...because of him. And there was nothing he could do about it. He had but one more lead, albeit a weak one—Akil.

Alistair handed the reigns of his horse to the stable boy and walked into the house. He passed Ismene's room and stopped to check on Alonah. She was sitting up, talking excitedly to Jabari. Making a move to walk on, he decided to give them their privacy.

"General!" Jabari called after him. "I have been looking everywhere for you!"

"Oh?" Alistair had not the time nor the patience to suffer flights of fancy.

Jabari stood and closed the distance between him and the general with a few long strides. "I know where the Lady Ismene is being held."

"What?" Had he heard the soldier correctly?

"A man gave this to me." He handed Alistair a slip of crumpled paper. "I think he died trying to get it to you."

Alistair examined the paper. The paper detailed directions to a place in the middle of the desert—a smart place, indeed, to set up a hidden fortress and keep concealed something as precious as a general's wife.

"Let us go at once!" Alistair moved back toward the stables, Jabari on his heels.

Once they arrived at the stable and the boy rushed off to saddle Alistair's horse, Alistair caught Jabari's eyes.

"I will ride on ahead. You round up Captain Ptah and his unit to meet me there."

Jabari stopped short. "You're going on your own?"

"Yes, but you will all be there soon after me if you hurry."

The stable boy brought Alistair his horse. Grabbing the saddle, Alistair mounted.

Jabari raised his fist to his chest, bowing toward his general, indicating that he would do as he had been commanded. With that, Alistair dug his heels in and the horse took off.

Alistair did not look back, driving the horse ever forward. Every step of the way, he tried to weigh every decision with the precision of a military commander. He knew that if he got there before his men caught up with him, there might be little he could do for Ismene, or worse, he might be ambushed and killed.

It wasn't that he feared death. No, that had faded long ago after carrying out countless military campaigns for his pharaoh. But the thought of his Ismene and their child surviving but not him left him with a cold fear he had never expected. He could now see that what he used to brush off as careless daydreaming about his bride had become committed love for his wife and unborn child. The thought of not being able to see to their every need for the rest of their lives scared him.

In this moment of crisis, everything was clear. Though there was a wall between them, he would go to any length to break it down so they could be rejoined. He didn't care if she agreed or not. What Alistair felt for his Ismene was not based on how she felt about him, but instead on true love and a strong feeling of commitment. She was his wife.

Alistair's mind was sifting through the options he could take. He figured the time it would take to rouse Captain Ptah and the rest of his troops, followed by saddling horses and catching up to him. In that amount of time, Alistair estimated he would reach the location, just a few miles outside the city, and gather enough information to mount a rescue.

He reviewed all of this with calm precision as he rode in the dark night. Then he stared up at the stars and saw the shape of Diana. Praying to whatever deity that would listen, he hoped that Ismene looked upon the same stars as well and that they would be linked together again.

After almost an hour of riding hard, Alistair approached the mouth of the cave system that was described on the scrawl of paper a man had died to bring him. He stopped several hundred feet away, and tied up his horse. Proceeding on foot, he began looking and listening for any hints of movement. As he approached, he noticed some flickers in the moonlight and discerned that two men were standing watch over the cave entrance. Alistair's eyes swept the rest of the area, and seeing nothing, he started to circle around.

That's when he found the body. It was clear the man had been struck down by an arrow, and not that long ago. There was still warmth in his body. As Alistair came closer, he saw movement. The man was still alive!

Alistair gently maneuvered the man to lay on his side. Though his face was bloody, Alistair could identify him as Ismene's evening rendezvous in the palace gardens. He pushed the emotions that swelled to the surface down. It was no matter—this man might have information that may help him.

The man's eyes sought Alistair's face. There was a glint of recognition there.

"I'm going to pull this arrow through. It will hurt," Alistair said without ceremony.

The man nodded as much as he could manage.

Alistair tore off pieces of his clothing to staunch the wound on both sides and jerked the arrow through. Then he was able to move the man to his back. It was clear to Alistair that his injuries were not limited to the bruised face and the arrow puncture.

"I'm not going to make it," the man said.

Alistair nodded, eyebrows furrowed. He would not dishonor the man by contradicting him.

"You have to save her." The man's plea was earnest.

Alistair nodded again. "Where is she?"

He listened as the man, with ragged breath, described a twisting path through the cave to get to Ismene. It became difficult for the man to breathe. Alistair knew that blood from internal injuries filled his lungs. He wished he could make him more comfortable. Even though he would say this man had wronged him, he didn't wish this death on anyone. Especially since this man may well have given him the key to saving his wife.

"Thank you." Alistair offered the only thing he had to give to this young man who had risked everything in an attempt to free Ismene.

"She..." he tried.

"Please, don't push yourself to talk further. It will only make it worse." Alistair pressed a hand to the man's shoulder in an attempt to comfort him.

The man shook his head. It was a slight movement.

"She didn't betray you," he managed to get out.

Alistair met his eyes then. "I know."

The man, pleased that he had accomplished all that he had held on for, closed his eyes and let his life slip away into eternity.

Alistair stayed with this man who had been so important to his wife in her early life until he was gone. Then Alistair removed his own cloak and laid it over the man. He wished that he could have taken the time to honor him with a proper burial, but he knew he must get on with his mission. Wiping his brow, Alistair promised to come back for him.

Shifting his attention back toward the guards overhead and to the right, Alistair began to form a plan. He crept up behind the first man positioned to guard the entrance. Drawing his dagger, he grabbed the sentry, and thrust his blade into his back before the man could utter a sound. Letting the body fall to the ground, he moved around the opening of the cave until he was behind the second guard. In one quick movement, Alistair grabbed him and held the blade against the man's neck. From Thelopolis's verbal map, he knew where Ismene's quarters were, but he needed to assure himself that she hadn't been moved.

"Where is the Lady Ismene?" His voice was calm, quiet. The man started to reach for his sword. Alistair's grip tightened.

"I wouldn't try that. Now where is the Lady Ismene?"

"I...I..."

Alistair, realizing the man couldn't speak, loosened the blade slightly.

"Inside the caves. Take the first left."

That was the first turn Thelopolis had told him to take. He looked down into the cave. "It's dark in there."

"There is a torch inside the entrance," the guard choked out.

"You have been useful. I may plead for Pharaoh to spare your life." Alistair then knocked the man out with the pommel of his dagger, and tied him up with a coil of rope he had brought.

"Well, I may plead, I may not," Alistair said to himself, still burning with anger at everyone who was involved with this plot to kidnap his Ismene. He climbed down to the entrance, and felt his way in. Farther into the cave, he found a lit torch and picked it up. The thought passed into his mind that he should wait for his troops, but as he wandered into the cave, he realized he couldn't stop now. Once he found a spare lamp, he lit it, and left it at the entrance to signal Captain Ptah.

Yes, he knew it was foolish, but he simply could not wait for Captain Ptah. He had to proceed, knowing full well there could be more men waiting just around the next corner to ambush him. Alistair had served Pharaoh through many struggles and protected him and his empire in combat. But nothing felt as personal as this. Whether or not Captain Ptah would understand his reasoning in this situation didn't matter.

Alistair made his way through the cave's twisting tunnels until he reached what had been described to him as Ismene's cell. It took little effort to get past the makeshift door. And there she was, lying haphazardly on a mat on the floor. He was on his knees next to her in a heartbeat. She was still—too still. With gentle fingers, he touched her face. Her skin was cold, but she stirred in response to his fingers on her.

He pulled her into his arms, fighting tears, not wanting her to see them.

She opened her mouth to speak, but nothing came out. She cursed the weakness that pervaded her body and dragged her heart.

"No, don't try to speak. Just nod if you can hear me." Alistair's voice was shakier than he'd expected.

She nodded, sliding a hand up to rest on his. "Alistair..." she managed to speak at last.

"Shh..."

"Alistair, please be real." She finished her thought out loud.

"I am." He stroked her hair. "And I'm here to take you from this place."

"Home," she whispered.

"Yes, home. To our home." His voice was but a whisper.

He felt her hand on his chest.

"No, I am home."

Alistair looked at her, drinking in the sight of her, the depth of her eyes. He held her to himself, sure that he would never be able to let her go. Breathing in the scent of her, he reveled in the security of the depth of her loving embrace. His lips grazed her hair, the side of her face, and then touched her lips. Using her hands, she drew his face back to her lips.

After only a few brief moments, he forced himself to break off the contact, remembering what she had been through and how weak she was. One look at her confirmed for him that she was fighting to hide it.

"Let me take you away from this place," he said, reaching out his fingers to graze her features again.

She nodded.

He shifted her to lift her, but his hand stopped over her midsection. His eyes fell to where his hand rested over the swell there. Alistair looked at her tired smile as he imagined the child within. Her hand rested on his. Remembering his jealous words, he became saddened anew by how he had hurt her.

Her eyes reflected the wear of her experience, but even still he could see her love and understanding forgiveness. She lifted her hand to cup his face and managed a smile for him. His lips caught hers once more.

His face became more serious. "We need to get out of here, we're not safe yet."

Then he lifted her. She clung to him with what strength she had left.

The trip back through the tunnels was less smooth. Their progress was halted when Ismene dropped their light and it snuffed out. She was weak and probably drugged, Alistair had decided. The main corridor had lights on the walls, but the passageway they were about to take was dark as night and they needed that light source. He sat her down so that he could get his hands free to attempt to relight it.

"Alistair, something's..." Her voice cut off.

"Something is what, Ismene?" He concentrated on his work.

She didn't respond.

He turned to check on her.

There in front of him was Ismene, her back pressed up against Prince Meleager as if she were a body shield. He held a knife to her throat.

"Well, well," Prince Meleager said with a sneer. "The great General Merenre, commander of Pharaoh's mighty army. A job that should have been mine."

"Pharaoh does not entrust his army and the protection of his kingdom to a traitor," Alistair spat.

"It is true that I have always been last among his concerns," the prince spoke as if they were conversing over a pleasant meal. Then his voice darkened. "He loves you as a brother, and you enjoy the merit and favor that are rightfully *mine*!"

"This is between you and me." Alistair leaned forward, holding his hands out toward the prince. "Please allow the lady to go. You have me and that is what you wanted."

"The wife my brother secured for *you*. She should have been mine, too." His stony gaze rested on Alistair. "But then, she has been mine."

Ismene's eyes widened and she gasped in renouncement. Alistair's eyes showed, only for a second, his surprise before they were serious again.

"Are you sure you want her back, Merenre?" He spoke Alistair's Egyptian name with disdain. "After she has prostituted herself to me and my men in return for better treatment?"

"No, Alistair," Ismene protested before Meleager pressed the blade more firmly against the side of her neck, cutting her off again. Tears of anger and shame at his implication slipped down her face.

Alistair's eyes were cold. The anger was not for his Ismene, but for this treatment of his beloved.

"Let her go, Meleager." It was no longer a question.

The prince's eyes were no longer on Alistair. He was looking at Ismene, his face so close to hers. He ran his free hand down her face and throat. She trembled.

"What's the matter, milady?" Her title was said as an insult.

She didn't answer, just closed her eyes and let the tears fall.

He boldly kissed her cheek where one tear was making its trail.

"Meleager," Alistair dared, not able to keep himself from stepping forward.

The prince glared at him and jerked her head back, preparing to cut the jugular.

Ismene cried out.

Meleager turned back toward her, running a finger down the length of her neck. "Does that scare you?"

"Yes," she whispered.

Alistair could feel a tear running down his face, having escaped his guarded features.

Prince Meleager moved the knife down, tracing a line down her body's outline. "What if I cut here?" He stopped with his knife pressed to her swelled abdomen.

"No!" She couldn't stop herself from crying out.

"Come now," he said, his voice low and taunting. "You didn't say *please*."

Another tear slid down Ismene's face. "Please."

"Please? Please what?" he mocked her.

"Please let her go." Alistair couldn't remain silent any longer. "I'm the one you want, not her."

"Wrong," the prince shot back. "You're the one I want to hurt."

Alistair racked his brain. They were at an impasse. Someone had to make a move. More than anything, he wanted Meleager's hands, and the knife, off of Ismene. "If you think you are every bit as capable as I, I challenge you to a duel. Prove it to me."

"I warn you, *General*." Meleager all but laughed. "I have been trained in swords by the best in all of Egypt. Are you sure you're willing to risk it all to attempt to prove something to me that we both know has been exaggerated from the start?"

"We'll let the swords do the talking."

Meleager tossed Ismene to the side. She crumpled to the ground. Alistair took a step forward to check on her, but Meleager drew his sword and pointed it at Alistair, stopping him in his tracks. Alistair responded by drawing his own sword and standing at guard. The two locked eyes, waiting to see who would strike first. Hearing Ismene whimper, Alistair darted his eyes in her direction.

At once, he felt Meleager's sword flying toward him. Without even thinking, he thrust his blade upwards and blocked the strike while at the same time falling to one knee. Then he took a short swing and knocked the prince's sword back, giving him the precious seconds to get back on both feet. They both started circling.

"That is what happens when you don't pay attention to your opponent." Meleager was gloating, and loving it. Alistair cursed himself. *This isn't some half-drunk corporal. This is indeed a sword master!* The tension was growing. After a few steps, Alistair slowed, feigning weakness and grunted.

"I heard you were ambushed by the mob. So sorry to hear that." While the prince jabbed, he took a timid step, and Alistair leapt in with a center thrust. Meleager was barely able to parry the attack and duck out of the way.

Sensing the prince being off-balance, Alistair continued his offense and swung his blade in several small circles. Meleager was startled, and the sudden shock in his eyes hinted to Alistair that he feared being hit.

"It seems you have had some training as well," the prince tried to speak with a confident tone of voice as he bounced between the balls of his feet.

And you are a talker! Those sorts of warriors were quite annoying, but Alistair didn't let this upset him. It seemed the prince drew strength from self-spoken taunts. If Alistair could distract him with a few swings...

Just as Meleager bounced onto his right foot, he made a daring sweep with his blade to the left. This caught Alistair by surprise, because he expected such a swing from the right, where Meleager's weight would best serve him. Alistair gripped his sword with both hands, pulling it upwards to block the stroke, and swinging back in anticipation of another pass from the prince. But because the prince had attacked from his weak side, there was no follow-on stroke. Instead, Alistair was swinging at air, and before he realized it, the prince had moved around to his flank side.

Alistair was just able to parry the first strike that came on his weak flank when he suddenly felt a cut on his left leg from a second strike. The pain from this light gash streaked through his body. His lack of fear in combat diminished. Up until now, the soldiers he had fought seemed to be real amateurs. He felt like he was being schooled by the prince, and the fear was starting to show in his eyes. A grin spread on Meleager's face.

"Don't assume your attacker will always come from the strong side, my *General*."

If only Alistair had anticipated that last swing, he could have taken the advantage it granted. In a sense of panic, he took a couple of steps back, trying to resist the distraction from the searing pain in his left leg. In this moment of retreat, the prince seized the opportunity to move in and swing a high blow with lethal force. Instead of blocking it, Alistair twisted down and to the left, partly due to panic, but partly out of some hidden instinct. Meleager's blade nicked Alistair's right arm, and generated another wave of pain, exacerbated as the sweat on Alistair's body embraced this fresh wound.

Alistair was being beaten back, and was starting to feel weak. The pain was growing, converging, and starting to tell him that he would die. Then the calm still voice of his master instructor from long ago rang in his head, "Pain is good. It means you're alive, but never let it dominate you or you shall soon be dead."

Pain. Pain was filling his body, but that voice also told him that pain would soon be visited upon Ismene if he failed. With renewed vigor, he started to circle again as Meleager jeered at him.

"General, I fear the Egyptian army may soon need a new commander."

As Alistair circled, he stumbled on purpose, trying to give no signal to Meleager of his determination but instead to keep up the ruse of his weakness.

Alistair weakly raised his sword to swing from the side. Meleager saw this as his opportunity for a kill strike, and parried the feeble attack. In smooth stride, he swung his own blade around in full circle, expecting to land a blow on Alistair's head. In the brief moment of his pride, he had looked up where his sword was, and as it came down, the general was gone! Anticipating the prince's counterstrike, Alistair had deftly moved to the prince's strong side. He took a short strike and hit the prince's hand.

Meleager, realizing that the general wasn't as weak as he appeared, was shocked as his right hand was hit by a blow. By sheer luck, he managed to hold on to his blade. Fumbling to react, he shoved his shoulder into Alistair, knocking him off-balance. He took those few seconds to back up and pivot to face the general.

The two swung at each other at the same time and were locked together. Each was trying to push the other with every ounce of strength left. Alistair noticed that the trickle of blood that had been running down his shoulder had covered his hand and was making the handle of his sword slick.

Ismene had found strength from somewhere deep inside and used the cave wall to pull herself up.

Meleager, sensing that Alistair's strength was failing, shouted out, "And now it is time to die!"

"No!" Ismene screamed.

Alistair felt the calm embrace of his master instructor fill his soul as he twisted his body, allowing the blood in his hand to provide the means to pivot to the ground while his sword slipped free. This caused Meleager's body to fall to the ground next to Alistair. Not being able to break his fall, the impact of the prince's full weight knocked the wind out of him. Before he could react, Alistair grabbed his blade and thrust it into the prince's back. He staggered back and gave out a huge sigh.

As the traitorous prince's lungs filled with blood, he somehow managed to roll over to his back. Blood was in his mouth and he coughed a few times.

"I...I..." was all that came out, before his eyes glazed over.

Ismene fell to the ground in tears. Alistair limped over to her, dropping his sword. He knelt in front of her and pulled her into his embrace.

"There, there, my love. It's all right, he can't hurt us now."

She nodded against him. Gripping the front of his tunic, she pulled him ever closer, clinging to him as if he were a lifeline.

Alistair, exhausted, adjusted them so he could lean against the cave wall for support and used his uninjured arm to cradle her. The pain in his limbs, in his whole body, seemed far away as he relished the feeling of having her in his arms. Safe.

That's when he heard voices in the tunnel, too many to be the small forces Meleager had pulled together. He heaved a deep sigh knowing it was his men. His relief, however, was short-lived.

Ismene's whole body tightened and she called out in pain.

"What is it, my love?"

"The baby! Something is...ahhh!" she cried out again.

His men were close; he could hear it.

"Hold on, Ismene." He was frustrated with his ineptitude. All he could do was sit there, helpless to do anything but hold her.

Captain Ptah, with a couple of men from his unit, rounded the corner just then.

"General!" Turning his head, he saw Meleager's body. His face betrayed his disgust at recognizing the mastermind behind this whole plot.

"Captain," Alistair pulled his attention away from Meleager's body. "The Lady Ismene is in need of a doctor."

Alistair did not wish to be parted from her again, but he knew that in order to get her to a doctor forthwith, this was just what must happen.

The captain nodded. "Chenzira, get the lady to a doctor at once."

Chenzira came forward to gather her in his arms.

"No!" Ismene said through her pain. "I want to stay with you!"

"I know, love," Alistair said. "I want that too, but we need to get you to a doctor. I'm worried about you and the baby."

"What about you? You need a doctor."

"I need patching, love. Any number of my men can do an adequate job of that."

Ismene nodded. She then allowed Chenzira to lift her from her husband's lap and carry her off down the dark corridor from which the soldiers had just come.

Now that Ismene wasn't relying on him for stability, Alistair collapsed against the wall. Ptah knelt by Alistair to examine his wounds.

"Captain, is there any vinegar water?" Alistair asked.

Ptah shook his head. "I'm sorry, General, we did not have time to gather proper supplies. But I don't think we can move you with wounds this deep. You will bleed out. We'll have to tend these and sew them."

Alistair nodded his understanding. Ptah was telling him that there was nothing for pain and there would be nothing to dull the pain of the stitching. But he did not fear the pain. His only concern was for the safety of his wife and child.

Alonah was stirred from sleep as a soldier, led by Rabiah, carried Ismene into the bedchambers.

"Milady!" she gasped, sitting up, tears of joy brimming her eyes. She had begun to fear that she would never see her mistress again. Alonah moved to get out of bed, limping.

Rabiah was leading him toward the bed, but Alonah could see Ismene's lips moving.

"She's trying to say something." Alonah attempted to stop the party.

They halted and Alonah was able to catch up, grimacing with the pain of every step.

"Milady, it's Alonah. What is it?"

"Alistair," she said, her voice weak as she was fighting uncon-sciousness.

"She is asking after the general." Alonah looked between the maid-servant and the soldier.

"I haven't heard anything from the captain or the general," the soldier said.

"Alistair," Ismene insisted, barely able to annunciate the word.

"She's delirious, I think," Rabiah said.

"No, I think she's trying to communicate something." Alonah thought for a minute. "I think she's requesting we lay her down in the general's bedchambers."

"Should we violate the general's private chambers without his permission?" Rabiah seemed worried about being chastised for wrong actions.

"We should do as our mistress requests," Alonah said, her voice a little harsh, leaving no room for discussion. "Follow me," she said to the soldier.

Alonah, though slow on her feet, led the way as they moved back out of Ismene's chambers. They were only able to move at Alonah's pace, but at long last they did arrive at Alistair's rooms. The soldier settled Ismene on the bed and Rabiah went about seeing to her comfort.

Alonah indicated that the soldier should follow her to the outer chambers.

"What can you tell me of the lady's condition?" Alonah's eyes met those of the soldier's.

"Captain Ptah's unit found the lady and the general in some caves some miles outside of the city where the lady had been taken. Lady Ismene was in need of a doctor. I was charged with getting her there. He said that her body was injured and under much stress. It had caused the child to try to come early. The doctor was able to stop the progress of the labor with these herbs." He pulled a pouch out and handed it to Alonah. "If she has the pain again, you are to make these herbs into a tea and have her drink it."

Alonah nodded her understanding. "I thank you for returning her to us."

"My charge to oversee the continued well-being of the Lady Ismene will continue until my captain or the general releases me. I will take up a post outside of the bedchambers. The doctor insisted she be allowed to rest." The soldier was all seriousness.

"Yes, of course." Alonah did not wish to get in his way.

The soldier moved to his post outside of the outer chamber's door and Alonah went to oversee Ismene's care.

Alistair was relieved to see the outline of his house on the horizon. After his ordeal, all he wanted was to see that Ismene and the child were well. It would only be a matter of minutes before they were at the house and he would find out what had happened to his beloved.

Would it be possible to gather her in his arms to sleep? While that might be uncertain, he did know that he would not be parted from her again for a long time to come. He would discuss with Pharaoh a leave of absence to be with his wife after this terrible trial they had come through.

The chariot stopped at the entrance to the house and Ptah assisted Alistair down. He did not wish to depend on his captain, but he did not wish to tear his stitches either. So he allowed himself to be helped, and he took his steps slow and steady while moving into the house. They were greeted by Fenuku. Alistair felt a pang of loss that it was not Neterka, but that was something he would have to get used to.

"Has the Lady Ismene returned?" Alistair was desperate to hear of her condition.

"Yes, General, all is well. She is resting in your chambers."

"*My* chambers?" That was a pleasant surprise. It also touched him. She must have wanted to be close to him, even in his absence.

Everyone matched Alistair's pace as he moved through the house toward his suite. Knowing that Ismene was mere steps away, it was easy to forget the pain. He was tempted to rush, but forced himself to continue his slow steps, being mindful of the stitches in his leg.

They met Chenzira at the door.

"How is the Lady Ismene?" Alistair wanted to forego the soldier who had done his due diligence, but he would acknowledge the man's faithfulness.

"Resting comfortably, General." Chenzira stood at attention as he spoke.

Alistair was thankful that he got the short version. There would be time later for the details.

"Thank you for your service, Chenzira. I shall see to it that you are given a commendation." A knowing look passed between Alistair and Ptah.

"You are dismissed," Ptah said, as Alistair moved into the outer chambers.

Moving farther into his receiving room, he could hear Ptah speaking to Fenuku in the hall. "Do you have some herbs for pain? The general could use a tea if you do," Ptah said.

"I will see to it," Fenuku said.

Alistair waited a moment to see if Ptah would follow him into the bedchambers, but he seemed to think better of it. This was fine with him; his mind was elsewhere.

Slipping into his inner bedchambers, Alistair could barely breathe. It was not his intention to wake Ismene, but he wanted to check on her, to see that she was safe. She was indeed where Fenuku had said, resting peacefully. Surely she had insisted on being put in his bed. That made him happy. He couldn't imagine her being across the house, recovering in her suite while he was in his.

Ismene stirred and opened her eyes, smiling as she took in her surroundings. She tenderly touched the place where he would have been lying and sighed. Only then did she seem to notice him standing over her.

"Alistair," she said in a whisper.

He came forward. "I'm here." Sitting on the edge of the bed, he took her hand in one of his, leaning over her. She tugged on his hand, indicating that she wished for him to lie down next to her. Alistair obeyed, curling up beside her and gathering her with his good arm. They lay there for some time, resting in the comfort found in each other's arms—the comfort each had longed for.

"Please, always stay here with me." Ismene placed a hand on his chest.

"Not even a hundred armies could pull me away."

Epilogue

Alistair paced outside of the birthing pavilion.
Hearing Ismene's cries, he knew them to be the normal cries of labor.
He would just have to wait it out. There was nothing he could do to
ease her pain or remove it. Taking this moment to reflect, he thought
back over the course of their marriage and all they had been through.
The trials of their early marriage seemed but a distant memory, almost
surreal, some three years later. So much had come to pass because of
those events.

Most of the members of the radical faction of the Alexandrian mob
were arrested that day so long ago. They were rounded up in the caves
by the soldiers that arrived to rescue him and Ismene. Did they get the
entire faction? There was no way to know. The members they did arrest
never talked, but they did imprison Sefu and Akil—two men they knew
to be directly responsible in the plot to kidnap and attempt to murder
his wife.

A contingency of soldiers had also been sent to the estate where
Alistair had faced off with the mob. Alas, it was abandoned and they
had not been able to track down anyone associated with that group. Not
even Neterka. He had disappeared, leaving behind everything. The only
thing the soldiers could bring back to Alistair was a blue robe. Neterka's

room had been raided a week after the incident and Alistair knew it must have been someone connected to the mob. But nothing ever came of that.

Fenuku had seamlessly replaced Neterka with Ismene's help. He had proven to be a competent and loyal valet. Alistair, however, had been changed by the event. No longer did he trust even his personal manservant with the kinds of information he had before. No, he had seen the folly of his ways. It was difficult for him to no longer have someone to use as a sounding board, but that was necessary for the security of Egypt.

Alistair was shaken from his thoughts as Alonah exited the birthing pavilion. He had been so lost in thought he hadn't noticed the screams of his wife subside to be replaced by the cries of their child. How had he missed that? Now that he recognized it, he knew it to be one of the most beautiful sounds in the entire world.

"She is asking for you, General." Alonah smiled, then she squatted. "And you too, young man."

Ismene glanced over at her handsome husband and their amazing son, Teremun, as they entered the room and came over to the bed where she reclined. Teremun had his mother's olive complexion and curly black hair but his father's bright blue eyes. He was a beautiful child. He bounded into the room and over to his mother, eager to meet his new sister.

"What are we going to call her, Mommy?" he asked as his father helped him up onto the bed so he could see his sister better.

"Well, she is precious to Mommy. Just like you. So why don't we name her 'precious.' Do you know the Egyptian word for 'precious'?" Ismene reached out to stroke her son's curls.

"Aziza!"

"That's my smart boy," Alistair said.

"But my name doesn't mean precious, Mommy," Teremun said.

"That's right, what does your name mean?" Ismene's eyes followed the bouncing movements of her son.

"That Daddy loves me!"

"That's right, 'beloved by his father,'" Ismene replied.

"Is she gonna have two names like me?" The young boy seemed rather concerned about his sister having proper names.

"I think she should. Let's think of a Greek name too. How about 'beautiful'?" Alistair spoke up.

"Adara!" Teremun said excitedly.

"Aziza Adara," Alistair said. "Precious and beautiful. Just like her mother." Alistair planted a kiss on her lips. "You are amazing, darling." He settled himself in a seated position at the head of the bed next to his wife.

Teremun jumped down off the bed and bounded around the room, examining the murals and statues around the birthing chambers.

Rabiah and Alonah returned, Rabiah with additional blankets for wrapping the baby, and Alonah with a cool drink for Ismene. For her part, Ismene surrendered her precious bundle over to her handmaiden, Rabiah.

Since Alonah had left her service to make her home with Jabari, Rabiah had proved to be almost as attentive and caring a servant and friend. But no one could quite replace Alonah. Lucky for Ismene, no one had to. Alistair had insisted Jabari allow him to offer assistance setting up a home for them as thanks for Jabari's role in bringing Ismene home. Their home was a fifteen-minute chariot ride away. Ismene was able to visit her friend as often as she wished.

Alonah had been sitting on the bed to offer Ismene the cool drink, but she stood, placing her hands on the small of her back and letting out a deep breath.

"It won't be long for you now." Ismene put a hand on Alonah's protruding stomach.

Alonah smiled. "I only hope Jehovah smiles down on me as He has you."

Crying out to Jehovah in the midst of her ordeal had been only the beginning of a long journey of faith for Ismene. She had become quite the eager pupil of the scholars and scroll-keepers at the library of Alexandria. The more she delved into the wondrous mystery of Scripture, with the foundation of her experience to build on, the more she came to believe.

Soon after, Alistair and then Alonah came to see the truth as she had. Alistair had even decided to give Teremun the second name of "Esaias," which was Greek for "God saves," as he began to believe that Jehovah had brought them through their ordeal and saved their lives.

Rabiah brought Aziza back over to Ismene, having swaddled her and calmed her. "She is going to have your eyes, milady."

Ismene took her daughter back and gazed into her eyes. She could see that, while her eyes were indeed a newborn blue, they were quite dark already. Certainly, they would get darker.

"Would you like to hold your daughter?" Ismene held Aziza out in Alistair's direction.

"Of course." He gathered her into his arms.

Having been startled to wakefulness, she began to cry. The practiced father started gently bouncing his new baby girl, holding her close to his body. It worked to calm her to sleep again.

He looked over at his wife and smiled. She couldn't miss the glisten in his eye.

"Thank you," he said, "for the two most precious children in the whole world."

She smiled back. "Thank you for the most amazing life."

Ismene sighed. Her life *was* amazing. It seemed as if it were a lifetime ago that she was being forcibly relocated to Egypt to marry this man who was a stranger to her, scared, skeptical, and disheartened. And now, this was home. This life was home. The love of this man was home.

Keep reading for a preview of the first book in the Cripple Creek Series!

Thank you, dear reader, for for reading along with me! If you enjoyed this story, I would sincerely appreciate if you would submit a review. It would mean so much to me!

Author's Note

This book was my introduction to writing a full length novel...and clean Historical Romance. It was the second book published, but the first one written. And, as such, it holds an extra special place in my heart. It started as a challenge to myself--placing a love story in this time period that just fascinated me: the Ptolemaic Period in Egypt.

The Ptolemaic Period, as you may have gathered from the Prologue and the story, is set after Alexander the Great's death. Ptolemy, one of his generals, took over Egypt and named himself Pharoah. This ushered in a time when there was Greek influence and a line of Greek rulers in Egypt.

One of the more difficult things for me was to determine which Ptolemaic ruler to place this story under. I decided to include the writing of the Septuagint. This helped me narrow it down to Ptolemy II Soter.

The existence of a Greek general or a marriage made with a Greek bride...is purely fictional. But the presence and actions of the Alexandrian mob were based on research. This group did not accept Greek rule and did what they could to make the lives of the Greeks in Egypt diffi-cult. The Diana constellation is my own creation, but is based on the stars in Orion.

All in all, this novel was an adventure. It both thrilled and challenged me. And I am so glad it is in your hands.

HOPE IN CRIPPLE CREEK

The stagecoach moved along, bumping and rocking as it went. Trees and other green scenery whisked by the window. Views of mountains and open plains were visible from the seat of the coach, vistas familiar to its occupant. Katherine Matthews was coming home. She returned to Cripple Creek, no longer the scared, unsure teenager who had left to further her education so many years ago with hopes and dreams of a new life in a new place. No, she had matured into a confident young woman who had grown in stature and in beauty. Her hair was no longer the mousy color she always hated, for it had deepened into the same beautiful chestnut brown she had always admired in her mother's appearance. She'd grown out of her awkward teenage features, and was now well regarded among her peers as a rather handsome woman.

Returning to Cripple Creek brought many rather-mixed emotions to the surface. Imagine, one of her first postings would be at the same schoolhouse where she received her educational start. When her mother wrote to her of the interim need, she was glad to help out. What an odd coincidence that the letter would find her, too, in transition. Would this turn into a permanent placement? Did she want it to?

The mountain scenery became more recognizable, and she thought back on her childhood. There were so many happy times here. Unbidden, her mind wandered to the day of the great tragedy that had marred her spirit—the day Ellie Mae died.

Even all these years later, she carried the scar in her heart. The events of that day had left her broken. Why must thoughts of Ellie Mae plague her so? And all the more as her return became imminent? She shivered as the images from her nightmares the previous evening flitted across her mind. They would not stop. These same visions visited her in sleep night after night. All the more frequently these last weeks.

Closing her eyes, the hazy images took form and became memory. It was as if no time had passed. She and Ellie, walking through the schoolyard just as they did every other day . . .

Hooking arms with Ellie Mae, Katherine stepped out of the schoolhouse and into the yard. A rather large group of students gathered off to the right near the old tree. It didn't bother Katherine. She turned her attention toward the path that would lead home.

"What do you think they're up to?" Ellie Mae whispered.

Katherine glanced in that direction and noticed Betsy Callaway at the center, flapping her jaws. Why would anyone listen to anything she said? But they did. The class at large seemed to adore Betsy. It didn't make sense. Clenching her teeth, Katherine grabbed for Ellie Mae's hand. "Whatever it is, we don't want to be involved." She pulled Ellie Mae along as she walked on, trying to pass the gathering.

"I know Miss Matthews couldn't do it," Betsy said loudly.

Katherine froze in her tracks. What had she just said?

The crowd of students parted and glared at Katherine and Ellie Mae.

"Let's keep going," Ellie Mae pleaded, tugging on Katherine's hand.

She should listen to Ellie Mae and not become a part of whatever game Betsy played. But she could not let Betsy get the best of her. What would everyone think of her?

So, she turned to face her accuser. There stood Betsy with Wyatt Sullivan, the most popular boy in school, right beside her. Betsy's blonde pigtails, tied back with perfect pink ribbons, shone in the sun. Her dress was no less perfect, pink with just the right amount of lace and even a slight puff to the sleeves.

"Do what, pray tell?" Katherine shot back. Her heart beat furiously in her chest.

"Go down through the mine shaft." Betsy folded her arms in front of her chest and raised an eyebrow.

Katherine's heart skipped a beat then, but she tried not to show her fear.

Ellie Mae's grip tightened on her hand.

"I assure you, Miss Callaway, it's not that I can't do it. It's simply that I have better things to do than to be traipsing about a mine shaft." She turned to leave and hoped that would be enough to silence Betsy.

"Prove it." Betsy's voice rang out after her.

Katherine's eyes slid closed. Was there any way around this? "I have nothing to prove to you," she called back over her shoulder.

"Fraidycat!" Betsy laughed.

The other students joined in.

Katherine's face burned. A fire had been lit within her. She was not afraid of anything! Releasing Ellie Mae's hand, she then whirled around. "I am not afraid!"

"There's only one way we'll believe that." Betsy's hands moved from her chest to her hips.

There was no way this would be a one-way challenge. "Are you going?" Katherine poked her chin out, putting her own hands on her hips, attempting to puff up her chest as much as she could.

"Of course," Betsy said, though her voice caught.

"Then, let's go." Katherine grabbed after Ellie Mae's hand and headed out in the direction of the old mine shaft. She hoped Ellie Mae didn't feel how her palms had started to sweat. Perspiration covered her whole body. How was she to keep up this façade?

The group of students followed, a din of voices behind. As they neared the cavernous opening, they became quiet as they halted several feet short of the forbidden place.

Wyatt pushed through the crowd once they had stopped. "Now, girls, this is foolishness. Talking about it is one thing, but you're not actually going down there, are you?"

Katherine glanced at the mine opening. It looked dark and ominous. Not what she wanted to see. Then she eyed Betsy. She had everything—the popularity, the most handsome boy in school ... But she would not have Katherine's pride, too. "I am."

"Then I am, too." Betsy stared at Katherine, matching her glare through slitted eyes.

"Kath-rine," Ellie whispered, tugging on her hand.

Katherine looked over at her friend. Ellie's eyes begged her not to go. Katherine wondered again at the danger. Her friend had every right to be concerned, she supposed. But it would not last. Betsy would go but a few steps in and give up. Katherine was sure of it. So, she would not be dissuaded.

Wyatt's eyes moved from one girl to the other. A couple of years older than the girls at their thirteen years, he stood a good head taller than Katherine. At last, he threw his hands up in the air. "Then I'm going too."

"And so am I," came Ellie Mae's quiet response.

Katherine leaned toward her friend. "Ellie, you don't have to go." Her eyes held Ellie's. What was she going to do? She couldn't take Ellie into that place. But something had eased in her when Ellie Mae volunteered to go. Was it selfish of her to want her friend to accompany her?

"Yes, I do." Her voice was firm, though her chin quivered. "I'm sticking with you."

A bump in the trail jolted Katherine from her reverie. The scenery outside became blurred. Or was it her? Touching her face, she felt moisture. She wiped at the tears. This would not do! Whatever happened when she returned, Katherine was determined she would face it with as much bravery as she could muster.

To read more, find *Hope in Cripple Creek* here:

https://saraturnquist.com/hope-in-cripple-creek/

Acknowledgments

I want to thank my editors for making this book what it is. Their input was both valuable and necessary. I also want to thank my irreplaceable beta readers Christina Horton, Stacy Shoenwetter, and Hillary Harvey, without whom this book would not be possible. Their insight and encouragement have added so much and pushed me through so many tough spots. As well, my writing mentor, Hannah Conway, deserves acknowledgement for pouring into me everything she can. And I want to give a shout out to my critique group members whose honest feedback and support are priceless!

I also want to thank the amazing cover artist, Cora Graphics, who is just phenomenal. I am impressed by both her talent and how easy she is to work with.

My photographer, Rachel Bull, is also one of the most talented people I know. I am grateful for her work as well.

And I want to thank Stephanie Taylor and Clean Reads for believing in me and giving me my start.

For my sister, you make me want to be better. For my parents, you make me feel so good to have achieved this dream of writing. And for my husband and kids, you give me every reason to smile.

Sara is a coffee lovin', word slinging, Historical Romance author whose super power is converting caffeine into novels. She loves those odd little tidbits of history that are stranger than fiction. That's what inspires her. Well, that and a good love story.

But of all the love stories she knows, hers is her favorite. She lives happily with her own Prince Charming and their gaggle of minions. Three to be exact. They sure know how to distract a writer! But, alas, the stories must be written, even if it must happen in the wee hours of the morning.

Sara is an avid reader and enjoys reading and writing clean Historical Romance when she's not traveling.

Please follow along with her journey through her newsletter at: http://saraturnquist.com/list

Happy Reading!

facebook.com/AuthorSaraRTurnquist

instagram.com/sararturnquist

x.com/sararturnquist

youtube.com/@SaraRTurnquist

pinterest.com/sararturnquist

Also by Sara R. Turnquist

CONVENIENT RISK SERIES

A Convenient Risk

An Inconvenient Christmas

A Less Convenient Path

A Convenient Escape

An Inconvenient Acquaintance

These Golden Years

A Less Convenient Arrangement

Ranch Hands Collection (ebook only)

CRIPPLE CREEK SERIES

Hope in Cripple Creek

Christmas in Cripple Creek

Faith in Cripple Creek

Love in Cripple Creek

~Prequels~

Leaving Waverly

Leaving Stoneybrook

LADY OF BOHEMIA SERIES

The Lady Bornekova

The Lady and the Hussites

The Lady and Her Champion

The Lady and Her Secret

RAILWAY ROMANCE SERIES

Laura, The Tycoon's Daughter

ACROSS THE YEARS SERIES

Among the Pages

Between the Lines

STANDALONE NOVELS

The General's Wife

Trail of Fears

Off to War